WHERE DUTY LIES

The minute Charlotte sees Meridan Avebury at a wedding, it causes such a sudden feeling in her heart that she believes it must be love at first sight. But Meridan is already engaged to the beautiful Phillipa, who is dangerously ill. And while they don't deny their feelings for each other, Charlotte and Meridan are unwilling to take their own happiness at Phillipa's expense. However, Meridan becomes troubled by divided loyalties and struggles to find where duty really lies.

SPECIAL MESSAGE TO READERS

PATRICIA ROBINS

WHERE DUTY LIES

Complete and Unabridged

LINFORD
Leicester

First published in Great Britain in 1957

First Linford Edition
published 2013

British Library CIP Data

Robins, Patricia, *1921* –
   Where duty lies. - -
   (Linford romance library)
   1. Love stories.
   2. Large type books.
   I. Title II. Series
   823.9′14–dc23

   ISBN 978–1–4448–1433–0

Published by
F. A. Thorpe (Publishing)
Anstey, Leicestershire

Set by Words & Graphics Ltd.
Anstey, Leicestershire
Printed and bound in Great Britain by
T. J. International Ltd., Padstow, Cornwall

This book is printed on acid-free paper

1

When the telephone rang, Charlotte rose slowly to her feet and went to answer it. Later she was to remember that she had had no premonition, no sudden inner warning that her life was to be changed completely by this one phone call. Somehow it seemed wrong in retrospect that she could have walked so slowly and carelessly towards her Fate.

'Charlotte, is that you? It's Bess, darling! Now listen, Charlotte, because this is rather important . . . you know I was to have been bridesmaid on Saturday to Angela Bates? Well, the other bridesmaid whom you haven't met . . . she was a friend of Angela's fiancé . . . she has just been carted off to hospital with appendicitis so Angela's desperate. It'll throw out all the arrangements because she needs two of us to carry the train.'

'I'm so sorry!' Charlotte said, wondering how she could help. She had been friendly with Bess for years but barely knew Angela except as an acquaintance at the tennis club with whom she'd once or twice made up a four.

'The thing is, you and Phillipa . . . the girl with the appendix . . . are just about the same build. Angela wants to know if you'd step into the breach and be the second train-bearer?'

'I . . . I suppose so!' Charlotte said a little doubtfully, her young mouth turned down from its usual pretty upward curve in momentary indecision. 'All the same, I shall be almost a stranger . . . and I'd have to have a rehearsal of some kind . . .'

'But of course, Poppet!' Bess broke in, giggling a little. 'I knew you'd help out . . . I told Angela not to worry. Now listen, can you come over to my house right away and try on the dress. Mummy says she'll do the necessary alterations this evening. We're to go to

2

the church to meet Angela . . . there's a full-dress rehearsal laid on for three o'clock, complete with ushers and everything. We can just make it if you fly . . . '

Having seemingly committed herself, Charlotte gave a slight shrug to her slim shapely shoulders and replaced the receiver. Bang went her plan for a leisurely half day from the office . . . and she'd wanted to wash her hair, too! And furthermore, she'd have to get permission to be off on Saturday morning as well. It was all very well for Bess who lived at home and didn't work . . . except doing charitable work on committees and women's institutes with her mother. They belonged to a different income group from Charlotte who had to help support a widowed mother and did a not uninteresting but routine job as secretary to an elderly solicitor in the City! Mr. Everwell wouldn't be a bit pleased at having to give her an extra half day although she would offer to make up time next half-day. If she didn't he'd certainly dock her pay packet and she couldn't afford to lose the money . . . not if the holiday she had planned for her mother this Summer was to materialize.

Although only twenty-two, the circumstances of her life which had forced Charlotte to be the family breadwinner ever since she left school at eighteen, had contrived to make her look older than her years. Although her creamy complexion was without lines or any marks of age, and her soft grey eyes brilliant and youthful enough, there was nevertheless a serious set to the line of her lips and a determined tilt to the curly dark head that sometimes made her look a woman nearer thirty than twenty.

This curious mixture of youthfulness and maturity gave her an attraction in addition to her natural prettiness. But it had not, however, brought romance into her life. She knew this was her own fault. Any of the young men who had tried to establish a slightly more intimate relationship at the tennis club dances she occasionally attended, or whom she had met at Bess's charity meetings, she had immediately discouraged so that they had soon ceased to telephone for dates. Her reasons for doing this were two-fold. For one thing she had promised the father she adored that she would take care of her mother who was a semi-invalid . . . and with her job to keep her busy during the day and her mother to keep company evenings and week-ends, she felt she could not manage to cope with the tangles of light romantic engagements; and perhaps the more important reason was that she had never yet met a man who seriously roused her to any feeling stronger than a mild affection. This had not worried her for deep down within her, she knew that one day, like the song, *he'd* come along; knew she would recognize him at sight and fall in love with her whole being. Until that happened, she fought shy of becoming involved for her own and her mother's sake.

Bess had put forward the view that if

Charlotte were less attractive she would be more concerned with finding herself a boy friend! That she could afford to sit back because she knew quite well that she had only to beckon a little finger and a choice of suitors would come running! This was by no means Charlotte's view for she did not consider herself either plain or attractive . . . just ordinary, but she did not try to argue with the good-natured Bess who was longing to marry her off to someone almost as ardently as she longed to be married herself. Bess, with her round friendly mischievous face was by no means lacking in attractions herself, and it amused Charlotte to see how Bess fell in and out of love as quickly as showers came and went in Spring. Every new boyfriend was *the* one — until about a week later, when she cheerfully admitted her mistake and set about finding the Right One as quickly as she could.

Having settled her mother comfortably in front of the television set to watch woman's hour, Charlotte hurried round to Bess's home. Her slight lack of enthusiasm at being a bridesmaid to a girl she scarcely knew, vanished when she tried on the dress. It was a cloudy billowy mass of palest tangerine net, beautifully cut and fitting her as if it had been made for her as well as the unfortunate girl with the appendicitis! Charlotte knew without being told that it was a very expensive dress and certainly the most beautiful she had ever worn. The two girls were also to wear tiny crowns of artificial violets and each was to carry a posy of fresh violets intertwined with orange-blossoms.

'Oh, Charlotte dear!' exclaimed Mrs. Hopkins, Bess's kindly mother, 'you look like the bride yourself. How well the colour becomes you!'

'And Bess, too!' Charlotte said, watching her friend adjust her own wreath. 'Those violets look perfect against your fair hair.'

Bess grinned cheerfully and gave Charlotte a careful but impulsive kiss.

'We must rush, darling! Angela's sending a taxi to fetch us at ten to three . . . no expense spared on this wedding I can tell you. I bet we'll meet dozens of glamorous eligible young men. There's to be a big party afterwards and after the bride has gone, we'll be the most important people there! Isn't it fun?'

Even the cool Charlotte felt a tinge of excitement run through her . . . not because of the dance or the partners she might have . . . but because she knew she had never looked lovelier and it was rather fun . . . such a change from the drab greyness of a London city office.

They were met at the fashionable church by Angela and her bridegroom-to-be, and half a dozen morning-suited young men who were to be ushers. Angela's brother, who was amongst these, immediately brought a little law and order into the chaos that reigned on their arrival. Soon the rehearsal was in full swing. Charlotte found that the part she had to play was quite simple and she enjoyed the afternoon almost as much as Bess, who had found time to nudge her and say that she'd really found the man of her dreams at last.

'The usher standing by the door, darling . . . next to Angela's brother . . . see him?'

But Charlotte did not see him. Instead, her eyes had gone to the man whom she had not noticed before, but who was now talking to the bride's father. Surely . . . surely she had seen him somewhere before? She could only glimpse his profile but something in the set of his shoulders, the turn of his head as he stood in the sunlight streaming through the open church door, struck a chord of memory deep within her.

'Bess, do you know who that is . . . talking to Mr. Peters?'

'Haven't a clue! Charlotte, will you please look the other way and see the man I'm going to marry!'

But Charlotte could not take her eyes away from Mr. Peters's companion. It was ridiculous to take Bess's chatter seriously and yet . . . yet her own heart was beating curiously fast, her own eyes were as fixed as Bess's . . . on the man *she* knew she was going to marry!

'I'm as silly as Bess!' she had time to tell herself before the dark head turned suddenly towards her across the emptying pews and she saw his eyes staring into her own. Then coherent thought ceased altogether and she had to put her hand out to one of the pews to steady herself as she saw him making his way towards her. She felt panic-stricken now she knew that she had never met him before; that he was a stranger to her and that she had been staring so outrageously that he must have imagined she was trying to attract his attention. The blood rushed to her cheeks and she wished herself suddenly a million miles away. Then he spoke, his voice deep-toned and rather hesitant.

'I'm afraid you'll think me rather rude . . . when I caught sight of you just now I could have sworn we had met before. I realize now I was mistaken . . . ' He broke off and gave her a sudden, quick, apologetic smile.

With rare impulsiveness, Charlotte flung her usual reticence to the winds and replied:

'As a matter of fact, I thought I had met you, too. My name is Charlotte Matthews.'

He took her hand and held it for a moment in a strong firm clasp.

'How-do-you-do! I'm Meridan Avebury. I saw you talking to Bess just now. Are you a friend of hers?'

'Yes!' Charlotte said, her words a little trembly from the queer inner exhilaration that seemed to have her in its grip. 'Perhaps we have seen one another at one of Bess's parties?'

He led her out through the church door into the sunshine, and for a moment, stared down at her . . . he was six feet tall, Charlotte only five-feet-five . . . his brown eyes looking into her grey ones.

'No, I don't think so. I'm quite sure I would remember if that were so. Besides, I would have made sure of an introduction to you.'

It was a plain statement of fact the way he put it and yet the compliment was as direct as it could be. The colour heightened in Charlotte's cheeks and she was glad that Bess came up at that moment, a fair-haired, sun-tanned young man behind her.

'Darling, this is Jeremy Patricks . . . Jeremy, one of my dearest friends, Charlotte Matthews . . . oh, hullo Meridan! Do you two boys know each other?'

Without giving them time to answer, she rushed on:

'Jeremy and I thought it might be fun to have a foursome this evening after all this hard work. How about you and Meridan joining us?'

Charlotte felt a swift rush of joy, followed immediately by a feeling of helplessness.

'Bess, I can't . . . much as I'd like to. I've left Mother alone all afternoon . . . I simply must go home this evening.'

She knew the man was watching her,

willing her to change her mind even before he said quietly:

'Couldn't you possibly make it? It sounds such an excellent idea?'

She wanted to go . . . desperately . . . in a way she had never felt before about anything. If she didn't go, she might never meet him again, and it had become the most important thing in the world that she should get to know him better.

Bess, seeing her hesitation, said cheerfully:

'Look, Charlotte, why not bring your mother round to spend the evening with my parents? They'd love to have her and then she wouldn't be alone. Have either of you boys got a car?'

Both men nodded their heads and Meridan said quickly:

'I expect you'll want to go home and change. Suppose I call about six-thirty to pick you up and run your mother round to Bess's house. Then we can all go on wherever we're going in my car?'

'That settles it!' Bess said enthusiastically.

'Will that be all right?' Meridan asked Charlotte.

Just this once, Charlotte thought . . . Mother can't mind.

She nodded her head.

It was only later, as her mother sat on her bed, questioning her while she changed into a ballet-length evening dress, that Charlotte fully realized how crazily she was behaving.

'But, darling, *who* is he? I know you said he was a friend of Bess's but what does he do? You really know nothing about him at all!'

'No . . . I suppose I don't!' Charlotte admitted as much even while she could not admit yet to her mother exactly how she felt about this stranger who had walked into her life and taken possession of her every thought. 'All the same, we shall be a foursome so there's no need for you to worry, Mummy. And as he's calling here to fetch us, you'll meet him for yourself. I'm sure you'll like him!'

It did not need Charlotte's spoken

confidence to reveal to her mother how important was this date. Charlotte was behaving in a manner so completely foreign to her usual behaviour that this point alone gave her away, even had it not been for the glowing cheeks and brilliant eyes with which she returned from the wedding rehearsal.

'She's falling in love!' thought Mrs. Matthews with a sudden, swift fear. 'Maybe this is the man she'll marry . . . and I'll lose her!'

She tried to hide her fear even from herself. She was not a selfish woman . . . only a very lonely one since her husband had died. She suffered such ill-health it was nearly impossible for her to leave the house, especially since they could not afford a car. She did not wish to spoil Charlotte's life by being a drag on her, yet the young girl's companionship and love and care for her had been so complete and unstint-ingly given, that until this moment, she had all but forgotten that she might one day have to lose her. That was a fear she had faced only rarely, sometimes when she was having a sleepless night and life seemed at its most difficult. Then she had always comforted herself with the thought that Charlotte was not like other girls . . . she had few boy friends and the ones she had meant very little to her. She knew her daughter had a warm, even passionate nature, but believed it to be of the kind that awakens late. So she had managed to convince herself that Charlotte wouldn't get married until she was at least in her thirties . . . and by then . . . well, the doctors had told her not to count on more than ten years . . .

'Mother, please don't worry. I promise not to be late. In any case, someone will have to bring you home and I'm sure Mr. Avebury will offer to bring us both back at a reasonable hour.'

Her own selfishness suddenly apparent to her in the face of her daughter's thoughtfulness, Mrs. Matthews said quickly:

'No, darling . . . there's no need for

16

that. Bess's father will get me a taxi and I shall be perfectly all right. Since you are going out at all, which you do so rarely anyway, you might as well enjoy yourself properly. Be as late as you wish . . . but don't forget you're working tomorrow!'

Her reward was a hug from the slim white arms of her daughter and a whispered:

'You are a wonderful Mum!' which was as unlike the cool reticent Charlotte as the rest of her behaviour in the last few hours.

'I'll leave you to finish dressing in peace!' Mrs. Matthews said, suddenly unwilling to face further for the moment the youthful glowing picture of her young daughter.

Alone, Charlotte sat down at her dressing-table and studied her face.

Was she really pretty? Bess always said so but then Bess made all kinds of remarks that were merely expressions of her own moods and had no foundation in fact! Was she the kind of girl men found attractive?

Her finger touched her eyebrows, traced the line of her cheek, the curve of her lips, touched the smooth skin of her neck and shoulders.

Well, at least she was not plain!

Suddenly, as she stared at her reflection, the colour flared into Charlotte's cheeks and she covered her face with her hands, her heart beating absurdly.

How mad was this kind of behaviour . . . these thoughts . . . all because she had had a few words with a man called Meridan Avebury, about whom she knew nothing . . . nothing, except that his hair was dark and grew into an attractive point at the back of his neck . . . that his forehead was wide and deep and intelligent, and the brown eyes . . .

'Charlotte Matthews . . . if you don't stop day-dreaming you'll be late!'

She finished her dressing with a sudden flurry of movement which only enheightened her colour and did nothing to smooth her nerves which seemed all on edge. When the front-door bell rang a few moments after six-thirty, she jumped so violently backwards from her dressing-table that she upset the bottle of *Toujours* perfume across the glass top and only just avoided it spreading to her black nylon net skirt.

As she hastily mopped up with pieces of cotton-wool, she heard the unaccustomed male tones in the drawing-room below and for an instant, she stood perfectly still, her thoughts suddenly crystallizing into a moment of stark truth. She was in love . . . for the first time in her life. Downstairs was the man she wanted to marry . . . every instinct told her so. This is why she had been waiting for so long . . . the man she had known with some inner consciousness was coming to claim her . . . to awaken her. For this she had been sometimes lonely, sometimes even a little afraid, yet knowing all along it would happen . . . that she would one day find herself no longer alone.

Meridan Avebury . . . he had a strange name. Who was he? What did he do? What kind of work occupied him? How had he lived his life all these years she had not known him? Which of the services had he served in during the war . . . Army? Navy? Air Force? Where did he live? What were his parents like? How old was he?

Suddenly, she smiled at the slim, eager-eyed figure in the looking-glass. She would know when she next came back to this room . . . she would know exactly what and who this man was. She would know whether he wished to see her again . . . whether her love was founded on rock or sand . . . whether . . . whether he could ever fall in love with her, too.

For a moment, she was afraid. It was not enough that she should be discovering this new person she knew herself to be . . . not enough to know she was no longer a girl but a woman in love as crazily and stupidly as Bess might fall in love! She wanted to be reassured that it was true . . . that she had not imagined it . . . that when she went downstairs, she would not look at him and wonder how she could have spent these last hours in so fantastic a day-dream.

'Don't let it be a day-dream,' she prayed silently as she switched off her bedroom light. 'Don't let me fall out of love! Let him be in love with me, too!'

Then she ran downstairs and joined her mother and the man who had in the space of a few moments turned her life and her reasoning upside down.

★　★　★

Bess and Jeremy were dancing. Jeremy had had one duty dance with Charlotte earlier in the evening when they had just finished eating, after which he had danced consistently with a happy, excited Bess. And after one dance with Bess and two with Charlotte, Meridan had preferred to sit out and talk in the intimacy of a crowded noisy restaurant where other people were bent on their

21

own amusement. They were no more aware of the young couple at the corner table than Meridan or Charlotte were of them.

In a brief while, Meridan had made Charlotte tell him about herself, her childhood in India with a father in the civil service whom she had loved dearly and a gay and attractive mother; how her father had contracted some tropical disease and they had been forced to come home to England where he had seen one specialist after another, gradually getting worse until at last, when Charlotte was eighteen, he had died; how her mother had suffered a stroke from the shock of losing him and recovered only partially, and how she herself had immediately taken a secretarial job to augment the tiny pension that was all they had to live on.

It had not taken long to tell these few tragic events of her life and yet he had been impressed by the uncomplaining way in which she spoke of these last five years . . . of her obvious devotion and sense of duty to her mother. There seemed to have been so little that was gay or full of fun for a young girl growing up.

'Don't let's talk about me . . . tell me about yourself!' Charlotte said. 'I really know nothing about you at all except that you are a friend of Bess's. I'm surprised she has never spoken about you.'

'I don't really know her very well!' Meridan admitted. 'I've met her once or twice because she is a friend of Phillipa's . . . '

He broke off, leaving the name on the air between them.

'Phillipa? The girl who was to have been Angela's bridesmaid . . . whose place I've taken?'

The man's face became curiously lined.

'Yes, whose place you have taken. Phillipa and my sister, Elizabeth, were at school together . . . they are very close friends. I have only the one sister, no brothers. I had the conventional upper middle-class upbringing and education . . . prep and public school and on to Oxford. When I left college, I joined the Air Force as a bomber pilot. After the war, I went into my father's business . . . paper manufacturing. The firm's done very well, in spite of restrictions and controls. My people live in Surrey and Elizabeth lives with them . . . she's mad about riding and keeps her own hunter. She's going to marry Phillipa's brother next year . . . John is by way of being an up-and-coming racehorse trainer so that suits Elizabeth down to the ground. I think they'll make a good match.'

'And Phillipa?' Charlotte asked the question that would not stay unanswered.

'Well, Phillipa was a deb. last year . . . she's nineteen now. It's always been understood that as soon as she was twenty-one, she . . . she and I would be married.'

'No!' Charlotte thought with a violence that made her feel almost

physically sick. 'No, it can't be true
. . . it can't.'

'Charlotte!' She remained perfectly
still, her head bent, her eyes fixed on
her hands clasped together on the table.

'Charlotte, please look at me!'

'I can't!' she thought desperately.
'He'll see in my eyes what it means to
me to learn he's engaged to someone
else. I mustn't give myself away.'

'Charlotte!' he said again . . . 'Please!'

She tried to compose her features
into an expression of unconcern yet
when she did raise her eyes to his face,
the look there destroyed any attempt on
her part to pretend.

'Charlotte, I know it must seem mad
to you to be talking this way . . . we've
only known each other a few hours, yet
because . . . because of the way things
are, I have to speak out now . . . before
it's too late. I've known Phillipa since
we were children. They've always lived
next door and as Pippa was only a year
younger than Elizabeth, it was only
natural that the two girls should be in

25

and out of each other's homes just as her brother, John, and I were constant companions. When we were growing up a bit, we made a stupid childish pact to marry each other ... Elizabeth and John, Pippa and me. It didn't mean anything of course and I think we all forgot about it ... we were like brothers and sisters, anyway, and were always quarrelling. John and I were ten and eleven years older than the girls. It wasn't until after the war, when both of us had served abroad for some years, that we came back to find the girls had suddenly grown up. Elizabeth became unofficially engaged to John when she was only seventeen. As you can imagine, Mother and Father were delighted, but they wanted her to be sure she knew her own mind, so they forbade a marriage until Elizabeth was twenty-one. Meanwhile, it became my lot to chaperone Liz and John when they went out together. Naturally, I took Pippa along as a four. She'd grown up, too, and was a pretty amusing girl, full of life and fun, and I enjoyed her companionship. I'd met a reasonable number of girls during the war, of course, but none I wanted to marry. Then one day Liz told me that Pippa was in love with me. It had never really occurred to me before to take her seriously . . . she still seemed so young to me. But I wasn't in love with anyone else and . . . well, I'd always had a deep and genuine affection for Pippa. Our friendship became a little less platonic and I found her attractive . . . '

'Do you really want to tell me all this?' Charlotte broke in, wondering how she could bear to hear from Meridan's own lips how he had gradually fallen in love with Phillipa.

'Please let me explain!' the man said. 'You see, I let myself believe I was in love. When Pippa told me she loved me, I asked her to marry me as soon as she was old enough. She was still only eighteen then and I was twenty-eight. So we drifted into an engagement, unofficial at first and then on Pippa's eighteenth birthday, officially. Our parents were delighted and so were Liz and John. It seemed to suit everybody. It wasn't until this afternoon that I realized what I had done . . . Charlotte, believe this, please, because it is the only thing I'm sure of any more . . . when I met you this afternoon, I knew for a certainty I was not in love with Pippa, that I never had been. As soon as she is out of hospital, I mean to tell her, to break off our engagement. I had made up my mind to do this before I called for you this evening. Charlotte, do you believe in love at first sight?'

'I do, I do!' Charlotte's heart told her, yet she could not bring herself to say so. Even while she believed without question every word he had told her, for it had the unmistakable ring of truth, she still retained sufficient clear thinking to be sure of two things. First, that he, as much as she, herself, could not be sure within a few hours of meeting one another that the mutual attraction they felt was really love. To fall in love . . . that could mean no more than an attraction of the senses. To love meant so much more . . . to respect, admire . . . to be in sympathy with . . . to share interests and understandings. And secondly, that she had no right to come between any man and the girl to whom he was engaged. If Meridan chose to break his engagement, it must be without her encouragement. She would not take another girl's man from her.

He looked at her anxiously, trying to read her thoughts. At last, unable to bear the silence, he said:

'I suppose you are thinking me quite mad. I know I must sound so to you. This is not the way I usually behave. How can I expect you to understand what has happened to me today when I can scarcely understand it myself.'

'I don't see how you can possibly break off your engagement because . . . because of me,' Charlotte said at last, her voice almost a whisper. 'We've only just met and we hardly know one another.'

'I'll admit that. But I am sure at least of this one thing . . . that I cannot possibly be in love with Phillipa if I can feel as I do about you. And if that is true, I have no right to go on with an engagement . . . for Phillipa's sake more than anyone's. I hate the thought of hurting her, but to live a lie would hurt her far more. Besides, she is very young . . . I think she will find someone else in time.'

'You judge her feelings for you very lightly!' Charlotte said seriously. 'If she really loves you, she might never get married to anyone else. Some people love only once in a lifetime.'

'Even if that were true of Phillipa, I could not marry her now that I realize I don't feel for her what a future husband should feel. Fondness is not enough. Surely you, as a woman, would agree that it would be all the more intolerable to love someone and have to live with them knowing they did not feel the same for you? This is nineteen fifty-six, Charlotte. I know it is not a nice thing to have to do, but whether you agree to see me again or not, I must do it. Dishonesty is something I dislike so much I could not be a party to it even if I believed it to be for someone's good.'

'He is right!' Charlotte thought. 'It is not a question of moral fibre or courage' . . . it took more of both to hurt someone than to give up what you most wanted in life . . . unless you were callous and indifferent to other people's feelings. Surely Meridan was neither of these things. Yet how could she know except by instinct? And could one's instinct not be warped by the intensity of one's emotions? She *wanted* to believe he was right . . . that he was acting from the best and most sensible of motives.

'Charlotte, I am not going to ask you if you will see me again. I want you to understand that except by accident, you are not responsible in any way for what I have to tell Phillipa. If you would prefer it so, I'll not make any move to see you until I am quite free.'

That was entirely fair . . . yet ought

she not to refuse to see him again . . . ever . . . no matter what happened? He might then go back to his childhood sweetheart.

'I cannot!' Charlotte thought. 'I know, somewhere deep down in my heart, that I belong to him . . . that he belongs to me. I knew it when I saw him by the door of the church. He knows it, too, just as surely as I do. How can I let him go out of my life?'

Yet to refuse to meet him again until he was free must surely mean an added incentive to get free. Would it not be better for all of them if she and Meridan were to see as much of each other as possible in these next few weeks and discover quite surely how they felt for one another? Then, at least, when he went to Phillipa to ask her to release him from his engagement . . . if it came to that . . . he would be sure he was doing the right thing.

'Please tell me what you are thinking!' his quiet, slow voice beseeched her. 'You sit there looking as if your thoughts were a million miles away and I had no part in them. You cannot know how important it is to me that you should understand how I feel, crazy as it may seem. Liz would tell you that I am acting quite out of character and that I am normally a steady, unemotional, unimpulsive kind of fellow.'

Charlotte seized on his own words to try to express her own feelings. She said:

'I do understand, I think. But you will agree that it is wrong to trust these . . . these kind of instantaneous attractions. You say yourself that you are acting out of character. That is true of me, too. I . . . I knew when I met you this afternoon that I wanted to see you again. But that does not mean we are in love . . . or even falling in love. I think it would be wrong to break your engagement until you are quite sure.'

'Charlotte!' Her heart leapt into her throat at the caress he seemed to make of the mere sound of her name. It pulsed there in soft breathless beats and she was glad that the room was filled with people so that he could not touch her. More than anything in the world, she wanted to feel his hand on hers, yet she was also deeply afraid of the emotions that might result since even the tone of his voice could leave her trembling. Shyly, she raised her eyes to his and in them he read the answer to his own feelings.

'Dance with me now!' he said, suddenly determined.

As if a dream, she got to her feet and moved out among the other couples. The orchestra was playing a slow foxtrot and the lights were soft and not too bright. Then Meridan's arms were round her and her body seemed to become one with his. An instant later, his cheek was against hers and his arms had tightened round her and she had, as she had known, no resistance.

'This is heaven and madness, both!' he whispered against her hair. 'To think that yesterday I did not even know you existed!'

For a moment, she was chilled by the thought. It could not happen like this . . . so suddenly, so surely, so irrevocably! Then she, too, felt the wonder of a Fate that had brought them together . . . a Fate that until today had kept them apart. And it was not too late. Engagements could be broken . . . they were not betrothals as they had been in the past.

Charlotte felt one instant of blinding pity for Phillipa, lying in hospital unknowing of what Fate held in store for her, and then her eyes closed and she gave herself unrestrictedly to the wonder of dancing in Meridan's arms.

2

They drove home at midnight in Meridan's car. Charlotte sat in a silence born not so much of fatigue, although she was tired, but from a sudden cooling of her senses. Dancing endlessly throughout the evening in Meridan's arms she had given up coherent thought or reason, and blindly admitted to herself that she had never been so happy, so delirious, so perfectly in love. They moved together as one person, in complete harmony, and she had been sure that the world could hold no more wonderful an evening than this.

She had known that Meridan felt the same way. Once in a while he would whisper something against her soft hair, telling her there were stars in her eyes, that he had never been so happy, that to dance with her for the rest of the time was all he asked of life. It must have been obvious for any other couple on the floor who cared to glance their way that they were in love, and certainly Bess had noticed. It was she who had brought Charlotte back to cold reality. As they joined one another in search of their coats before leaving, Bess put a hand on Charlotte's arm.

'Don't think I'm being a tell-tale, darling, but . . . but before this goes any farther, I do think you should know Meridan is engaged to Phillipa Bates.'

'I do know!' Charlotte said, a sudden tiredness sweeping away the radiance. 'I know Phillipa is a friend of yours and this must seem rather horrible to you, Bess, but what else can I do? I can't pretend to Meridan that he means nothing to me. I did try but I don't seem to be very good at pretending . . . Meridan took one look at my face and saw for himself. Bess, you know so much more about being in love than I do . . . it's the first time for me. Do you think it would be wrong for Meridan to break his engagement? It's what he wants to do.'

'Darling, how should I know? Any fool watching you two this evening could see what was happening. Frankly I did wonder what Meridan was up to, although I was quite willing to withhold judgement on him. He isn't the sort to go round flirting with girls when he's engaged to someone else. I've known him on and off for some years and I like him awfully . . . he's a thoroughly nice type. All the same, it does seem a bit tough on Pippa . . . she worships the ground he treads on . . . has for ages and ages.'

'Couldn't it be a kind of childish hero-worship?' Charlotte asked a little desperately. 'I mean, he's a lot older than her. Do you really mean you think she mightn't get over it in time?'

Bess shrugged her plump shoulders and suddenly smiled.

'I don't know, really I don't. But I do know this, Charlotte . . . you aren't the type to lose your heart twice in a lifetime. For goodness' sake go carefully. It's so *unlike* you to fall in a heap in the space of a few hours! It's high time it happened and I always knew it would . . . but all the same, I wish it hadn't been Meridan!'

There had been no further time for confidences and they had quickly found their coats and made up their faces and rejoined the men. Even after the cheerful good nights had been said as the two couples separated on the pavement outside the restaurant, Bess's 'I wish it hadn't been Meridan' ran with a chilling persistency through Charlotte's mind.

'A penny for them, Charlotte!'

She jumped and turned her attention to the man driving beside her.

'I don't think you will really want to hear what I was thinking . . . ' she said hesitantly, and then with a rush: 'Oh, Meridan, I've been thinking of Phillipa. Can two people be happy at the expense of someone else?'

For a few moments, Meridan did not answer. Then he steered the car into the grass verge and switched off the engine.

He made no move to touch her and stared out of the windscreen, not looking at Charlotte's white, strained face.

'Look, Charlotte, even if you told me now that this evening had meant nothing at all to you . . . that you were just having a good time, flirting with me if you like, and that you'd prefer never to see me again, it wouldn't make any difference to what I have to do. So long as I believed I loved Philippa, then our engagement was a good thing, right for both of us and right for her. But *I* wasn't 'having a good time' this evening in the sense that I was just amusing myself with you. I wasn't flirting with you or playing a game. This evening has been the most wonderful of my whole life. I've fallen in love with you, Charlotte, and I could never marry any other woman now. Beyond everything else that might lie in the future for either of us, I could not in all good conscience marry Phillipa now. Surely you can understand that?'

His words were reasonable enough and yet still she could not let it rest there. The thought of the other younger girl lying in hospital not knowing that her dreams were so soon to be shattered, would not leave her free.

'Meridan, you cannot possibly be sure you love me. You know so very little about me . . . or I about you . . . I mean, what we're really like deep down inside ourselves. I'm not sure I even know myself! Tonight . . . the whole day, I've been a different person from the Charlotte my mother, Bess . . . my friends, have known in the past. You say this has never happened to you before and I believe that. But should we trust something that is so new to us both? Is it right to make someone else unhappy at this stage? Perhaps in a few days . . . weeks . . . we'll feel differently. This might not last . . . and then you will have hurt Phillipa for nothing.'

He turned then to look at her in the faint light of a distant on-coming car.

'I could never go back to believing

myself in love with Phillipa . . . not after this!' he said with a conviction she could not doubt. 'But if it would make you happier, darling, I'll say nothing for a few weeks. But I'll have to speak to Pippa as soon as I see her again. I could not pretend to her . . . surely you see that. And I think, anyway, she might guess. I'm not a good actor. But the last thing in the world I want is that you should reproach *yourself* for what I have to do. You are only indirectly involved.'

For a moment or two, Charlotte did not speak. She was trying to put herself in Phillipa's place . . . to understand what it meant to give your heart to a man who did not love you; to be married to someone to whom you were only a burden. How awful it must be to make some loving gesture, only to have it pass unnoticed or carefully avoided! It would be better to be alone . . . to know at least that you could give the man you loved happiness by giving him his freedom. Would Phillipa see it that way? She and her brother were, in Meridan's own admission, his oldest friends . . . and those of his sister, Elizabeth. She would be sure to meet them. If Phillipa hated her, Charlotte, for taking Meridan away from her, it would make it difficult for everyone concerned. Meridan had said he owned a small bachelor flat in town but he spent every week-end and holiday at home. A complete break from Phillipa would hardly be possible since she lived so near his house.

'Charlotte, *darling*!'

'I don't want him to kiss me!' Charlotte thought wildly a moment before his arms went round her, drawing her close against him. Then, as his lips touched her mouth for the first time, she knew that there was nothing she desired so much. Feelings of which she had been unaware until this glorious awakening, stirred her to a passionate response that was really her true nature. When she drew away from him at last, her cheeks were flushed, her eyes shy as she smiled at him shakily.

Meridan, too, was deeply disturbed. Her obvious innocence had forced him to keep a strong curb on his own emotions; passions which he, too, was discovering for the first time in himself. His life in the forces had not been devoid of amorous affairs but they had never touched him deeply, and afterwards he had always felt a little ashamed of his part in them. With Phillipa, it had been different. He had been attracted to her with a faint stirring of emotion that paled into utter insignificance beside this feeling Charlotte aroused in him. He had not known when he asked Pippa to marry him that he might feel one day like this for another woman, and his affection for Phillipa had been easy and satisfying, remaining as it did on a light, almost casual plane. He had kissed her good night once or twice after a dance, sat talking to her for a while with his arms round her, in a kind of friendly intimacy that had no connection at all

44

with the fierce exaltation and burning desire that Charlotte aroused in him with one kiss. Every part of his body and mind was touched alight with this new miracle and he knew without any shadow of doubt that he was really and truly in love with her . . . that he wanted her for his wife and that he could only love her more as he grew to know her better.

'I think I'd better take you home!' he said at last, reluctantly. 'You have to work tomorrow, don't you?'

She nodded, knowing that tired as she was, she would willingly stay here with him until dawn if he asked her. Free will seemed to have deserted her utterly and she wanted only to feel his lips on hers again. But he did not take her back into his arms until they were outside her house, and then only for one last good-night kiss.

'Parting from you is like a physical amputation!' he said with a smile she tried to emulate. 'I'll ring you tomorrow, Charlotte. Perhaps we could lunch together if you're going to be in the City?'

'All right!' she said breathlessly, and gave him her office number. Mr. Everwell would not like it but she didn't care! Nothing mattered but that she would see Meridan again so soon.

Partly because she was tired but mostly because she was waiting for Meridan's phone call, Charlotte was unable to concentrate on her work next morning. Mr. Everwell had to correct her three times for unnecessary errors and ended by asking her if she felt unwell. Usually she was so reliable and sensible.

Then the phone call came while she was taking dictation.

'It seems to be for you, Miss Matthews,' he said, his hand over the mouthpiece. 'You know I don't like personal calls in office hours!'

But he gave her the receiver, wondering at the bright colour that had spread suddenly to her cheeks.

'Charlotte!'

She wanted to say 'Darling, darling, darling . . . ' so great was her joy at hearing his voice, but Mr. Everwell's severe gaze reduced her to a brief:

'Oh, hullo!'

'Charlotte, I suspect that you are busy so I won't keep you now. Can you meet me at the Hungaria at one?'

'Yes, I'll be there!' Charlotte said. 'Good-bye now!'

After that, concentration became easier and she managed to complete the morning's work to Mr. Everwell's satisfaction. At a quarter to one, she hurried off to catch a bus to the Haymarket. She had hoped to be there before him so that she could go and tidy herself first, but he was waiting for her by the door. Catching sight of him before he saw her, Charlotte all but halted in her path. She had wondered so much how she would feel when a new day replaced the magic of the old one . . . how she would explain if in fact nothing of last night's miracle lived through this second meeting. But the fears and doubts were swept away in a second as she saw him and she felt only shyness . . . and a faint unease at the seriousness of his expression.

'Charlotte!' he greeted her, the pressure of his hand on hers warm through her glove. 'I'm glad you're early . . . there is so much to talk about!'

For a moment he studied her face, her eyes, and then his expression changed and he smiled and said:

'How beautiful you look! This morning I woke up and told myself I must have dreamed it all . . . that when I saw you again, I would wonder what could have happened to me.'

'And now?'

'Now I know my heart was right . . . that you are beautiful and that I love you!' he said quietly. 'Come, darling, let's find our table. I'm afraid I have some bad news to impart!'

Having ordered a drink for them, he turned to her and again his face was serious and anxious. He came directly to the point.

'It's Phillipa! She's very ill. Liz phoned me this morning to tell me. Apparently the appendix burst when she was on the operating table and now they think peritonitis has set in. They've asked her parents to stay in the hospital to be near her.'

All Charlotte's happiness vanished at his words.

'I'm sorry! How . . . how serious is it?'

'I don't know. Liz thinks I should stay by in case I'm wanted. Charlotte, you realize that this makes a bit of difference to us for the time being? I'd hoped to take you out tonight . . . or if you felt you ought not to leave your mother, to visit you at home . . . at least to be with you some way or other. Now I'll have to stay home in case a call comes through. Liz thinks Phillipa may ask for me. Besides, neither of us could enjoy ourselves very much knowing she was so ill.'

'Of course not!' Charlotte agreed, hating herself for the question that had risen despite herself to the forefront of her mind . . . how much did this matter to Meridan? How much did he really care?

As if in direct answer to her thought, he said:

'No matter what happens, I'll always be fond of Pippa . . . she's like a very special younger sister to me. I hate to think of her in any kind of pain.'

'I understand!' Charlotte said. 'You'll let me know how she gets on? I'll be worrying, too.' And strangely enough, that was true. She might never have met Phillipa, and yet already the younger girl had assumed a personality for her, part rival, part friend.

'Well, meanwhile, let's eat!' Meridan said, trying to shrug off the immediate worry. He beckoned the waiter and at Charlotte's request, ordered for both of them. While they waited, Meridan said suddenly:

'You haven't changed . . . since yesterday? It's still the same for you, too?'

She knew what he meant . . . knew so exactly how he had wakened to doubt the reality of what had happened to them both. She smiled at him and shook her head.

'It's still the same, Meridan. I'm afraid it must show on my face. I'm sure Mr. Everwell noticed a difference . . . my work suffered abominably!'

'Good!' said Meridan smiling. 'Oh, darling, I wish I could tell you how happy I am . . . despite everything. Just to be sitting here with you is peace and perfection. To think I could have lived for twenty-eight years without knowing you. I suppose all lovers feel this way. I grudge every moment of your life that I know nothing of. Tell me more about yourself. Were you a very serious, thoughtful little girl?'

Charlotte laughed.

'No! A bit of a dreamer, Mother tells me . . . but I was naughty enough. I don't think I started to be what you call serious or thoughtful until Father got ill. I suppose it was partly growing up, too. Now I think about it, I feel rather like the Sleeping Princess . . . as if I'd been asleep these last six years and you have brought me to life again.'

'Life is only just beginning . . . for both of us!' Meridan said earnestly. 'We're going to have such a wonderful future, Charlotte . . . lots of times like these to get to know each other. Then, when you are sure, we'll be married and start a home together. Where would you like to live?'

She hadn't thought about the future in such definite terms. Something in her rejoiced that he should be thinking already of marriage and a home together, and yet another part of her was suddenly sobered at the thought. For one thing, there was her mother. She could never leave her alone. And there was Phillipa . . . they had no right to be discussing a future together while *her* future lay in the balance. She felt a sudden wish to meet Meridan's sister, Elizabeth; as if by knowing a relation of his, she could see more objectively the man sitting beside her. She asked Meridan on the spur of the moment and saw his surprise.

'But of course you'll have to meet Liz!' he said eagerly. 'I know she'll want to meet you . . . at least, I'm sure she will . . . ' But now that he stopped to think about it, he was by no means sure. Liz and Pippa had been friends since they were tiny children. Liz would be almost as upset as Pippa at the broken engagement and in no mood to welcome Pippa's successor.

Then, as he looked at Charlotte, feeling only his own overwhelming love for her, he rejected the idea that Liz might not like her. How could anyone fail to love Charlotte? Manlike, he could not see beneath his own immediate emotions.

'Liz will probably come up to town to see Phillipa when she's convalescent!' he said. 'I'll arrange for us all to have lunch together. You'll like her, Charlotte!'

'Yes, I'll like her,' Charlotte thought,

'but will she like me? I'll like her because she is related to Meridan and dear to him. But how can she like me when I'm coming between her brother and her dearest friend?' How would she feel if she had a brother engaged to Bess and then some strange girl caused him to jilt Bess who was really like a sister to her?

'I'd hate her!' Charlotte thought. But, fortunately, the arrival of their lunch put an end to such unhappy thoughts and it was only as Meridan said good-bye to her, promising to ring her that evening at her home, that she felt again that chill of apprehension.

★　★　★

In the private room of one of the big London hospitals, Mr. and Mrs. Bates sat by their only daughter's bedside, their faces distraught with worry. Both of them knew that she might die. The surgeon had been perfectly frank with them, for which they were grateful. The poison from the burst appendix had spread over her whole body. They were hoping that the constant penicillin injections would gradually get the poison under control but until now, the girl did not seem to be reacting to the drug. There were other drugs and everything that could be given her would naturally be available. The next forty-eight hours would probably decide the issue. Meanwhile Phillipa lay in a semi-coma, sometimes delirious, a nurse constantly in attendance.

There was nothing her parents could do except pray. They sat for a while at the bedside, staring down at the flushed fevered face, hearing the incoherent mumbling and growing more anxious with every moment. Only the nurse seemed calm and unmoved, although her face clearly showed her concern for the parents.

Phillippa was of medium build, with a round, rather childish face, and fair hair that curled naturally above a straight, youthful brow and hazel-green eyes. She and her brother, John, had the same colouring and were alike in many ways as well as in feature. Both were thoroughly nice, good children of which any parent would be proud, although neither had any distinct talent or academic ability. Both lived for their riding and horses and, since the family were reasonably well off even in these times, there had been no necessity to train Phillipa for a job. In any event, she intended to marry Meridan before long, and so a short domestic course had followed the end of school, and now she was just filling in time till she married and settled down.

Mrs. Bates liked Meridan but she had sometimes thought he was a little old for Pippa . . . and a little serious. Pippa was always laughing, always gay and full of fun. Even in their late teens, she and dear Liz still giggled just as they had used to do as schoolgirls when anything struck them as particularly amusing. Meridan's attitude to Pippa was rather that of an older brother but maybe this was simply due to the fact that they had been, in a way, brother and sister for so many years. There was no doubt that Meridan was very fond of Pippa and would make an excellent husband for the young girl. Mrs. Bates knew her own husband approved of the match. But the two young people had been in no great hurry to marry and she herself believed a fairly long engagement to be a good thing under the circumstances. Pippa was always meeting young friends of her brother's down at the racing stables and it would give her time to change her mind about Meridan if she were going to do so ... not that her mother really believed she would. Pippa had idolized Meridan ever since she had been tiny, and she could see nothing wrong in him. That childish hero-worship had grown into a girl's adoration and Meridan had only to make a statement for Pippa to be convinced that it was right just because Meridan said it!

Now the future she had thought so

much about was in question and for quite different reasons . . . Pippa, her only cherished daughter might die! Mrs. Bates could not bear the thought. Over and over again she said to her husband that nowadays people just did not die from something so ordinary as an appendix.

Yet one glance at Pippa's bed, surrounded by tubes and bottles and charts, and with that young nurse sitting so quietly on the far side, was sufficient proof of the seriousness of her condition.

The nurse looked up and saw the older woman's eyes. Kindly she said:

'It must be nearly lunch-time, Mrs. Bates. I know you probably don't feel like eating, but you don't want to get ill yourself at this juncture.'

'Nurse is quite right,' said Mr. Bates, rising and helping his wife to her feet. 'Come dear. We're doing no good here, anyway!'

After they had gone, the nurse looked again at the temperature chart and felt again with skilled fingers for the racing pulse. She did not, herself, have very high hopes for this patient. She had, of course, grown used to death in her six years of nursing, yet somehow the thought of the young girl dying touched her beyond her usual immunity and she felt pity stirring her. She wished that there were something *she* could do, and knew exactly how helpless poor Mrs. Bates must be feeling. She wondered, too, about the fiancé. She had noticed the ring on her patient's finger, and knew that he had phoned daily to inquire for her. If things got worse, he'd be allowed to visit her. Meanwhile, the patient was in no state even to be aware that he was there. He must be worried, too, thought the nurse. For a moment, worry for other people oppressed her and she was glad when the door opened and another nurse relieved her while she went for lunch. When she came back, the patient's condition was worse and outside the door, the surgeon and doctor were in consultation, discussing how they might yet save the young girl's life.

3

Meridan was surprised and pleased to find Elizabeth waiting in his bachelor flat when he got back from the office, more particularly because a lonely evening awaited him while he stayed home for news of Phillipa. He greeted Elizabeth with a brotherly hug.

'I'll get you a sherry!' he said. 'You look worn out!'

'I'm so wretchedly worried about Pippa!' Elizabeth said, sitting back in the comfortable leather armchair. 'She's worse and there's talk of another operation. I gather there's some doubt as to whether she's in a fit state to face the operating table. You must be out of your mind yourself with anxiety.'

Meridan made no reply but came back with sherry for Elizabeth and a whisky-and-soda for himself. He sat down opposite her and gave her a worried glance.

'I'd no idea things were so serious!' he said at last. 'Liz, they don't think . . . she'll die . . . do they?'

Liz bit her lip.

'It looks as if that's possible!' she admitted. 'Aunt Jo was in tears when I spoke to her this afternoon but Uncle Bill told me it was touch and go. What did they say to you?'

'I was waiting to get back here to phone,' Meridan told her. 'I'll ring the hospital now.'

He went out to the tiny lobby and dialled the number Liz called to him. He decided not to question Pippa's father but to speak to her surgeon. Unfortunately, he was operating, but Meridan gathered from Matron that they had postponed any decision about a further operation until morning; also that there was no point in him going round to the hospital himself.

'Gosh, I'm sorry, Merry!' Liz said as he sat down again, his face tired and white with strain.

'I'd no idea it was so desperately

serious until you told me just now,' Meridan said thoughtfully. 'It seems rather awful to think of it, but I . . . I was out dancing till the early hours last night!'

'Dancing? You? But whoever with?' Liz asked incredulously.

'With a girl I met at the wedding rehearsal . . . as a matter of fact it was a friend of Bess's who was called in to take Pippa's place as bridesmaid.'

'You mean for Angela's wedding on Saturday?'

Meridan nodded. The incredulity in his sister's voice had unnerved him a little. He decided to be frank with her.

'Liz, I've got something I want to say . . . to explain. I suppose it'll seem a bit callous talking like this when Pippa is so ill . . . but well, I must talk to someone.'

His sister gave him a look of pure surprise. What could have happened to Meridan? He was undoubtedly in deadly earnest about something . . . and worried, too.

'You know I won't split!' she said, using a childhood expression for promising secrecy.

'It isn't a question of that!' Meridan said, smiling for an instant at the phrase. 'Everyone will have to know in due course. But it's becoming rather complicated just for the moment . . . because of Pippa being so ill. Liz, I've fallen in love!'

'You've *what?*' his sister asked, her brows drawn down in complete amazement. 'What *are* you talking about, Merry?'

Meridan slowly lit his pipe before replying. He sensed intuitively that Elizabeth was not in the mood to receive this particular confidence and yet he had to tell her. He could not spend the evening in her company without speaking of Charlotte.

As briefly as he could, he told her about the wedding rehearsal . . . the meeting with Charlotte when they had both thought they had met somewhere before; how Bess had persuaded him to make up a foursome with herself and Charlotte and Jeremy Patricks; how the evening had ended.

'I thought when I woke up this morning that I must have imagined the whole thing. It seemed so improbable,' he ended his story. 'Then I met Charlotte for lunch and I knew it was a fact. I want to marry her, Liz. I'm really and truly in love.'

'But Pippa . . . you're going to marry Pippa!' Elizabeth cried. 'You can't possibly turn against her at a time like this!'

'It isn't a question of 'turning against her'!' Meridan said almost angrily. 'I'll always be fond of Pippa . . . and I hope very much we'll always be friends. But I discovered when I met Charlotte that I just don't love Pippa the way a man should love the girl he's going to marry. Whether I marry Charlotte or not or even whether I'm in love with her or not isn't important . . . not to my decision, I mean. I have to break off the engagement because I'm not in love with Pippa. *I know now I never have been.*'

Elizabeth sat in stunned silence. She adored her older brother and since they had both been grown up, seldom ever disagreed with him, let alone quarrelled with him. Very like him to look at, with dark hair, and dark eyes and an olive complexion that together gave her a slightly Italian type of beauty, Liz Avebury was also like her brother in temperament . . . warm, loyal to her friends, an implacable enemy to those who deceived or let her down. She was young enough to believe that the world held only two points of view, right or wrong, and was seldom in her own mind in doubt as to which was which. This tendency to dogmatize was over-looked by those of her family and friends who loved her because if she discovered herself mistaken, she was the first to admit it . . . the first to apologize for her mistake. Meridan, who had lived ten years longer and had a much wider experience of life, had tempered his views now to a more factual acceptance of life . . . that there could, and more often than not were, as many 'greys' as blacks or whites. But, like his sister, he had only to be convinced that he was right in his own mind for him to go wholeheartedly for what he believed in. He was as incapable of dishonesty as Elizabeth and both had been in trouble at times for their refusal to dissimulate or prevaricate.

Watching his sister's face, Meridan guessed a little of her thoughts. He had expected that she would remain loyal to Pippa . . . that it would be a great personal disappointment to her too, if he did not marry her future sister-in-law. Yet he believed she would understand that he had no alternative. One could not possibly pretend a love one did not feel, and marriage without love on both sides surely seemed as wrong to her as it did to him.

'Merry, you'll break Pippa's heart . . . she'll never get over it!'

Meridan bit on the stem of his pipe.

'I think that's a little dramatic . . . and not quite true,' he said quietly. 'I believe now that we just drifted into this engagement as much because everybody else wanted it as because we wanted it ourselves. I don't think Pippa knows the meaning of the word love any more than I did until last night.'

'That's untrue and unfair!' Elizabeth cried hotly. 'Pippa has loved you ever since she was a tiny girl. When she grew up, that love developed into a more adult emotion and I knew years before you even guessed that she hoped one day you'd ask her to marry you. She confided in me when she was only sixteen that she would never marry anyone else.'

'How could she judge what she wanted at sixteen?' Meridan argued sensibly. 'That's exactly what I am trying to point out to you, Liz. She's never really been around with anyone else. In time she might meet and fall in love with someone who'll make her a much better husband than I could.'

Elizabeth looked at her brother with a mixture of instinctive belief in his judgement and dislike for what he was saying.

'I can't think how you can bear to talk this way when Pippa is so ill. Who is this girl who can have such a horrible effect on you?'

'That's cruel and quite unjustified, Liz!' Meridian said sharply. 'Charlotte has nothing at all to do with my decision. When she agreed to join the foursome last night, she didn't even know I was engaged. She is only indirectly responsible in that I happened to understand for the first time through her what it meant to be really in love. If you could forget Pippa for a moment, I'd like to tell you about her. I feel sure you'd like her, Liz, and I hoped you'd be able to meet.'

'I've certainly no wish to meet her!' Elizabeth cried hotly. 'It would be completely unfair to Pippa to side with you against her. I love Pippa even if you don't! As to forgetting her for a moment . . . how *can* you, Merry, at a time like this?'

'You're being childish!' her brother said flatly. 'We'd better end this discussion and go and get something to eat. We can get a quick meal at the restaurant downstairs. Are you going home tonight?'

'Yes! I drove up this afternoon,' Elizabeth said more calmly. And then, changing her mind, she added: 'Perhaps I might stay at the club overnight, just in case Pippa is worse tomorrow. Merry, promise me you won't speak of this to anyone . . . anyone at all, until she's better?'

'But how silly you're being, Liz!' Meridan said. 'As if I would!'

'Well, I've no doubt *she* is pressing you to get your freedom as quickly as possible!'

'Liz!' Meridan said sharply. 'I've no need to answer such a silly remark, but just to put you right, Charlotte is very much against my breaking off my engagement in a hurry. She is trying to persuade me to wait. In fact, she has very sensibly agreed to our seeing as much of each other as possible these next few weeks so that I can be sure about the way I feel. She thinks I might discover when I know her better that I'm not in love with her at all.'

Elizabeth digested this slowly. Either this girl was a very decent type or else a very clever one. She knew a sudden curiosity to meet her . . . yet at the same time, she was sure she could never like her . . . never forgive her for what this would do to Pippa. It had all been so perfect until now . . . she, herself, to marry John, and Merry and Pippa . . . they could have teamed up for holidays and family reunions would have been perfect since they had always seemed like one family anyway. John would be terribly upset, too. He'd looked forward to having Merry as a brother-in-law. Oh, if only her mother and father had agreed to them marrying before Merry met this girl.

Yet, even as the thought flashed

across her mind, Elizabeth was honest enough to admit two things to herself . . . that Merry and Pippa had been in no great hurry to get married, and that it would have been terrible to discover when there was no hope of freedom that you did not love the woman you had married, or that your husband did not love you.

Merry was right in a way . . . it was better not to marry unless you were absolutely sure you were in love. But how could he possibly be so certain that he wasn't, just because of one date with a different girl? Unless he really had fallen in love with this Charlotte . . . love at first sight. It was something Elizabeth did not fully believe in. After all, she had never experienced the emotion herself. Her love for John had come gradually through the long years of knowing each other, growing from a childhood friendship into the firm, steady devotion they now felt for one another. It seemed to her to be the only perfect way to come to marriage . . . knowing all there was to know about each other's faults and failings and accepting them, just as one loved the good qualities. It was so safe. There was nothing they could discover about one another after marriage to spoil everything. Theirs was a love that could only grow deeper as it was fulfilled in its physical union, and by the shared experiences of marriage.

Softened by her thoughts, Elizabeth stood up and impulsively linked her arm through her brother's.

'Merry, do be careful, won't you? You and Pippa have always seemed so right for one another. Please think it over a long while before you break her heart. I do see that you can't marry her if you don't love her . . . but at least be quite sure you don't! Are you certain you aren't confusing love with physical attraction? That what you feel for this other girl isn't just a kind of new excitement? Naturally, that doesn't exist between you and Pippa after all these years of knowing each other, but what you feel for Pippa might be more real and lasting than this other affair.'

Softened in turn by her more reasonable and understanding remarks, Meridan said truthfully:

'I know it must be difficult for you to appreciate, Liz. To be quite frank, I find it hard to believe myself. All I am quite, quite sure of is that what I feel for Pippa isn't enough for marriage. It isn't just a matter of physical feeling. I can suddenly see quite clearly . . . just as if a picture had come into focus after being a blurred outline . . . that I have only a fondness for Pippa . . . almost the same feeling I have for you, Liz. I agree that we do have many things in common . . . share many interests, but then we were brought up to the same way of life and it is bound to be so. But Pippa and I have never been really close to one another's thoughts. I don't think I've ever tried to get close to her that way . . . we've just had a good time together. With Charlotte it is quite different. Strangers as we are to one another, I seem to know intuitively what she is thinking . . . feeling . . . just as she seems to guess at what lies in my heart. I told you before that when we first caught sight of one another, we were each sure we had met somewhere before. In fact we had not. It was a kind of spiritual recognition. Liz, dear, do say you will meet her . . . then you will perhaps understand what I'm trying to tell you.'

'All right!' Elizabeth said hesitantly. 'But not yet. Merry . . . not while Pippa is so ill. It's all going to be terribly difficult, isn't it? Pippa will be home convalescing and she'll be a great deal in our house with me. You'll want to bring this other girl down to meet Father and Mother, and that means she and Pippa will meet.'

'I know!' Meridan said, biting his lip. 'But I hope that Pippa will be able to accept this fairly lightly . . . once she gets used to the idea. Perhaps we could have a kind of weekend house-party when I first bring Charlotte home, so that we aren't paired off quite so obviously. I'll find someone really attractive to bring down to squire Pippa. You can make it easier for all of us if you're willing, Liz.'

'It isn't going to be easy for me!' his sister said doubtfully. 'Pippa's my dearest friend. It won't be easy for me . . . or for John . . . to make Charlotte welcome. I doubt if Mother or Dad will want to, either.'

Meridan did not press the point for he could see how divided his family's loyalties must be under the circumstances. Pippa was like their own daughter to his mother and father. Then his face cleared. For how could anyone fail to love Charlotte when they knew her? There was something so very obviously good and sweet and gentle about her . . . no trait that he had so far discovered that could grate on their nerves or cause them to feel antagonistic towards her.

He remembered suddenly that he had promised to telephone her and decided to wait till Liz had gone home or to the club. He knew he could not talk naturally in front of his sister and he did not want Charlotte to think that he had changed in any way.

'Come on, let's forget our worries and eat!' he said, shrugging his shoulders and reaching for his coat. But although Liz ate a surprisingly large dinner, he found his own appetite quite gone. It was not going to be so easy to forget one's worries after all.

Elizabeth remained in London for three days. During that time, neither she nor Meridan saw Charlotte although he phoned her each evening. The reason was that news from the hospital was very grave indeed. Infection had set in and spread to the lymph glands, and it had been decided that there was no alternative if Pippa's life was to be saved but to perform a partial hysterectomy. The doctors had reached the decision reluctantly, knowing what this must mean to a young girl. While she might lead a normal married life in every other respect

76

she would never be able to have a child. Since she was engaged to be married, this must inevitably be a very difficult thing for her to accept although she was as yet far too ill to be told about it. But there was, perhaps fortunately, no alternative, and therefore no heart-rending decision for her parents to make. The operation had to be done and immediately. Mr. and Mrs. Bates gave their consent for at this moment, they thought only of saving their daughter's life. It fell to Elizabeth to tell Meridan and to explain exactly what the operation meant. She was nearly in tears as she did so.

'Merry, don't you see what this will mean to Pippa when she finds out what they've done to her? She'll believe that you've broken the engagement because of it. It'll make her feel a kind of cripple all her life. She'll never marry. I know that's how I'd feel. It would be different if you'd broken the engagement before. Then she couldn't possibly believe that it was because she couldn't bear you a child. The fact of being sterile isn't too hard to accept if you're not in love and haven't any plans to be married anyway. It's happened before to lots and lots of girls. But for it to happen this way . . . Merry, you just *can't*!'

For quite five minutes, Meridan sat lost in thought. Then without explanation, he stood up and said abruptly:

'I have to see Charlotte. I probably won't be back till late so don't wait in for me, Liz. Go to a flick or something. I'll see you tomorrow.'

Meridan ran down the three flights of stairs, not waiting for the lift. He hurriedly got his car out of the garage, and drove with exaggerated care and thoughtfulness through the crowded streets and out to the suburb where Charlotte lived with her mother. He had no idea what he would say to her . . . no certainty even that she was at home. But his whole being was crying out for a need to see her and he felt that if only he could do so for a few moments, somehow the nightmarish quality of this new problem would vanish.

It was nearly nine o'clock when he drew up outside the house and rang the doorbell. Charlotte opened the door to him, wearing light-weight black slacks and a pale blue cardigan over a crisply ironed white cotton shirt, for although it was officially Spring by the calendar, the evenings were still very cold.

Her dark hair had been caught back off her face with a pale blue ribbon and Meridan's first thought was that she looked incredibly young and unsophisticated. When he had last seen her, at lunch in town, she had been wearing a neat grey tailored coat and skirt with a tiny petunia-coloured hat perched on her head, and she had looked the part of a competent woman secretary. Now she looked sixteen and with the bright colour rushing into her cheeks at sight of him, he knew himself to be as captivated by this new Charlotte as he had been by the girl he'd carried in his mind since last he saw her.

'May I come in?' he asked.

'Mother's gone to bed. I was cleaning

the silver!' Charlotte was suddenly shy. 'There's a fire in the sitting-room. I'll get you a drink!'

He followed her into the tiny hall . . . remembering again the night he had come to collect her before the dinner-dance. Charlotte's home, so much smaller and unpretentious than his own family house, was nevertheless tastefully and attractively furnished, and impeccably neat and tidy. The rooms smelt faintly of lavender and he associated it with the small frail woman who was Charlotte's mother. He was glad now that she had gone to bed and that he would have Charlotte to himself.

'I'm afraid there's only sherry!' she said, preceding him into the sitting-room. 'We've never re-stocked the drink cupboard since we ran out after Father died . . .'

Her voice died away as she felt his arms go round her from behind her where he stood. He turned her slowly round and then within a brief second, their lips met.

'Charlotte! I love you so much!'

Only after he had kissed her again was she able to whisper back her own love for him. And how surely she knew it now. Not seeing him these last few days had been a kind of torture for her . . . bearable only because of his phone calls in the evenings. The thought of them bore her through the long day and even longer nights when she could not sleep for thinking about him. She knew that Phillipa was dangerously ill . . . knew that Meridan had his sister in town with him . . . and that for the time being at least, it was impossible for them to meet. She had understood and yet she had craved for just a glimpse of him. Now, to be here in his arms, pressed tightly against his heart, was to realize all her dreams in one glorious instant.

Meridan moved slowly and drew her down beside him on the deeply cushioned settee, where she lay cradled comfortably in his arms. His lips were against her forehead, planting little kisses there and murmuring endearments. For a brief while, they were both ecstatically happy. Then Meridan placed a finger beneath her chin and turned her face towards his.

'Charlotte, darling! If you could only guess how much I've longed for this moment . . . how terribly I've missed you. Does it seem absurd to you that anyone could talk of missing someone whom until a week ago they lived quite unquestioningly without?'

'It's the same for me!' she told him honestly. 'I've tried to understand how my life was bearable until I met you! How I could have gone on from day to day without knowing what I was missing. How was I ever happy before I knew you, Meridan?'

The man's face was suddenly drawn and lined.

'Darling, if I could only promise you that this happiness could last. I suppose I ought not to have come to you like this . . . but I had to see you. I felt as if everything in the whole world was conspiring to keep me from you.'

'Is . . . is your sister very disapproving?' Charlotte tried to guess at the reason for his sudden loss of certainty about the future.

'It isn't really Liz . . . I suppose you'd call it Fate . . . ' Meridan said huskily. 'Charlotte . . . I want to do what's right . . . what I know in my heart to be best for everyone. I know I'm in love with you . . . desperately in love. I believe you love me, too, although we have known each other so short a while. I know, too, that I'm not, and never have been, in love with Phillipa. While there were only those facts to consider, the future was simple enough although the prospect of breaking an engagement is never very pleasant for a man to have to face. But now there is more in it than that.'

'Tell me!' Charlotte said quietly, her heart suddenly chilled despite his assurance of love.

'Pippa is desperately ill!' Meridan came straight to the point. 'If she doesn't have another operation tomorrow morning, she will certainly die. But that operation will make it impossible for her to have children. Charlotte, Liz thinks that Pippa will believe this to be the reason I'm asking her to release me from our engagement . . . that she'll suffer all her life believing it to be so. What in the name of Heaven am I to do now? I can't marry her . . . not feeling the way I do about you. I can't!'

Charlotte sat unmoving in stunned silence. Right from the start she had hated the idea of being the cause of another girl's unhappiness. Yet she had seen, too, that for Meridan to marry Phillipa when he did not love her, might hurt her more than a broken engagement would do. But now . . . to allow her to believe that she had ceased to be loved or wanted because she could no longer bear a child . . . that would be an unpardonable cruelty. Meridan's sister was right when she said it might affect Phillipa for the rest of her life. She herself would feel bitter and hopeless if the same thing happened to her. Phillipa would need extra love, extra care and understanding to help her accept the result of this operation.

It suddenly reached Charlotte's consciousness that this must surely mean an end to her love for Meridan . . . his for her. So unbearable was the realization that she turned to him with a little cry and was caught back into the strong, desperate clasp of his arms.

Neither spoke, for their lips had met again in kisses that were full of fear and desperation, as if they knew already they must be the last. Then Meridan drew away and said shakily:

'It's no good, Charlotte. I couldn't pretend! It isn't in me to live a lie. Even if I said nothing, Phillipa must guess the change in me. However hard I might try to deceive her, I don't think I could succeed. I can see that I must go on with the pretence for a while . . . at least until she is fully recovered. But surely if she meets you . . . sees us together . . . she will see for herself that we're in love . . . offer me a release from our engagement of her own accord. If she knows there is someone else I love, she cannot attribute it to this operation. Had I loved her, it would have made no difference to me, much as I would like a family one day.'

Hope, desire, conscience warred in Charlotte's tortured heart. What Meridan said could be the truth. If Phillipa saw them together and guessed for herself that they were in love, she could not believe Meridan had changed because of what had happened to her in hospital. In time . . . in time, Meridan would be free to marry her, Charlotte. Yet conscience said as clearly: 'Had you and Meridan not met on Monday, he would have been by her bedside, comforting her, sustaining her, believing he loved her!'

Tomorrow was Angela's wedding. Only five days since she and Meridan had turned their heads to see each other across the church . . . five days in which to fall so hopelessly and irrevocably in love . . . to bring so much unhappiness to three people. If she were to go out of Meridan's life after tomorrow . . . never see him again, wouldn't he, in time, begin to believe those five days had never existed. *She* might not forget . . . never again could she feel this terrible glorious emotion for any man . . . but he might go back to his first love. He must have loved Phillipa in a way, and Phillipa's need of him was surely as great, if not greater, than her own?

'No!' cried Charlotte's heart. 'No one could need him as I do. I love him. I cannot let him go.' Where . . . where did her duty lie? One could not love freely at the expense of one's conscience. Others had proved that was so and she knew it to be true. How could she and Meridan be happy together knowing they had between them ruined all chance of happiness for the other girl.

'There is one way!' Meridan cried suddenly. 'If only Liz will help. Charlotte, if you come to our house often . . . as Liz's new friend . . . surely in a little while, Pippa will see how we feel about each other. Once Pippa knows I love you, she cannot want to keep me tied to her . . . I'm sure she would not. If the break is gradual . . . and as much of her making as mine . . . then she cannot believe anything else but that, quite simply, I've fallen in love with you and wish to be free to marry you.'

'If I go to your home as your sister's friend, we would be deceiving her!' Charlotte said weakly.

'But only for her sake . . . to save her pain!' Meridan argued. 'Charlotte, don't let us allow anything to come between us. I cannot believe it would be right to do so . . . not just because I want you so badly. I know in my heart I could not hope to make Pippa happy now I've met you . . . now I know what love can mean. It is as much for her sake as for ours. It would be a useless sacrifice.'

'Is any sacrifice useless?' Charlotte questioned miserably. 'You say you cannot make her happy because you would not love her. But you are fond of her . . . you must be after all these years. If she has never known anything different, she will not necessarily know she is losing something . . . something precious and beautiful. Her life could still seem complete to her . . . just as ours did to us until we met!'

'Even if that were true . . . and I don't believe it, what of you, Charlotte? And me? I shall never cease loving you for as long as I live . . . even if I never see you again in my life. Will you forget me so easily? Find someone else to love . . . to marry . . . to give you children?'

'Meridan!'

She was in his arms again, her need of him, her love for him transparently written across her face, shining in her eyes.

'There could be no one else . . . ever!' she whispered.

'Then try my suggestion!' Meridan begged her desperately. 'If at any time we seem to cause Phillipa unnecessary

89

pain, then we'll talk again of what is right and wrong for us to do. Pippa and I were not to have been married until next year in any case. She is still so young it is possible she will herself change her mind. It could happen. Engagements are not betrothals as they used to be. Had it not been for this wretched operation, I would have had no doubt as to what to do. Charlotte, dearest darling Charlotte, tell me you'll wait . . . wait to see what happens. Don't walk out of my life now.'

'All right . . . I'll wait!' Charlotte promised weakly. But in her heart, she felt that her decision was wrong . . . that she should go out of Meridan's life now . . . before harm could come to the poor girl who had such a heavy burden to bear.

Then Phillipa was forgotten as Meridan took her once more into his arms and love, passion, desire, claimed them both in its oblivion and forgetfulness.

4

'Merry, darling, how *lovely* to see you!'

Pippa's large eyes stared at him from a pathetically white, thin little face. How ill she looked! It was ten days since her second operation and yet there was not a suspicion of colour in her cheeks. Her soft fair hair was tied back from her face with a pink ribbon matching the fluffy bedjacket she wore. She looked pathetic, young . . . very feminine and appealing. All Meridan's resolve to face Pippa with courage and even ruthlessness (for her sake even more than his own and Charlotte's) dissolved in a helpless feeling of protectiveness. How could one say anything to bring distress to someone who was still so obviously very weak and ill . . . whose eyes, even while they smiled their warm welcome to him, were sad and puzzled, like those of a hurt child.

'Pippa, my dear!'

He took the hand she held out to him and held it for a moment in his two large, warm ones, noting anxiously their thinness and the dry texture of the skin.

Suddenly, without warning, tears began to run down the girl's cheeks. Pity again surged through him in warm waves.

'Pippa, darling, please don't cry! You're going to get well now. There's nothing whatever to cry about!'

The first lie! How easily it had come to his lips . . . yet what man could have prevented himself from speaking so.

'Oh, Merry! Don't you know? Haven't they told you what they've done to me?'

The girl watched her fiancé anxiously through eyes still clouded by tears. In fact she had not been particularly distressed for herself when she had been told she might never have children. The maternal instinct was not strong in her, although perhaps in time it might have been awakened, and she had never felt any particular wish to have children although, when she had thought about it, she had supposed that she and Merry would raise a family some time or other. But she was still far too young to consider such a thing . . . still very immature for all her outward sophistication . . . and she had not even been in any great hurry to marry. The future had stretched before her in a bright, gay ribbon, hers to gather in at will. Meantime, she had everything she wanted, Merry to squire her round to dances and parties, horses to ride, John and Elizabeth for company when Merry was in town during the week working, and a large allowance from her parents which more than catered for her need for pretty clothes and perfumes and feminine trinkets.

It had never occurred to Phillipa that she was spoilt . . . that she had never yet in her nineteen years had to forgo anything she had seriously wanted. Life had been good to her and she had taken her good fortune entirely for granted. Now the first blow had fallen. Her mother, who had told her about the consequences of her operation, had also told her she must tell Meridan.

'But why?' Pippa had asked, suddenly afraid. 'You don't think he'll stop loving me because of it?'

'Darling, of course not! But children may be very important to him . . . some men want an heir as much as they want a wife. He'll have to know . . . it's only fair that he should. But I'm *sure* he wouldn't dream of letting it make any difference.'

Pippa had pondered the question with an unfamiliar thoroughness. Normally, she did not by temperament let any problem disturb her for long . . . she simply shelved it until time or Fate took care of it for her. But this was a little different. For one thing she was still not feeling well enough to read . . . nor was she allowed visitors except for her mother. Time hung heavy on her hands and despite herself, her thoughts kept turning to Meridan.

Somewhere, far in the back of her

consciousness, she knew that if she were to be truly unselfish, she would offer Merry his freedom . . . offer it in such a way that he could take it if he wished. But she never allowed that thought full rein, for suppose Merry did mind about the children and allowed her to break the engagement! No! she could not contemplate that even for a moment. Merry was hers . . . and she wouldn't let him go without a fight. Merry was decent and honourable, and he wouldn't break his side of the bargain or do anything to hurt her.

She toyed with the idea of keeping it a secret from him, but realized that he might quite easily learn the truth from someone else. Liz knew . . . she may have told him already! Merry hated any kind of deceit. There was only one course open to her . . . and that was to throw herself on his mercy. Somehow she did not think Merry would fail her. After all, he did love her . . . he'd said so often in that slow, husky voice of his, an affectionate smile in the dark eyes, a gentle squeeze from his strong fingers. It might not be a very passionate kind of love, but she never doubted its sincerity. Merry had always loved her, ever since he'd been a small boy and she a tiny girl. He'd always protected her from John's brotherly teasing and practical jokes and tried to get her excused from the punishments that followed their childish escapades, taking the blame on himself rather than allowing her or Liz to suffer.

He was really much kinder, much nicer than John! John liked his own way just as she, Pippa, did, and they often squabbled even now, when their interests conflicted. Merry never argued. He seemed quite pleased at any time to fall in with their wishes or plans. Yet he wasn't weak! There was some quality in him that made them all, even John, look to him for leadership. Perhaps it was just that all three of them had a very healthy respect for Meridan . . . recognized in him a finer character than they possessed themselves.

Now Merry was here, beside her, and she watched his face to try to read from his expression how much it mattered to him that she couldn't give him children.

'Yes, Pippa! Liz told me. I'm terribly sorry for your sake. But never allow yourself to think it could make any difference to . . . to the way I feel about you!' (How difficult it was to find the right words . . . to reassure her without further lies.)

'Then you won't stop loving me . . . because of what they've done?'

'Pippa, you mustn't be so silly! That could never be a reason for any man ceasing to love a girl . . . how could it?' (For he knew that if this had happened to Charlotte, he would have wanted her to marry him as much as ever. If only he could say the same to Phillipa who needed his love!)

With a tenderness born of his compassion for her, Meridan took out a large handkerchief and gently dried her tears. She smiled at him tremulously.

'Darling, I'd begun to wonder if I

ought to give you back your ring!'

Her fingers went to the diamond circlet on her left hand. Merry felt his heart come to his throat and turned abruptly away from her, walking over to the window where he stared out over the tops of the yellow-green new leaf on the plane trees waving there.

It was so near . . . freedom . . . freedom to go to Charlotte and say: 'Will you marry me? I can ask you now!'

Yet how utterly impossible it was to take advantage of the opening Pippa had given him. Liz had been right, of course. Even if he were to tell Pippa now all about Charlotte, she would believe it was really only an excuse and not the real reason.

It was barely a year since he had given Pippa that ring . . . and remembering how they had gone together to choose it, he realized how insignificant the gesture had seemed at the time. They had nothing to do one wet afternoon and Pippa had suggested they drive up to town.

'We might do a matinée!' she suggested. 'Maybe Liz and John would like to come!'

But Liz and John were going riding so they had driven up alone. Over lunch, they had discussed Liz's and John's engagement and Meridan had said casually:

'I expect both our parents will be delighted when we follow their example!'

There had, after all, been an understanding between them for some months now.

'I know they will!' Pippa agreed eagerly. 'When are we going to announce our engagement, Merry?'

He'd smiled at her and said:

'Well, we've an hour to fill in before the matinée. Suppose we go and choose a ring?'

It had all been so casual . . . so matter-of-fact. Pippa had been thrilled with her ring and the family, when they had added their unsurprised congratulations, duly admired it. Pippa's father had opened a bottle of champagne at

99

dinner that night and the atmosphere had been gay, friendly, contented. Everyone was pleased and happy, and Merry had been content, too. If only he had known that love lay just around the corner . . . real love; that what he felt for Pippa was no more than a strong affection, an almost brotherly emotion which had no comparison to the soul-stirring depth of his feeling for Charlotte. He had had no sense of 'tying himself up', of losing his freedom, for he had no reason then for wishing to be free . . . nor had Pippa shown any inclination to tie the knot tighter . . . on the contrary, they had decided not to get married for at least a year or so.

Maybe that would save him now. If their engagement were perforce to continue . . . it was possible that within a year, Pippa might change her mind.

'Merry!'

Her voice pulled him back from his thoughts.

'Merry, if you're quite sure this

doesn't make any difference to you, can we get married soon . . . this year?'

'But, Pippa!' he said desperately. 'You said you wanted a long engagement! And your parents . . . they wanted you to wait till you were twenty. Why rush things now?'

There was an expression on Meridan's face that Pippa . . . in her present sensitive mood, quickly perceived. Her remark had been made without fore-thought . . . merely to test him, but now, seeing the uneasiness in his eyes, she persisted:

'But why not, Merry? The doctor said I would need a good long holiday in the sun somewhere to convalesce. We could combine a trip abroad with our honeymoon.'

A reasonable enough suggestion and yet Meridan was searching frantically for excuses.

' . . . not a good thing after you've been so ill . . . time to get quite well first . . . busy at the office anyhow!' The words spilled from his lips and he hated himself, knowing them all for lies. Had it not been for Charlotte . . .

He was rescued by the entrance of the nurse.

'I'm afraid you'll have to leave now, Mr. Avebury. Doctor said only ten minutes . . . but you can come again tomorrow!'

He bent and kissed Pippa's hot, dry cheek with a tenderness that was born of guilt at his gladness to be escaping the issue . . . at least for another day. She clung to him a moment, disregarding the nurse, and whispered:

'You do love me, Merry? Nothing's changed, has it?'

But even for her peace of mind, he could not tell so deliberate a lie. He kissed her again, on the lips, and knew that this was a lie, too, for she smiled at him and let him go, content.

Elizabeth had at last agreed to meet Charlotte, and Meridan had arranged for both girls to come to his flat that evening before dinner. Charlotte was to go straight from the office and Meridan had expected to be there to meet her. He hoped he would have about half an hour alone with her before Liz arrived.

But owing to the phone call from Phillipa's mother, saying he might visit Pippa that same evening at six, he was in fact not home when both girls arrived.

The embarrassment of their meeting was eased a little by explanations for Merry's absence. He had phoned Charlotte, telling her he would be late and to get the porter to let her into his flat so that she could open the door for Liz. She had been waiting only a few moments before his sister arrived.

'Well, if we have to wait, we might as well have a drink,' Elizabeth said, a little put out by her first glimpse of Charlotte. She was not in the least as she had imagined her to be! Her main feeling was of surprise ... that Charlotte was not more stunning ... to use the only appropriate word she could think of. She had expected her to be a raving beauty beside whom poor old Pippa's rather doll-like prettiness paled into insignificance. But although Charlotte was nicely turned out . . . and undoubtedly possessed a certain type of warm beauty, she did not seem to Elizabeth's first critical glance to have anything so special about her as to be the cause of this upheaval.

'I'm afraid I don't know where Meridan keeps things,' Charlotte said shyly. 'I've never been here before!'

'No, of course!' Elizabeth said, getting up to see to the drinks herself.

Charlotte, in turn, had quickly summed up Elizabeth and found her not unlike the girl of her supposition. She was very like Meridan to look at, but a feminine version of her brother. She was beautifully and expensively dressed, and to Charlotte, seemed at first meeting to be older than her twenty years. She had a sophistication that spoke of expensive finishing schools and plenty of money. And as Charlotte had anticipated, Elizabeth showed no sign of friendliness towards her!

Elizabeth came back from the kitchen with two glasses of sherry.

'That should revive us!' she said casually. 'I wonder how long Merry will be with Pippa!'

The other girl's name hung between them until the silence became unbearable . . . at least to Charlotte. She said impulsively:

'Please, may I tell you something? It's about . . . about Phillipa . . . ' She saw Elizabeth's eyebrows go upwards but the dark head remained bent over her glass and she could not see her eyes although she guessed them to be antagonistic.

'If I thought it was best for . . . for her . . . I wouldn't be here now. Please believe that. I'm not sure myself that Meridan is right about the . . . the whole thing. I don't want to hurt Phillipa . . . nor does he . . . but he feels convinced that it would be wrong to marry her now. He . . . he and I . . . we've known each other so short a while. I've felt that maybe if I went right out of his life now . . . before it's too late . . . well, that he might settle down again. But he swears to me that is impossible and that whatever I do, he won't go through with this marriage. He hopes eventually that Phillipa will herself break the engagement.'

'Yes!' Elizabeth said shortly, her voice unencouraging.

Charlotte struggled on.

'Please, can't you help me? You know your brother probably very much better than I do . . . and you know Phillipa. Tell me what *you* think? Do you believe that if I stepped out of the picture, Meridan would go back to her?'

Despite her loyalties to Pippa . . . despite her preconceived ideas about Charlotte and her inner wish to dislike her, the younger girl was impressed in spite of herself. There was no doubting Charlotte's sincerity. She was not playing a game . . . her voice, her words . . . even the nervous gestures of her hands . . . showed her in her true light.

Elizabeth knew now that she had

agreed to meet Charlotte in the hope that somehow she could persuade her to leave Meridan alone . . . go out of his life completely; that she would have stooped to anything to achieve this. But now, quite suddenly, she was no longer at all sure.

She looked up and for a moment, the two girls stared into each other's eyes.

'You love him?' Elizabeth said at last.

'Yes!' Charlotte agreed quietly. 'But not so much that I would come between him and someone else who loved him, too. Does Phillipa love him . . . very much?'

Elizabeth bit her lip. What, after all, did she know of Pippa's feelings! They had been friends for years and Pippa had always loved Merry, yet was this the same kind of love of which Charlotte now spoke? She was, herself, so young, that she knew herself unequipped to answer that question honestly. What was love? The kind of friendly companionship she had always had with John? The certainty that she wanted to be married to him and live with him all her life? It was one kind of love . . . but there might be others . . . such as this girl had for Merry . . . such as Merry professed to have for her.

'I think Pippa needs Merry . . . more than ever now!' she said at last. 'Frankly, I don't see what . . . what any of you can do. I . . . I hoped you didn't really love him . . . that if you could be made to keep away from Merry, it would all come right eventually. But I can see I've been wrong about you . . . and about Merry, too. I didn't believe he loved you. I thought it was just a kind of infatuation . . . after all, it did happen very suddenly, didn't it?'

'Yes!' Charlotte agreed instantly. 'At first I didn't trust my own feelings myself . . . or Meridan's. But deep down inside me, I know I do love him . . . so much that I'm not considering my own happiness . . . I'm only concerned with his.'

'She means it, too!' Elizabeth thought, surprised. It would be easy to convince her that Merry's happiness lay with Phillipa, and then it would all be resolved. Yet she couldn't do that . . . had no right to come between them. Besides, there was Merry to consider, too.

'I don't see what chance of happiness he has either way!' she said thoughtfully. 'I know my brother well enough to be quite sure that he won't be able to hurt Phillipa and forget about doing so. But if he really loves you . . . and not Pippa . . . I see that he can't possibly marry her either!'

It was at this moment that Meridan joined them. His face looked white and tired, and Charlotte instinctively started to her feet to go to him, but restrained herself and sat down again. Meridan, however, ignored his sister's presence and bent and kissed Charlotte's cheek, bringing instantly to her face the tell-tale rush of colour he loved to see.

Then he sat down on the settee beside her and turned to his sister.

'Hullo, Liz. Glad you two have met at last.'

'I'll get you a drink, Merry!' Elizabeth said, anxiously surveying his face. He really did look worn out. Had his visit to Pippa been so hard for him then?

When she returned with a whisky-and-soda, she asked him.

'Pippa wants us to be married as soon as she's out of hospital ... to combine the holiday abroad the doctors have recommended she have with our honeymoon!'

All colour left Charlotte's face and she bit her lip to keep back the cry that had risen from her heart.

As if sensing her reaction, Meridan took her hand and held it for a moment tightly in his own as if to reassure her.

'It was so much more difficult than I had expected, Liz!' he went on. 'I'd thought if there was some way it could be done, I'd tell her ... but it was out of the question. I couldn't do it, Charlotte.'

'I understand, darling!' the endearment slipped out unnoticed except by

Elizabeth, who felt suddenly and for the first time, the full force of love that existed between these two. There was no doubting it any longer . . . it was there, like some visible bond between them.

'You didn't . . . agree?' she asked her brother quickly.

Meridan shook his head.

'Fortunately the nurse came in and saved me a reply. Liz, you've just got to help me . . . find some way of persuading Pippa to let things drift for a while. If she presses me on the subject, I'll have to be honest with her . . . I just can't lie. Yet at the same time, I don't think I could bear to see her face if I had to do it. God, what a mess.'

'I suppose I could persuade her to wait a while!' his sister said thoughtfully. 'After all, it would be silly to go on your honeymoon if you didn't feel well or strong enough to do all the things you'd like to do. And she's bound to feel terribly weak for a while after she comes out of hospital. I understand she'll be in there for at least another five weeks. She'll be a semi-invalid when she first comes home.'

'Will it help at all, anyway?' Charlotte forced herself to speak her thoughts. 'It won't be any easier to break her heart when she is home convalescing, than it can be now. Meridan, I honestly believe we ought to . . . to forget about ourselves.'

'Forget that I love you? That you love me?' Meridan cried, forgetting his sister again. 'Charlotte, I couldn't . . . I just won't consider it. Be patient a little longer, darling. I'll find a way somehow!'

'It isn't a question of being patient!' Charlotte said, in her turn forgetting Elizabeth was listening to them across the room. 'You know I'd wait ten, twenty years for you, if that would help matters. But it won't, Meridan. It would be quite different if she didn't love you.'

Meridan felt suddenly inexpressibly bitter. Did Phillipa really love him? He did not question the fact that she *thought* she did, just as he had believed he loved her until he met Charlotte and learned what it really meant to love. In his heart, he knew that neither he nor Pippa had ever experienced together or apart that greatest of all emotions . . . the kind of love that was purely selfless, asking only the other's happiness. He could not let Charlotte go for something so comparatively meaningless as affection. Yet he *had* asked Pippa to marry him . . . had led her to expect that he would one day make her his wife . . . that he loved her. Engagements might not be binding but in a way, they were bonds, promises, vows, and if he wrote them off as meaningless, he would indeed be a man without any sense of obligation or duty . . . more especially since Pippa would undoubtedly misconstrue the reason.

'Please, Meridan, let me go!' Charlotte said suddenly, her hands covering her face. 'I cannot bear to see you so torn . . . you know as well as I do what we ought to do. We simply can't be happy at . . . at her expense!'

Any antagonism Elizabeth had felt for Charlotte vanished completely as she heard this cry wrung from the girl's heart. She felt suddenly, deep within her, that Merry was right. Charlotte was more than worthy of his love . . . and she knew suddenly that Pippa could never have been so unselfish as to deny herself for someone else as Charlotte begged to be allowed to do. Her loyalty to Pippa was completely overshadowed now by her admiration for Charlotte . . . and her belief in the love she had for Merry, in his for her.

'Don't make a needless sacrifice, either of you!' she said into the silence that had fallen. 'Maybe there is a way . . . maybe Merry's idea isn't such a bad one. If Charlotte comes home and we invite some other people as well, Pippa's bound to notice how you two feel about each other. Just so long as she understands that you're leaving her for someone else and not because . . . because of her operation ... then I think you're entitled to your freedom, Merry. I can see that you've little chance of making Pippa happy anyway, feeling as you do about Charlotte. It would be crazy to ruin three people's lives for the sake of ... of a sense of duty to one of them.'

'Liz, darling, thank heaven you see it my way!' Meridan said warmly. 'Believe me, I don't want to hurt Pippa ... there's nothing in the world I want to avoid more. But I do believe that given time, she might see for herself that our marriage wouldn't work. Then she can be the one to break the engagement. Charlotte says she'll wait ... bless her, and while I deplore the necessity for deception meanwhile, I think it could all be worked out in the end.'

'We can try!' Elizabeth said warmly. 'Cheer up, Charlotte. You can trust Merry, you know!'

'It isn't that I don't trust him ... the way you mean!' Charlotte cried. 'But I can't help feeling that something will go wrong . . . that this isn't the right way . . . '

She broke off, unable to give expression in words to the nameless apprehension that filled her. Then Meridan's touch on her hand, and Elizabeth's sudden warm friendly smile, eased the doubts, and for a moment, she was happy. She wanted so much to believe that they were right!

5

Phillipa lay on the sofa in what had once been the schoolroom in their house, but since the children had grown up, had been converted into their private sitting-room. Whenever she and Elizabeth and John and Meridan got together, they nearly always came up to this room which was as familiar to them as it was comfortable and informal. Almost the identical room existed in Elizabeth's and Meridan's house for as schoolgirls, Phillipa and Liz had wanted everything just the same. When one schoolroom had been converted, Elizabeth had persuaded her parents to agree to their doing the same, and the girls had chosen the same furnishings for chair-covers and curtains.

Relics of childhood lay about the room . . . a toy dog on the window-seat, John's sports trophies on the mantelshelf (although his riding cups had a place of honour in the dining-room downstairs); the old gramophone with a pile of old dance tunes to which they occasionally danced when they felt in the mood; photographs of all four of them, mostly group pictures, at various stages of growth.

Phillipa's hands were idle and there was a bored, rather petulant expression to the still pale face. John was busy polishing some stirrups he'd just bought in an old antique shop; Liz was doing some embroidery on a face towel intended for her guest-room when she was married. It was now nearly three months since Phillipa had first been rushed off to hospital and she was by no means fit yet. The doctor had forbidden her to ride for at least six months, maybe longer, and she tired quickly, which meant that any outings, such as a point to point, were not advisable, even if she went by car. An afternoon rest, early nights, lots of sleep and very little exercise; such were the doctor's orders and Phillipa was bored to the pitch where she wanted to scream. She made no effort to hide her feelings from the others and they had listened for the last half-hour to her rather high-pitched, petulant voice complaining.

Elizabeth tried to curb her own impatience. Everyone was sorry for Pippa and had been doing their best to keep her company ... to keep her amused. She and John had frequently denied themselves some enjoyment just so that Pippa should not be left alone. Pippa's parents had given her every-thing money could buy ... even to a new television set which had just been installed in the schoolroom since the downstairs' one was an old model not converted to Commercial and Pippa had professed herself bored with the 'same old thing day after day on the B.B.C.'. But nothing seemed to put an end to Pippa's complaints and demands. Even John, who had tried his best, had lost his temper with her only yesterday, and told her to get a hold on herself and try to make the best of the situation for all their sakes.

If Pippa had been at all shaken by her brother's criticism, and she had indeed burst into a storm of weeping which had lasted half an hour, there were apparently to be no lasting results from it. Now, even the patient Liz felt she could stand very little more. Unfortunately it had poured with rain the entire morning and it was still pouring even now, nearly tea-time. None of them had been able to go out.

'I do think Merry might make an effort and come down once or twice during the week!' Pippa's voice droned on. 'I know he's working hard and all that but surely he could sacrifice himself once in a while.'

'Dash it all, Pippa, he comes every week-end. I don't think you can expect him to do more.'

'Well, Daddy went up and down to town every day for years!' Pippa pointed out.

'Yes, but he knocked off from the office at four-thirty in those days and he was home by half-past six. Meridan doesn't get off till six most evenings as you well know,' her brother replied.

'Then they should let him off . . . he should tell them I'm ill!'

'But, darling, you're not really ill any more . . .' Liz began unwisely for Pippa dissolved immediately into the ready tears that were now so frequent they had almost ceased to take notice of them.

Wearily, Liz put down her sewing and went to the girl.

'Now, please, Pippa, don't be a silly goose. I know it's terribly dull for you . . . but if only you'd . . . well, *try* to feel better, I'm sure you'd pick up quicker. Dr. Nivan says you're getting along very well.'

'I'd be completely well again by now if only Merry hadn't been so stubborn about our going abroad. I know I'd have been all right by now if we had. And it was as much your fault as his, Liz. You agreed with him.'

Her irritation with Pippa vanished as Liz felt the now familiar pity and loyalty wash over her. It was true enough that she had supported Merry when he refused to rush into a wedding when Pippa came out of hospital. Merry had had the doctors behind him, of course, which made things easier for him . . . he stuck to his excuse that Pippa simply wasn't strong enough. No tears or pleadings from Pippa had been able to move him and when she had appealed to Elizabeth to talk Merry round, she had refused, saying she believed he was right. But of course, Pippa's health was not the real cause for the whole thing as Liz knew only too well and she had begun to wonder if it would not have been kinder after all to tell Pippa the truth.

Poor Meridan! Liz thought as she recalled her brother's tired, strained face. He had put himself into a hopeless position. On weekdays, he managed to get a few hours with Charlotte, but from Friday evening to Monday morning, he was chained to Pippa's side and Pippa was not exactly a congenial companion these days. She had Meridan running round her like a servant, fetching and carrying and attending to her needs, and she constantly demanded his attention. She had never been particularly demonstrative with him in public but now she seemed to make a point of having him hold her hand, no matter who else was in the room, or sitting close beside her with an arm round her shoulders while she snuggled up against him. It was clear to Elizabeth, who knew the reason, how Meridan dreaded these moments of intimacy. Even John, who did not as yet know the truth, had remarked to his sister:

'Do stop pawing Meridan, Pippa! You can see he doesn't like it!'

White-faced, Pippa had said nothing, but a hard determined expression had come into her eyes and Liz had wondered for a moment whether Pippa had begun to guess at the change in Merry's feelings. But she rejected the idea as impossible. How could Pippa have guessed? No one but she and

Merry in Pippa's circle knew of Charlotte's existence; and Merry was outwardly as devoted as he had ever been during the week-ends he spent so exclusively in Pippa's company.

What neither Liz nor her brother guessed was the heightened intuition that had come to Pippa as she lay idle so often with nothing but her thoughts as company during those last weeks in hospital. With little else to consider but herself, she had chewed over Merry's refusal to get married quickly and had come to the conclusion that however much he might deny it, he was no longer sure he wanted to marry her. It had naturally not occurred to her that there might be someone else . . . but the more she thought about it, the more convinced she became that the operation she had had did matter to him . . . had somehow changed him.

Now, because for the first time in her life she felt herself to be up against something she could not control, Pippa began to desire her own way feverishly and to the point where it had become a kind of complex. She had been in no great hurry to marry Meridan until she sensed his own reluctance to marry her. So it became of the utmost importance to her to marry him now, *at once*. But try as she might to persuade him, he remained adamant, simply quoting again and again that the doctors advised against it and he could not agree to anything they had not advised.

'You don't love me any more!' she had wept and stormed at him, but it had had no effect. He had said only:

'That's not the point, Pippa. Before anything else you must get well again.'

Pippa did not know how often it had been on the tip of Meridan's tongue to tell her the truth. He had been sorely tempted both when she was at the hospital and since she had gone home. But pity for her, and an awareness of her need of him at this particular time, held his tongue as much as Charlotte's repeated requests that he should say nothing.

'You cannot do it now . . . not yet, Meridan. Be patient!' she had begged him over and over again. But even Charlotte could not fully understand how impossible it was for him to dis-simulate; did not know how demanding Pippa could be, or how difficult it had become for him to show her affection by any physical terms. His love for and need of Charlotte had seemed to grow and expand with every day that passed, and he knew that she felt the same way about him. The all too brief moments when he held her in his arms had become for them both a kind of bitter-sweet torture. They longed to give full rein to the emotions that enthralled them and yet were forced to exercise a control that became harder as time went by. He knew that the situation could not remain as it was for very much longer. There were dark shadows beneath Charlotte's eyes and no colour in her cheeks. She looked far worse than Pippa! And he knew himself to be tired to the point where he could no longer sleep at night.

But Pippa seemed to be making so slow a recovery. The family doctor seemed delighted with her progress but whenever Meridan saw Pippa, she was lying down, looking wan and complaining of a headache or some illness. Until she was better, how could he further his own plans? Clearly Pippa was in no state to support a house-party and the first move he had planned was to fill his home one week-end with a crowd of young people, including Charlotte . . .

It was Liz who managed to arrange it after all. On that wet afternoon, searching for something to amuse Pippa . . . to liven her up, she said spontaneously:

'I know life has been rather dull for you lately. Merry and I had thought of giving a party one week-end . . . it's ages since we had a house full. But we didn't want to arrange anything until you were strong enough to join in. When do you think you might feel up to it, darling?'

The change in Pippa was immediate.

The colour came into her cheeks and she sat up, her eyes bright and full of animation.

'What fun! I'm sure I'm well enough now . . . after all, I needn't dance much . . . maybe we could have charades or paper games or something I could join in, too. Oh, Liz, why didn't we think of it before. It's a splendid idea! Let's make a list of the people to ask.'

John gave his sister a half-affectionate, half-irritated glance.

'You are a fraud, Pippa!' he said bluntly. 'One moment you're the dying swan . . . the next moment you're all agog for a party!'

But Pippa paid no attention to her brother and, jumping to her feet, went in search of paper and pencil.

'This week-end!' she said to Liz. 'Do let's make it this coming week-end. I couldn't possibly wait another ten days!'

That night, Elizabeth phoned Meridan to give him the news. She sounded full of hope.

'Pippa's thrilled with the idea of a

party, Merry . . . she's a changed girl . . . you wouldn't know her to see her this afternoon. I have a feeling it may all come right . . . if only we can get hold of some attractive young men to replace you!'

'There is one young chap in the office . . . ' Meridan said doubtfully. 'It's rather short notice but he might come. And we could ask Angela's friend, Bess, and that new young man of hers, Jeremy someone or other. According to Charlotte, Bess has cooled off a bit so she wouldn't mind if he made a bee-line for Pippa. But I can't think of anyone else.'

'Well, that's probably enough for house guests,' Elizabeth said sagely. 'John and I can ask some of our local friends in just for Saturday night when we have the actual party. You'll bring Charlotte?'

'I'll phone her right away!' Meridan said. 'And thanks, Liz! I don't think I could have coped with another week-end like the last!'

'Nor do I!' his sister laughed. 'Even John is fed up with the gloom.'

Since she was not meeting Meridan that evening, Charlotte decided to slip round and see Bess whom she knew was in. She had not been able to bring herself to confide in her mother although she was fully aware that her mother was only too anxiously awaiting her confidences. But she did not want to worry her. Charlotte knew that if her mother were aware of the fact that Meridan was engaged to someone else, she would strongly disapprove of her daughter meeting him. Of course, her mother must have guessed that she and Meridan were in love. He came round after dinner twice a week and twice a week she stayed in town after office hours to meet Meridan for dinner.

It had been impossible to hide from her mother how she felt about Meridan. But she could not bring herself to tell her more than that she was in love and that they would certainly not be getting engaged until they knew one another very much better.

Content with what she considered very sensible behaviour, and because she herself was not yet ready to face the thought of losing her daughter, Mrs. Matthews let things be. She liked Meridan and, in her heart, definitely approved her daughter's choice of a husband. But she still knew very little about him and was far from reassured by Charlotte's white face and shadowed eyes. There was no questioning the fact that Charlotte was in love ... but whether she was happily in love was another question. Meanwhile, she did not question her, knowing Charlotte would speak when she was ready to confide.

It was from Bess, Charlotte felt the need for advice. At least, from someone other than her parent who would worry so much if she knew the truth. And Bess had met Meridan, liked him, and might understand. There had been only one brief meeting between the two girls since that foursome together ... at the wedding itself, and no chance then for a private talk.

Now, Charlotte felt she could not keep her problems to herself any longer. Meridan had phoned asking her to go down to his house with a party of young people, to include Bess, and she had said she would go. But much as she longed to do so . . . longed for the chance of seeing him for two whole days uninterrupted, she knew that she was also going under a false flag; that she and Meridan would have to conceal their feelings for one another. And foremost of all her fears was the thought that she must at last meet Phillipa.

'What a mess!' was Bess's blunt comment when Charlotte finished her story. 'And to think that I never knew all this was going on! I've been so busy rushing around with Jeremy, I never gave another thought to you and Meridan. Though now I come to think of it, I did notice he was particularly attentive to you at Angela's wedding.'

'I wish I knew what was the right thing to do!' Charlotte said despairingly. 'I can't help feeling horribly responsible!'

'I'm the one who is really responsible,' Bess said comfortingly. 'I made you take Phillipa's place at rehearsal, remember? If you'd said no . . . '

'But I didn't!' Charlotte broke in. 'Bess, what would you do? If Meridan had never met me, he might be married to Pippa by now. I've asked him to let me go . . . suggested we stop seeing each other . . . but he says it won't make any difference . . . that he'll never marry Phillipa now. I know he does love me but he might forget about me in time.'

'But you love him, too, don't you!' Bess said flatly. 'It's written all over your face. It's a bit different for me . . . I fall in and out of love regularly. As a matter of fact, I would have sworn a week ago that I was in love with Jeremy. Then I woke up one morning and knew quite certainly that I wasn't! But seriously, I know what I've felt for all my past boy-friends isn't really love at all . . . not the way you feel, anyhow. I think if I did feel like you do . . . really serious and quite sure too, that the man loved me . . . then I'd hang on. After all, it's crazy for people to marry when they are not in love, isn't it? It just isn't necessary these days.'

'I suppose not! But there is something else that comes into it, too, Bess . . . one's consideration for other people's feelings. Meridan is one of the kindest people I've ever met. I know he couldn't hurt Phillipa and be happy. What chance would our marriage have on such a beginning?'

'Well, he'd hurt her far more if he married her without being in love with her!' Bess said sagely.

'Then you believe I'm right to go on seeing Meridan? You don't think I should refuse to see him any more until he is free?'

'Well, that seems rather like blackmail, doesn't it? I mean, it'll act as an incentive to the wretched man to get free as quickly as he can. If you both think Phillipa will see reason eventually, then I imagine the present way is best for everyone. I do see that it would be pretty wretched for her right now ... that she's bound to feel Meridan is only using you as an excuse to break off the engagement because of her op. I don't know her very well, of course ... she's more Angela's friend than mine. But I've met her once or twice and from what I saw of her, I'd imagine she'd get over anything in time ... she's not a very deep person ... not like you, Charlotte!'

'I wish I were different!' Charlotte said impulsively. 'I wish I could wake up one morning and be sure I didn't love Meridan, just the way you're sure you don't love Jeremy! But I do love him, Bess. I'd do anything in the world to make him happy ... even give him up.'

'Then stop worrying, ducks!' Bess said, smiling. 'Let things work out by themselves . . . they do, you know. If you don't take any action, you can't do the wrong thing! Or am I taking the easy way?'

'I think you are!' Charlotte said with a half smile. 'It's so much easier just to let things go on as they are than to be the one to put a stop to them.'

'Well, I think it's for Meridan to decide . . . though I'm glad I'm not in his shoes!' Bess commented. 'What does your mother say, Charlotte?'

'I haven't told her . . . although she's guessed I'm in love with Meridan. She likes him, of course, but she'd be desperately worried if she knew all the facts. I think she'd tell me to stop seeing him. I wish I didn't feel she would be right!'

'Well, maybe this week-end will bring things to a head. Maybe after meeting Phillipa, you'll feel differently. Or maybe she'll guess from seeing you two together what's up. She might even tackle Meridan about it and bring things to a head that way. Or you might hate the sight of Meridan's family!'

'I've met his sister, Elizabeth. I liked her very much indeed!' Charlotte said, with a wry smile. 'I think she liked me, too. Meridan says she did, although she'd made up her mind not to because Phillipa is almost a sister to her and her loyalty is naturally towards her rather than to me.'

'Well, don't go on worrying till you get ill . . . you look ghastly!' Bess said with friendly concern. 'You've lost weight by the look of you.'

'Only five pounds!' Charlotte admitted.

'Well, let's go down and raid the kitchen!' Bess said with a rueful glance at her plump figure. 'We'll put a few pounds back on you for the week-end. How will you go down Charlotte?'

'Meridan wanted me to go down with him on Friday evening, but I'm working Saturday morning so I can't. Could I go in the car with you and Jeremy on Saturday afternoon?'

'Of course!' Bess agreed. 'Jeremy is

really rather a poppet although I know I could never marry him now. What about your mother, Charlotte? She's not going, too?'

'No! But she says she'll ask Aunt Ethel to come for the week-end ... they haven't seen each other for ages ... so she'll be all right. Mother never lets me feel she is a drag on me if she can help it and she knows how much I want to go.'

And, of course, it was true. Rightly or wrongly, her whole being longed for the week-end, longed for the mere sight of Meridan, for the chance to be in the same room with him, to hear his voice, feel his touch, to know that he was sleeping under the same roof. It would be a kind of torture, too, having to conceal their wish to be near to one another ... he might not even have a chance to kiss her. And hardest of all to bear would be this meeting with Phillipa ... with the girl she ought to hate for standing between her and happiness, yet whom she could only pity because Meridan no longer loved her; the girl who was so much on her conscience and whom she had, and must again, deceive. 'If she loves him, really loves him, she will offer him his freedom,' Charlotte thought for the hundredth time. 'As soon as she guesses he is in love with someone else, she won't want him any more. That's how I would feel. I couldn't bear to hold on to a man who did not want me!'

She did not . . . could not . . . reckon for a nature so different from her own. Phillipa had never had to go without . . . had never had to sacrifice her own desires for someone else's. Easy-going, light-hearted, immature though she might be, she had an inner core of stubbornness that could and would persist until her desires were gratified. They always had been before and she had no doubt that they would be now. Right now she had but one thought in her mind . . . to get Merry to marry her as soon as ever she could. And she saw that she had been going the wrong way about it. Meridan had said time and again that he would not contemplate a wedding until she was quite well. She had thought that by playing the invalid, she might appeal to his natural kindliness . . . that he would give way to anything to have her get better. But now she saw how silly it was. Far easier to show him this week-end how well and strong she was and then he could not put off their marriage any longer.

It never once occurred to her that sooner or later she would not have her way.

6

Charlotte's first impression of Meridan's home was one of luxury. She had known he was well off but had never stopped to consider if he were actually rich. Now she knew that his family must be very wealthy, for not only was the house itself vast in comparison to her tiny suburban home, but filled with beautiful furniture and furnishings, so that at first, she felt nervous and ill-at-ease in these surroundings. She was glad she had Bess there to keep her company and that they were sharing one of the large guest rooms.

Meridan had greeted her warmly on their arrival ten minutes earlier and although he had not kissed her as he usually did now when they met, the pressure of his hand told her how glad he was to see her. Elizabeth also gave her a warm greeting and had brought the two girls up to their room to unpack and tidy up before tea. Of Phillipa, there had been no sign, and Meridan's parents had also still to be faced.

Sitting on the pale blue quilted spread, Charlotte said nervously:

'I wish I hadn't come, Bess!'

Bess turned from the mirror where she was combing her hair and gave her a reproving look.

'Don't lose your courage so early in the day!' she chided her. 'What's there to be afraid of, anyway?'

'I don't know exactly, but I am afraid!' Charlotte admitted. 'It's different for you, Bess. You lead this kind of life in town. I'm not used to it. I never realized it would be like this although I suppose I should have guessed. People with small country houses don't have half a dozen week-end guests!'

'Silly goose!' Bess said kindly. 'Just because the Aveburys are rolling doesn't mean you need be afraid of them . . . or their way of life.'

'I . . . I suppose Phillipa's home is

142

like this, too?' Charlotte said, thinking: 'She has been brought up to the same standards . . . she'll be at ease in these surroundings . . . will know what to do and when to do it . . . she'll be beautifully dressed, too . . . '

She thought dismally of the ballet-length evening dress she had already worn twice in Meridan's presence and which he must surely recognize. She only possessed one other . . . her tangerine net bridesmaid frock, and she had felt unable to wear it this week-end since it had really been made for Phillipa and she would surely recognize it! As to buying another one . . . well, that had been out of the question. She and Mother could barely make ends meet on the tiny pension and Charlotte's salary combined. Small as it was, the cost of running their tiny house seemed to eat up all the money and Charlotte had to save carefully to buy even a new pair of shoes.

She had never felt the need of money before . . . at least not money for her own adornment! Now she wished passionately that she had been able to go to someone like Digby Morton for a country tweed for this week-end, to Balmain's for an evening frock.

She surveyed the soft mauves in the plain Harris tweed she was wearing and stood up quickly, realizing that the skirt had probably been creased enough on the car journey.

'Bess, do I look all right?' she asked anxiously.

'With your figure, you'd look all right in a sack!' Bess said comfortingly, and glanced down at her own plump form in its dark wool dress. 'I wish I had your looks and your figure, Charlotte!'

Slightly comforted, Charlotte agreed that she was ready to go downstairs and join the others.

She walked with Bess along the thickly carpeted landing and down the wide staircase. Jeremy, Elizabeth, Meridan and two strange men and a girl they did not recognize, stood in a group in the hall below, laughing and talking. Instinctively, Charlotte's hands clenched at her side. It was obvious to her that the pretty fair girl standing with her hand possessively on Meridan's arm must be Phillipa. She gave a pretty bell-like laugh at some remark of Meridan's and then clearly, Charlotte heard her voice saying:

'But I'm feeling wonderfully well, darling. Isn't this fun!'

Bess gave a pull on her arm and as if in a dream she went downstairs, her legs moving her in one direction, her whole being longing to turn and run back to the privacy of her room. She just had time to wish even more passionately than before that she had not come, when she felt Liz's hand on her arm and heard her voice saying:

'There you are. Now let me introduce you to everyone. Jeremy you know . . . John, this is Charlotte . . . and Bess; and Peter Barnes, and John's sister, Phillipa . . . '

Charlotte glanced at each face . . . liking John's open suntanned slightly weather-beaten face, attractive in a firm masculine

way; not quite so sure about Peter Barnes
. . . presumably Meridan's bachelor friend
from the office. He was very dark, almost
swarthy, with a small black moustache
and brilliant blue eyes in which she read
approval and interest in herself. She suspected that he held her hand a moment
too long, but forgot him in the next
instant as Elizabeth spoke Pippa's name.

The younger girl was far prettier than
Charlotte had supposed, even in her
most imaginative moments. The baby
fine fair hair curled softly like a little
girl's around her shoulders. She had a
camellia-like skin which showed off to
their best large hazel-green eyes fringed
with surprisingly dark lashes. There was
a soft rose colour in her cheeks and the
small, prettily shaped mouth curved
upwards in a half-smile.

'I've been looking forward to meeting
you!' she said easily. 'Liz told me you'd
be coming . . . you're the one who took
my place as bridesmaid!'

'Yes!' Charlotte murmured, not daring
to glance at Meridan who was standing

a little behind Phillipa and, as she knew, looking at *her*.

'So you already know my handsome fiancé!' She linked her arm again through Meridan's and turned away from Charlotte to speak to Bess.

As Peter Barnes stepped forward to talk to her, Charlotte's thoughts were wild and chaotic. This was so much worse than she had imagined! There was not just Phillipa's beautifully cut green tweed dress and gorgeous amethyst brooch and bracelet to compete with; not just her absolute rightness in these surroundings; not even her unexpected prettiness and charm. But there was her unmistakable possession of Meridan.

' . . . never expected to find so many beautiful girls when I accepted the invitation!'

Hastily she brought her attention back to the man at her side, catching only the last words. She was saved a reply by Meridan, who had released himself from Phillipa's hand and stepped forward to take her arm.

'Come into the drawing-room and meet Mother and Father!' he said. 'I expect tea is nearly ready, anyway!'

The group moved into the drawing-room that seemed to Charlotte to be vast. There must be space here for fifty people at least to move about without touching one another. Heavy silk-brocade curtains hung from the great windows and her feet trod on the richness of dark Persian carpets covering a very beautiful polished parquet floor. Meridan's father, a handsome, rather leonine man, was standing by the fire, for Autumn had come suddenly upon them and the weather was cold for September. He greeted Charlotte kindly and then she was being introduced to his mother, who was yet another surprise for Charlotte. She was tiny . . . almost to the proportion of a girl of ten. Yet although she stood with the top of her beautifully coiffeured grey head barely reaching Meridan's shoulder, there was a chic about the dainty figure that spoke of maturity and self-confidence and graciousness.

If the quick bright eyes, so like Meridan's and Elizabeth's took in the quality of Charlotte's clothes, they rested eventually on Charlotte's face without criticism. Her voice was warm in its welcome. Charlotte knew she liked Meridan's mother.

'Give the rope a pull, Merry darling!' she said to her tall son. 'I expect Miss Matthews is longing for a cup of tea after that tiresome drive.'

'Please, call her Charlotte!' Meridan told his mother with a smile. 'Otherwise you'll make her feel she's back in the office!'

'Oh, you work then?' the cool voice asked, but not disparagingly.

'I'm secretary to a solicitor in the City!' Charlotte said, obediently sitting down on the sofa beside Mrs. Avebury.

Within a few moments she had put Charlotte quite at ease and at the same time, extracted from her a surprising amount of information about her home and family. Then a man-servant brought in a heavily laden silver tray and their conversation became general as the party helped themselves to afternoon tea.

Having done his duty as host by handing round sandwiches and cake, Meridan returned at once to Charlotte and sat on her other side. He gave her his warm, loving smile, and for a moment, everything in the world was all right for Charlotte. Then Pippa's bell-like laugh sounded from across the room and Mrs. Avebury said to Meridan:

'Pippa seems to be very much better this week-end. I think she wanted cheering up more than rest!'

'I'm sure of it!' Meridan said. He, too, had noticed a remarkable change in Pippa. She was no longer playing the invalid but was full of life and fun . . . quite her old self, in fact. He would have been relieved had it not been for another change in her from the casual, friendly companion he had once known. During the whole of yesterday evening, when he and Liz had dined at their house, Pippa had been prettily and yet quite obviously possessive of him. It was almost, he thought guiltily, as if she had guessed by some sixth sense, his reluctance for any kind of intimacy between them and was trying the harder because of it to tie him with invisible bonds.

Speaking of it to Liz on the way home, he had asked her opinion.

'Well, I did notice it, too, but I think you're exaggerating, Merry!' his sister said. 'She's just glad to be feeling better and to see you and well, at least let's be thankful that she is so much better.'

'Do you think I could . . . could speak to her this weekend?' Merry asked, a little desperately. 'I do so hate this pretence, Liz. It's getting me down. To have to listen to Pippa talking about this or that which will happen when we are married knowing full well I've no intention of marrying her! It seems so deceitful!'

'I know, Merry. I feel pretty uncomfortable about it myself. After all, I'm in on it as much as you are. She *is* better

. . . but we don't want a kind of nervous crisis to send her back into the glooms she's had until now!'

'It isn't going to be easy for Charlotte either!' Meridan said thoughtfully. 'Look after her for me this week-end, Liz . . . if I'm not able to myself, I mean.'

'Just keep up the pretence a little longer, Merry darling!' Liz said sympathetically. 'I'm sure it won't be long now before Pippa is completely well again . . . and then you can speak out.'

But it wasn't proving easy. His reluctance to have Pippa lay claim to him was heightened with Charlotte's arrival. He had been acutely conscious of Pippa's hand on his arm when Charlotte had come downstairs; embarrassed, too, when Pippa spoke of him, almost pointedly, it seemed, as her fiancé. The look of distress in Charlotte's eyes . . . even of fright, had not escaped him, and he had come to her as soon as he could, hoping by nothing more than a look or brief touch to reassure her of his love for her and his sympathy with her feelings. Difficult as it was for him, he knew that it was as hard for her, too.

Tea over, Elizabeth took Phillipa upstairs for a rest on her own bed before the party, so that she would not be overtired. John went home because he wanted to get down to the stables to see one of the lads before he went off duty. Bess, who seemed to be getting along famously with Meridan's father, was taken by him to see his library, and Jeremy and Peter Barnes had gone to the billiard room for a game of snooker. With the departure of his mother also to rest, Meridan was left alone with Charlotte. At once, he took her upstairs to the schoolroom and even before the door had slammed behind them, he had taken her in his arms.

For a few moments, she allowed him to hold her, knowing for the first time since she had come into his home, a feeling of peace and contentment. But it could not last long. She drew away from him with a little sigh, saying:

'Meridan, I can't . . . not behind her back!'

For a second, it almost seemed as if Phillipa's bright, slim ghost stood in the room between them.

Meridan walked away from Charlotte's side and stood in the half light by the window, the sky dark behind him showing through the uncurtained windows.

'I know! I'm sorry, darling. Come and sit over here by me on the window-seat so we can talk!'

Obediently, trustingly, she went over to him and did not draw away her hand when he took it in his own.

'It's . . . not easy, for either of us!' he said slowly. 'But I'm sure we are doing the right thing, Charlotte. Phillipa is better . . . miles better, than when I saw her last week-end. Mother and Liz have both noticed a change in her and I think it will only be a very short while before I can speak to her. If you could have seen her last week-end, pale, tearful, lying on the couch scarcely moving and so depressed, you'd understand why I haven't been able to speak to her before.'

'I do understand!' Charlotte cried. 'But it's somehow worse now I've met her . . . know her. She's happy right now, believing you love her . . . eager for the party tonight . . . it's dreadful to think of how she will feel when you tell her about *us*!'

'You must not let yourself think like that, Charlotte! It will be bad for a while, I expect . . . but I am convinced she will get over it . . . find someone else. And that reminds me, I don't like the way Peter looks at you! I'd hoped he'd be interested in Pippa!'

Charlotte smiled a little.

'I'm sure there is nothing to be jealous of! I've certainly no interest in him, anyway! Besides, I can't believe he wouldn't be more interested in Pippa if he didn't know she was your fiancée. I'm unattached and therefore available. Pippa isn't!'

'How logical, dearest! But you may

be right. All the more reason for me to speak to Pippa soon. I very nearly told Peter the truth when I brought him down yesterday but it seemed . . . well, disloyal to Pippa, to tell anyone else before her. It's a nasty position to be in but unavoidable. Charlotte, you do trust me?'

She gave him her soft, lovely smile.

'Yes, I trust you, Meridan!' she said. 'But it doesn't make me any happier about what has to be done . . . or certain we *should* do it. I know it's silly to consider any other way . . . that it'll be best in the end for Pippa, too. But I just can't be happy about it. It's silly of me,' she repeated, 'but I have a stupid premonition that it just won't work out as you intend.'

'But what can happen?' Meridan said anxiously. 'Pippa can't hold me to the engagement . . . I cannot believe she would try to do such a thing. Nothing *can* happen, darling.'

For a moment, silence lay heavy between them. Then Charlotte said:

'I wonder what your parents will say, Meridan. They don't know, do they?'

'I've said nothing yet . . . nor has Liz. But I have a feeling Mother will guess. She knows me too well.'

'Will she mind . . . very much?' Charlotte asked unhappily.

'No, of course not . . . how could she!' Meridan lied for he knew his parents were devoted to Pippa and would be bitterly disappointed. But because he loved the girl beside him so much, he could not conceive that they might feel anything but love for her, too. Liz had liked her so much in spite of her obvious intention of doing otherwise! It would be the same for his mother and father.

'I beg you, dearest, not to keep worrying. If I can, I'm going to talk to Pippa this week-end . . . get it settled once and for all. I won't have you worrying yourself or being unhappy . . . not even for Pippa's sake.'

But this was not what Charlotte

wanted . . . for it made her feel doubly responsible, doubly guilty, to think that Meridan might act prematurely for her sake. Hastily, she pretended a return of good spirits and light-heartedness and was glad to see the smile return to Meridan's eyes. Only after she had gone to her room to bath and change for dinner did she realize that deceit had a way of spreading . . . like a fungus . . . that she had had to pretend even with Meridan to whom she thought she could never, never lie.

Pippa's dress was a beautiful cascade of pure white lace, cut very low in the bodice, accentuating the pretty curve of her bosom and the creamy colour of her skin. Two tiny white rosebuds caught back the fair hair from her forehead and long elbow-length white lace gloves completed the picture of what might have been a society bride.

It was a new dress, bought from the most expensive shop in the nearby town . . . and chosen deliberately to attract Meridan and to suggest a bridal gown.

Somehow, tonight, she meant to fix a date for their wedding . . . to announce to the company that they planned to be married on a certain date. She knew that she looked her loveliest . . . that it was unlikely Meridan, who was also so compliant, would fail to be roused from the hesitant lethargic attitude he had shown her of late. Oh, he had been attentive enough to her needs, fetching and carrying and bringing her flowers! But there had been a lack of response inside himself . . . an evasiveness that she could not help but notice. It had to end . . . and her return to good health and spirits and her careful attention to her dress and appearance were all part of her campaign to change all that.

Sparkling, vivacious, buoyant, she ran down the stairs at the pre-dinner gong, hoping since she had started to dress before the other girls, for a moment alone with Meridan before cocktails were served. Merry would be down early, she knew, because on such occasions, he always mixed the drinks himself.

Meridan was, in fact, alone in the drawing-room. His thoughts were, as automatically he mixed drinks in the cocktail shaker, with Charlotte. He heard no footsteps on the soft carpets, and when from the door, Pippa said softly:

'Darling!' he spoke without thinking, from his heart:

'Is that you, Charlotte?' And as he turned to greet her, he saw his mistake too late. The colour rose to his cheeks and his hands remained poised on the shaker as he stared at the girl in the doorway.

The smile froze on Pippa's face. She was not a fool and the implications of their brief exchange of words did not escape her. She had called Merry 'darling' and since he had thought she was this other girl, Charlotte, it was obvious that *she* called him darling, too! Now, suddenly, the pieces of the puzzle fell into place. Meridan's strange behaviour of late was clearly enough explained. There was someone else

. . . another girl . . . the girl called Charlotte.

The thoughts and emotions that flashed through Phillipa in the brief second or two before she moved, were not revealed on her face which was still smiling. It had taken no longer than a moment for her to accept what had happened and to decide that for the moment anyway, she would act as if she had heard nothing.

'Like my dress?' she asked coquettishly, twirling round so that the full skirt flared into a circle around her slim waist and the fair curls danced on her bare shoulders.

It was on the tip of Meridan's tongue to speak out. He had been horribly conscious of the import of his blunder and now only surprise held him from telling Pippa there and then about Charlotte. Surely Pippa must have heard . . . must have guessed . . . yet she appeared to have noticed nothing. Her face, as she came towards him, was still smiling, and her voice still light and provocative as she said:

'It was chosen especially for you, Merry. Do say you like it!'

'It . . . it's very pretty!' the man said lamely. 'You . . . you look very pretty, too, Pippa. Look, Pippa, I . . . '

'Now, Merry, I won't be put off with that for a compliment after all the trouble I took to make myself beautiful for you,' she broke in quickly. 'Aren't you going to kiss me?'

Her face, innocent and artless so it seemed to the man, gazed up at him appealingly. He felt a stab of utter misery. What a ghastly situation he had got himself into. How could he disillusion this young girl about his feelings for her? Yet it would be bound to happen . . . just as it had happened a minute or two before . . . that he should give himself away again. Far better to speak out now . . . at once . . .

But Fate was playing the game on Pippa's side. Even as she flung her arms round Meridan's neck there was the sound of voices behind them and

Charlotte, Jeremy and Bess came into the room together.

Meridan felt even more wretched than before. Charlotte must have seen Phillipa in his arms even while he was not actually kissing her. Now her dark head was bent downwards so that he could not see her face, but he could well guess at the pain in her heart.

Phillipa was as pleased by the turn of events as Meridan was unhappy. Let Charlotte see for herself that Merry was *hers* . . . that she wasn't going to give him up without a fight! True, she knew little as to what had actually happened between Merry and Charlotte . . . how deeply they were involved; but she was not a fool where her own interests were concerned, and Merry's evasions and strangely unloverlike behaviour was now satisfactorily explained to her. He believed himself in love with Charlotte, whether the girl knew it or not. And before the evening was out, Pippa intended to find out exactly what she was up against. Never once did it occur to her that the honourable, unselfish thing to do would be to speak to Meridan and offer him his freedom if he wanted it.

'Well, well, well!' Jeremy was saying, waving a hand at the couple by the window. 'What a handsome pair you two make, to be sure!'

Pippa quickly linked her arm through Meridan's and smiled up at him.

'Aren't I lucky?' she said sweetly. 'There aren't many girls with a fiancé as good-looking as mine!'

It was Bess who came to the rescue, saying with a bluntness she would never have permitted herself had it not been for her feelings for Charlotte:

'Meridan, I'm dying for that cocktail you promised me!'

With immense relief, Meridan made his escape from Pippa's embrace and turned back to the table where he had been mixing drinks. Pippa followed him across the room and looked prettily at the two girls.

'How nice you look, Bess dear!' she said. 'That dark green is very becoming. And your dress is pretty, too, Charlotte!'

Never had Charlotte been more conscious of her short-comings. Beside Pippa's radiant white figure in its glorious gown, she felt drab, dowdy. And in her heart, the same dispiritedness reigned. Seeing Pippa in Meridan's arms had been shock enough but Jeremy's words, following close upon it, had upset her more. For while she realized that Meridan might have found it difficult to avoid proximity to the girl who was, after all, still his fiancée, there was no questioning the fact that they made a wonderful pair . . . that they looked the perfect complement of one another . . . that in appearance as well as in fact, they belonged.

'I should go away . . . leave them alone!' she thought with a conviction even more telling than she had felt it before. 'I ought not to be here. I can't stand it!'

Not even the look in Meridan's eyes,

as he came forward to offer her her glass, could comfort her. It had in it an appeal for understanding, for forgiveness for hurting her, his eyes openly revealing to her his love for her. Yet even that had not the power to make her feel welcome here, or that she had any right to be in this house while he remained engaged to another girl.

The arrival of Elizabeth and John and Peter Barnes, together with Meridan's parents, brought the conversation to a gay, lively level in which Charlotte tried desperately to join. But she felt completely out of her depth here for mostly they spoke of the coming hunting season and their horses. Had it not been for Peter Barnes, who had attached himself to her side, she would have felt more than ever out of place and character.

Dinner in the great oak-panelled dining-room was a sumptuous meal, served by a parlour-maid and a man-servant in pre-war style. The right wines were produced for each course and even the near out-of-date practices of using finger-bowls after dessert and leaving the men alone to pass round the port, were observed.

Back in the drawing-room with the ladies, Charlotte tried to disguise her own apprehension and unhappiness. But Pippa now sat beside her, engaging her in a conversation that could not be less than sheer agony for Charlotte, for she spoke continuously of Meridan.

'You've no idea how wonderful he has been to me all these weeks I've been ill!' the pretty, bell-like voice shrilled its message through the older girl's mind. 'And so patient with me. I suppose I have been a bit of a trial to everyone, but you know, it was a horrible shock . . . being so ill and . . . well, having to accept the facts of my operation. I suppose you know I can't have children now. It doesn't matter to me very much because I've never been very fond of babies anyway. But I minded desperately for Meridan. Naturally, I'd have broken the engagement if he'd wanted me to . . . but he didn't. Don't you think I'm lucky to have someone who loves me enough to put up with me even as I am now? But then Merry always was a darling . . . and so unself-ish . . . even as a little boy. You're aware, of course, that we've known one another for years and years?'

Charlotte was not to know that Pippa was choosing her every phrase with careful calculation, staking her claim to Merry, drumming in as hard as she could that he belonged to her . . . always had and always would. She was not ignorant of the effect her words were having on Charlotte whose sensitive face all too clearly revealed her state of mind.

'So she does love him, too!' Pippa thought. 'Well, let her try to take him from me!'

Yet somehow she did not think Charlotte would. She was not really afraid of losing him. In her own mind, she was far prettier than Charlotte . . . and she held all the trump cards in *her* hand.

'We hope to be married quite soon!'

she said aloud. 'I think the Autumn is a lovely time for a honeymoon. If you're going abroad as we are, it's not too hot. Merry and I both want to go to Spain . . . we've neither of us been there. Have you travelled much, Miss Matthews? I mean, Charlotte?'

'I spent all my childhood in India . . . but I've never been to Europe,' Charlotte said, knowing instinctively that Phillipa was not really interested in her life . . . that she merely wished to talk about her own.

'Liz said you worked in London in a solicitor's office. Isn't that terribly dull?'

'Well, it can be interesting sometimes!' Charlotte said, but knew that compared with the kind of things Pippa filled her day with, even the more interesting legal aspects of her job would seem dull by comparison.

'I often used to think I'd like a career!' Pippa said lightly. 'But then, I've known ever since I was in my teens that I'd marry as soon as I was old enough, so there wasn't any point in it.

I took a cookery course at the *Cordon Bleu* just so I could cook for Merry if we ever had to do without servants or the cook gave notice or something. But I didn't really enjoy it. I'm not very domesticated but Mummy says that won't matter. The kind of wife Merry needs is someone who can entertain for him and run his house. I'm very good at doing the flowers. Did you notice the ones in the hall? Liz and I did them together yesterday . . . '

'She's right!' Charlotte thought miserably. 'I can cook and sew and darn and type and I might make quite a good wife for a poorer man. But Meridan isn't poor . . . at least, it doesn't seem so . . . and he'll need someone with just Phillipa's background to run his home. I wouldn't begin to know how to cope with a big house like this!'

By nine o'clock, even the big house seemed to be over-flowing with people. Couples, whole families, arrived in their large cars and the young people were already dancing to the beautifully toned radiogram in the morning-room which had been turned into a ballroom the previous day. Charlotte soon lost sight of Meridan and Pippa ... of all the house-party guests in fact except Peter Barnes who clung tenaciously to her side. She still did not like him very much but was grateful to him for partnering her and for saving her from being the complete wallflower she now felt. At the same time, she was very much aware that her partner was holding her hand far too tightly and that everything he said was a subtly veiled compliment ... that he was, in short, flirting with her. She supposed it was partly her fault for agreeing to dance with him so consistently, and she found her efforts to strike a balance between gratitude and evasiveness very trying and tiring.

Her relief when Meridan finally stepped from amongst the crowded dance floor, firmly claiming her for the next waltz, was so acute that despite her intentions, she clung to him with desperation as he took her in his arms and swept her away from Peter Barnes's view.

'Darling, *darling!*' Meridan whispered. 'You know I came as soon as I could. People have been arriving for the last hour and as joint host with Liz I've just had to stay near the door to welcome them. You do understand?'

She swallowed, trying to dispel the lump that had gathered in her throat, the horrible threat of near tears assailing her.

'Charlotte, my darling, look up at me!'

But she couldn't do so. As they danced, he felt her trembling against him and knew that she was upset. Quickly, he guided her to the edge of the room and then, taking her hand, led her along the brightly lit hall and into the darkness of the billiard room. There, as he closed the door behind him, he gathered her quickly into his arms.

'Charlotte, darling, darling Charlotte!'

The tenderness of his voice, the indescribable relief of being alone with him, weakened her for a short while. She clung to him, returning his kisses, the tears now falling unheeded down her cheeks.

He could not see them in the darkness but he felt their salt taste against his lips and drew away from her in dismay.

'Charlotte, dearest, what in God's name is wrong? What has happened? Why are you crying?'

Filled with anxiety, he drew her across to the window-seat where the moonlight now flooded through the uncurtained windows, touching to diamonds the tears on her cheeks. He had never loved her more utterly, more tenderly, more protectively than he did at this moment when she was unhappy, afraid, and in need of him.

'I love you, Charlotte . . . with my whole heart! I cannot bear to see you cry. Has someone hurt you? Peter . . . he hasn't been bothering you?' He felt sick with anger and jealousy at the thought.

'It . . . it isn't really that . . . him . . . '
Charlotte said wretchedly. 'Though I
don't like him, Meridan. I wish he'd
leave me alone!'

'You shouldn't be so confoundedly
attractive!' Meridan said with a light-
heartedness he was far from feeling
himself but in the hope of cheering her
up. 'To tell the truth, I don't know him
awfully well myself. We never meet
socially but in the office he seems a
decent enough chap. What's he been
doing, Charlotte? I'll send him packing
if . . . '

She put a hand on his arm, shaking
her head.

'No, it isn't really his fault. I've been
dancing with him all evening and I
suppose he thinks I like his company.
Meridan . . . ' her voice took on a new,
more serious tone. 'Meridan, I can't
stay here. You must let me go home
. . . tomorrow.'

'Let you go home? Not stay here?
But Charlotte, darling, why? Peter can
go first thing if that's the trouble . . . '

'No, no, it isn't that at all!' Charlotte cried from her heart. 'It's because I don't belong here, Meridan . . . I don't belong here. Can't you see, this is all wrong . . . from every point of view? It isn't only Phillipa . . . though mostly it is, I suppose. But I've got to make you see the truth, Meridan . . . a truth I've only realized myself since coming here. Even if we love each other, it isn't enough. I'm not the right wife for you. Phillipa is!'

'It's not true, Charlotte!' Meridan cried, shaken beyond coherent thought by the revelation of her state of mind. 'You cannot say such things . . . this is my home, I know, but not the place where you and I will live when we are married. If you don't like this . . . well, we'll choose whatever you do like . . . the kind of place in which you feel you do belong.'

'Meridan, *please*! Can't you understand? I don't live in your world . . . Phillipa does. She loves you and she can't talk of anything but you and your future together. To her, it's a fact . . . and I can see now that she is right.'

'Right? *Right* . . . when I love you?' Meridan cried. 'What has she been saying to you, my darling? What's happened to make you feel like this? Can't you understand that I don't want anyone else for my wife . . . only you! You said just now that love wasn't enough. How can it fail to be if you love me as I love you? You haven't stopped caring for me, Charlotte?'

She might have lied to him but the desperate anxiety in his voice proved too much for her. Besides which, when she was with him, her doubts and anxiety receded and the only sure certainty of her love for him . . . of his for her . . . supplanted every other thought.

Her own suffocating feelings were revealed to him in the desperate little cry she gave as she flung her arms round him and pressed her face against his cheek.

'There, my darling, stupid girl!' he

said. 'How can you be so silly, dearest Charlotte? This is where you belong . . . here in my arms. Nothing else in the world matters!'

But it did . . . Phillipa mattered, and even as their lips met, the thought of her lay in each of their minds . . . Phillipa in her white dress . . . gay, brilliant, happy, in love . . . in love with Meridan to whom she was still engaged.

'Nothing can be right between Charlotte and me until I've broken my engagement!' Meridan thought desperately. 'It cannot go on like this. She is unhappy, and my position is intolerable. I must find a way of speaking to Pippa . . . tonight!'

The resolve made, he felt happier in his heart and more able to deal with this strange, desperate mood of Charlotte's. He sent her off to tidy her hair and re-make up her face, and waited in the hall for her until she came down. Then he took her back to the dance floor and uncaring of what anyone in the room who was observant enough to notice, he danced with her until late supper was announced. Then Charlotte, painfully aware that Phillipa, as she danced by with a variety of other partners, had noticed she was Meridan's constant companion, told Meridan that he must, for formality's sake, take Phillipa to the buffet.

'It isn't fair to humiliate her in front of your guests!' she reminded him.

'You're right!' Meridan said. 'All the same, I'd rather stay with you!'

As if he had been waiting for the moment for Meridan to absent himself, Peter Barnes appeared at Charlotte's side and, unable to refuse, she was led by him into the dining-room where a vast buffet refreshment lay waiting for the guests.

'I was watching you and Meridan dancing together,' he said, bringing the colour (not unnoticed by him) in a swift rush to her cheeks. 'Your steps match very well. I'd no idea he was such a good dancer!'

'Or that he's head over heels in love

with you!' thought the man. It was a pity the girl reciprocated the feeling as he could see quite obviously she did. He found her extraordinarily attractive, and was not used to having his advances met in so chilling a manner. Now he knew the cause, he did not feel so badly about it. Earlier, he had been peeved by her obvious reluctance to flirt with him.

Fully aware of Meridan's engagement to Phillipa Bates, he was by no means giving up the chase. To him, Charlotte had far too much attraction to let her go from his life so easily. There was something about her that caught and held a man, and he could quite understand how Meridan Avebury was so smitten . . . even to the point of forgetting his engagement to the pretty Phillipa. The younger girl might be prettier in the picture-book way, but Charlotte's face had more in it than mere prettiness . . . just as he guessed that her heart and emotions were capable of greater depths of feeling than

Phillipa even knew existed!

Peter Barnes, son of a Lancashire cotton man who had once been very wealthy, had been brought up to expect a certain standard of living. He had gone to the best schools and come away from them, realizing that his family were now socially beneath him. His father was a self-made man and only his money made him accepted in the society in which they moved. Not really through any fault of snobbism on Peter's part ... but because he had grown away from them an estrangement had grown up between him and them, and now he seldom saw them. He had seen the cotton slump coming and got out before the crash, starting again as a junior in Meridan Avebury's office immediately after the war.

He had brains and a native cunning in his north-country blood and he did well. Now he was making sufficient money to marry the kind of girl he wanted, and for the last few years it had been a question of finding the right girl.

He knew he would not be content with a Lancashire lass . . . such as his father had married. He wanted a wife with breeding, even if not with money. In fact, Charlotte exactly fitted the picture for she could hold her own in company such as this. Yet he knew from his earlier conversations with her, that she lived simply at home and was thoroughly domesticated as well as being an efficient secretary . . . just the wife for a man like himself who meant to get to the top. Charlotte could climb with him and when they had reached this kind of living . . . the Avebury home being his ideal . . . then she would be equally well able to act as gracious hostess as she could cook for him and mend his socks meanwhile!

It was entirely in keeping with Peter Barnes's character that he should have summed up the reasons for his finding Charlotte so attractive before he allowed himself to do so. Quick and shrewd, it had only taken him an afternoon to find out what he wanted and before dinner, he had resolved to marry her. It came as a bit of a shock to find she was in love with Avebury, but he was not discouraged. Clearly Avebury was going to marry Phillipa with both families' approval. No doubt the girl had money, too. Avebury would be a fool not to go through with it since Pippa had cash to add to his own! Were it not for the fact that he knew a girl of Phillipa's background would never consider marrying a mere two thousand a year, he might have made a play for her himself. Besides, even if her parents permitted such a wedding and she herself consented, he knew very well that she would soon run away with what cash he had. She had no doubt always had the best of everything . . . and she'd expect him to give it to her. No, Phillipa was not for him. But Charlotte . . .

For Peter Barnes, the best antidote for a setback with one girl was an affair with another. Mistakenly, he attributed the same feelings to others. He supposed that Charlotte could most easily be made to forget Meridan Avebury by his own skilful attentions. So far, she had certainly not reciprocated when he had tried to draw her a little closer as they danced, or to put his cheek against hers. Well, that he could understand. Half the time, her eyes were searching the room for Avebury and her attention was far from himself. But after supper, he would find a way to bring all of her attention to himself. He had no doubts as to his capabilities in the art of making love and he would be kissing Charlotte . . . really kissing her . . . before midnight.

He had no idea as he handed Charlotte plates of food she scarcely touched, that the Fates were conspiring to assist him. On the far side of the room, Phillipa was talking in an urgent voice to Meridan.

'Darling, can't you see what a good chance this is? I mean, all our friends are here and you know how booked up they get. Besides, it would add a nice flip to the party and I know Daddy will order up a case of champagne. Do let's, Merry . . . *please!*'

She was pleading with him to allow her to announce the date of their wedding. Desperately, Meridan sought for the right words to refuse her. He could not possibly tell her the truth at this moment, here amongst all these people, but somehow he must prevent her making things worse for them all.

'No, Pippa, please! I'm sorry to . . . to spoil the fun but it's quite out of the question. I don't know how things will be at the office and we can't begin to fix a date until . . . '

Phillipa pouted and put her hand against his mouth.

'I shall begin to think you're just making excuses, Merry. Never mind about the old office . . . you know your father will fix it for us. Let's say November the fifth . . . Guy Fawkes night. That would be fun . . . we might fix a firework party for them after we've gone away.'

'No, Pippa . . . *no!*' Meridan said

firmly. But with a gay little laugh, she had run from him and he watched her threading her way through the guests towards his father and mother. As if in a nightmare where his feet were rooted to the floor, paralysing him from action, he saw her whispering in his father's ear, watched the smile spread over his face as he in turn leant to whisper in his wife's ear. Then he patted Pippa on the shoulder and stood up, clapping his hands. Within a few seconds it was done . . . too late for Meridan to move forward to stop him. Silence fell and all faces were turned towards Mr. Avebury.

'Friends, I have something nice to tell you all . . . ' Feverishly, Meridan sought amongst the faces and at last, his eyes met Charlotte's. They never faltered while the kindly, happy voice went on . . . 'Phillipa and my son, Meridan, have now fixed a date for their wedding . . . a month from now . . . November the fifth. They want you to know you will all be invited to the wedding. Meanwhile, let's drink to their health in champagne . . . '

'Charlotte, Charlotte . . . I couldn't help it . . . she acted against my wishes . . . I couldn't do anything . . . ' But Charlotte's dead-white face was turned away from him. He saw her nod her head as the man beside her addressed her and follow him quietly out of the room.

7

It was a full ten minutes before Meridan could escape to find Charlotte and explain. His friends were crowding round him on all sides, thumping him affectionately on the shoulders, shaking his hand, questioning him about the coming wedding. In vain, he tried to push through the circle but they would not let him go. Phillipa edged in beside him and clung to his arm. Once he looked down at her and with a little stab of fear, she saw that the dark eyes were full of reproach . . . and bitter anger.

'Have I gone too far?' she asked herself. 'Have I pushed him too quickly?' But she quickly reassured herself. After all, they were engaged. And if November really didn't suit Meridan, it could always be postponed a while longer. Nevertheless, he had given office work as an excuse and his own father had said it was nonsense . . . that it was quite a quiet spell and Merry could get away for three weeks if he'd a mind to.

But her reassurance did not last long for it soon became obvious to her that Meridan was paying no attention to the remarks made to him, but was trying hard to get out of the circle surrounding them. A thin, stubborn line turned her pretty, smiling mouth down at the corners. He should not go! He should not!

But she could not prevent him without a scene. Quietly but firmly he at last detached her hand from his arm and, despite the occasional curious glance of an observant onlooker, broke away from Phillipa and went quickly to the door.

The arrival of the champagne saved Phillipa's face but she was horribly conscious of Merry's absence when her father called the toast.

'Where's the boy gone?' he called

across the room.

'He was wanted on the phone!' Pippa lied, her eyes smiling gaily but her heart heavy. Where had Merry gone? Her eyes searched the room and within a moment, had noticed Charlotte's absence. Feverishly, she wondered what to do now. Follow him? Perhaps find him in some compromising position which she could not possibly feign to ignore. No! Let him go for the time being. Sheer good manners demanded that he return soon . . .

Out in the moonlit drive, shivering uncontrollably, Charlotte was held in a tight embrace. As yet, Peter Barnes had not attempted to kiss her. He had grabbed his chance when Meridan's father made his little speech and suggested in a whisper to Charlotte that the room was far too hot and would she not like some fresh air? Desperately grateful for this chance to escape, Charlotte had agreed. She would have agreed to anything then to get away from the cheering, happy friends, and Meridan's betrayal. He *must* have known what was going to happen! Phillipa would not have dared to have such an announcement made without his approval. Not even the appeal in Meridan's eyes as they held hers across the room, could soften the moment for her. However much he might be disliking what was happening, he could have spared her the shock . . . the humiliation . . . the despair . . .

'Charlotte . . . let me drive you back to London . . . now, tonight?'

'So Peter Barnes knows . . . he has guessed!' Charlotte thought wearily. 'Well, I suppose it must be pretty obvious to him.'

She tried to draw back from his arms but he held her tightly, and because she was so cold and miserable, she did not fight against him for long.

'I'm sure I could hire a car . . . even at this hour of the night!' the man was saying. 'Wouldn't you like to go home?'

Yes! More than anything in the world she longed for the blessed peace and quiet and ordinariness of her little room

. . . her mother's kind, comforting presence . . . to be away from this house . . . from Phillipa . . . from Meridan himself.

Yet some remnant of pride remained to her despite the shock she had endured. She would not run away. She would stay it out . . . show Meridan that her mind was quite made up. After what had happened tonight, she could not possibly go on seeing him.

'I can go home tomorrow!' she said quietly. 'I'm all right now, thank you. Please . . . let me go!'

But he wasn't prepared to give her up so easily. His arms tightened round her and a moment later, she was twisting her head away to avoid his kiss. She heard his short, hard laugh, and then with one hand at the back of her head, he turned her almost brutally to face him, and his mouth came down on hers. She struggled violently, hating him and loathing this embrace more than anything in the world she had ever experienced. Had her mouth been free, she would have cried out.

But there was no need. Before either of them knew what was happening, Meridan had wrenched Barnes away from her and pushed him viciously to the ground.

'If you ever go near Charlotte again, I'll . . .'

'Meridan, please!' Shaking uncontrollably, but still sufficiently in charge of her senses, Charlotte laid a restraining hand on Meridan's arm. His face, white in the moonlight, was distorted with anger . . . with many other emotions, too. It would only make matters worse if there was a fight between the two men.

Slowly, Peter Barnes got to his feet. His instinct was to hit back . . . physical blows that would salve his pride. But beyond even pride, there was caution in his make-up. Upon Meridan Avebury he depended for his job . . . his career. If he hit him now, he'd be bound to lose his job.

'I . . . think . . . you owe me an

apology, Avebury!' he said slowly.

'An apology!' Meridan was almost shouting. 'Couldn't you see she didn't want your damned kisses?'

Peter Barnes took a chance. Turning to Charlotte, he said evenly:

'That, surely, is for Charlotte to say. She came out here quite willingly with me and allowed me to . . . well, to hold her in my arms. Naturally, that led me to suppose she wouldn't object to a kiss or two.'

'He's quite right, Meridan!' Charlotte admitted tiredly. 'It was probably my own fault!'

'Well, damn' well don't try it again!' Meridan said furiously.

'Again, I imagine that is for Charlotte to say!' Barnes retorted coolly. 'After all, she isn't exactly your property, is she?'

Meridan had never felt more impotently furious in his life. What this man said was all too true . . . Charlotte was not his. Moreover, he had no right to interfere between her and another man.

He decided suddenly to tell Barnes the truth . . . he would know sooner or later in any event. Calmer now, he said:

'Naturally, you are not aware of the position. I'm in love with Charlotte and she is in love with me. I hope to make her my wife . . . as soon as I'm free to do so!'

Peter Barnes pretended complete surprise.

'But surely that's fantastic!' he said innocently. 'Just now . . . I heard your father announce your wedding date . . . to Phillipa Bates? Forgive me if I made a mistake.'

'No, you didn't!' Meridan said, his tone icy. 'But Phillipa spoke in ignorance of the true position, and without my permission. I'm going to tell her tonight, when the party has broken up. Now, if you'll be good enough, I'd like to speak to Charlotte alone!'

'No, Meridan!' Charlotte broke in. She felt she could stand no more of this. He must be made to understand somehow that she could not go on with it. She could not . . . would not stand in Phillipa's way. 'Please, I'm terribly tired. I'm going indoors . . . to my room.'

'Charlotte, please!' Meridan begged her, uncaring of the man standing watching them, a secret smile playing about his lips.

'No, Meridan!' Charlotte said again. 'Let me go!'

'I'll take you in!' Peter Barnes broke in smoothly. 'And please let me apologize for what happened just now . . . I had no idea . . . '

There was no alternative if she wished to escape from Meridan but to go with Peter. In any event, she felt sure he would not try to force his attentions on her now. And she dared not stay here alone with Meridan . . . allow him to weaken her resolve again.

'Charlotte!'

'I'm sorry, Meridan. I just can't stand any more!' she said, her voice near to tears.

Meridan let her go. After all, there

was nothing he need say to her now. To make fresh avowals of his love was not necessary and probably wouldn't be welcome to her in her present state. When he saw her tomorrow, he would be in a far happier position . . . free to speak his heart. He'd tell Phillipa tonight that it was all over . . . tell his family, too; and in the morning, he'd take Charlotte back to London . . . away from it all.

He lit a cigarette and smoked slowly until his nerves were back to normal. He felt calm and quite determined. Nothing . . . no one should prevent him speaking to Pippa tonight.

The conviction that what he was about to do was the right course remained with him only a few moments. As he turned to go back indoors, a girl came running across the drive, calling to him. It was his sister, Elizabeth.

'Merry, what *are* you doing out there? We've been searching the house for you. Come in right away . . . Pippa's ill again . . . she's fainted!'

'Oh, God, no!' Meridan said in a hoarse cry.

Thinking him to be concerned about the younger girl, Liz said reassuringly:

'It's not all that bad, Merry. She has come round and is asking for you. She's wrapped up in blankets in Father's big chair in the library . . . the guests are all going home. What an end to our party! I suppose Pippa has been overdoing it . . . we ought to have taken more care of her. Mother has sent for the doctor and he should be here soon.'

'Let's go in by the garden door!' Meridan said, anxious to avoid the now-departing guests.

'You go that way! I'd better go and see everyone off. I'll say good-bye for you!' Liz said kindly. 'Do hurry, Merry. Pippa's been asking for you for ten minutes or more.'

Even now, Meridan did not guess at Phillipa's duplicity. It never once occurred to any of them that she had skilfully pretended the faint when Meridan remained away so long. Had it not been for her anxiety about Meridan out there alone with Charlotte, she might very much have enjoyed the commotion she caused when she fell back against the people pressing round her, her champagne glass slipping from her hand and breaking dramatically into a hundred pieces on the polished floor!

She lay now, huddled in the chair, her eyes closed, waiting for him. Merry could not very well be angry with her while she appeared ill!

He came into the room and stood there looking down at her. The beautiful white gown was covered in a tartan rug, the brilliant colours accentuating the pallor of the girl's face. She looked young and defenceless and for a moment, his courage failed. How could he tell her what he *must* tell her when she looked as she did!

'Merry! Darling, I'm so terribly sorry to have spoiled the party for you. Are you very cross with me?'

She held out her hand to him appealingly. By force of habit, he made to move towards her, then abruptly, turned away.

'Of course you couldn't help it, Pippa. I'm not cross about the party . . . only because of what you did . . . said . . . '

This was far more difficult than Pippa had imagined. She had expected that Meridan would come to her and take her in his arms.

'Oh, Merry . . . you mean about the wedding date? But your father told me it would be perfectly all right for you to leave the office and you'd said it was only because you might not be able to get away from work . . . '

Her voice broke and the tears spilled easily down her cheeks. He knew she was crying and had to fight with himself to say what he must say . . . no matter how ill she might be.

'Look, Pippa . . . try to understand that . . . that . . . ' he had turned to face her but the sight of her tear-drenched face unnerved him completely.

'I'm beginning to think you don't want to marry me at all . . . that you

199

don't love me any more!'

It was the opening Meridan wanted and he moved impulsively to her side, taking her hand in his own.

'Pippa, please listen to me. I *must* talk to you. It isn't that I'm any the less fond of you than I ever was . . . but I don't . . . I *can't* marry you now.'

The enormous blue eyes stared at him through a mist of tears. Her voice was barely audible as she said:

'You mean . . . because I can't give you children?'

'Pippa, no!' Meridan said frantically. 'I swear that had nothing to do with it.'

'But it must be that!' Pippa said quickly. 'You say you still love me . . . that you haven't changed towards me. If that's true, why don't you want to marry me? I don't understand!'

Helpless, Meridan turned away from her.

'Pippa, I can't marry you . . . because . . . because I'm in love with someone else!'

For a moment, silence held the great

room in its grip. Then Pippa's voice, high-pitched, almost hysterical, cried:

'But that can't be the truth . . . you're engaged to me . . . you just said you loved me! Merry, tell me you didn't mean it . . . you were just trying to punish me . . . to make me suffer because of what I did!'

She had struggled out of her chair and he had to force her down again, but could not disentangle her hold on his arms. The tears were pouring down her face now, genuine tears for she was frightened at last. She had never believed that Merry would speak out like this . . . that he was beyond appeal. She clung to him unashamedly, without a shred of pride. And beneath her desperation was a stubborn determination not to let him go.

'Pippa, please try to calm yourself . . . you'll make yourself ill,' Meridan said wretchedly. 'I promise you on my word of honour that it has nothing to do with what happened tonight. I'd have told you weeks ago if you had not been so ill. I'm in love with someone else, Pippa. It wouldn't be right for me to marry you now.'

'But you said you loved me . . . you just said so!' Pippa cried.

'I'll always be fond of you . . . always love you . . . but not as I love Charlotte!' Meridan said more cruelly than he had intended. 'I'm sorry to hurt you like this, Pippa, but it just happened . . . to both of us. Please, try to understand!'

'I can't . . . I *don't!*' Pippa wept. 'What has Charlotte to do with it? It's just a . . . an attraction between you . . . not love. I *know* you love me, Merry. You can't stop loving me now when I need you so much!'

'Pippa, please!' Meridan cried help-lessly. 'You mustn't talk like that . . . '

'But it's true, it's true!' Pippa broke in. 'You know how ill I've been . . . how terribly upset because of . . . of what they did to me. If you leave me, I'll never believe it isn't because of that. And you promised me, *promised* me it didn't make any difference to you. I'd have let you go there, in hospital. I was too ill to have cared then. But you swore it didn't matter and I began to hope again. It's only the thought of your love for me and your wish to marry me despite what happened that has got me well again. If you leave me now, I'll kill myself . . . I swear I will!'

'Pippa!'

She had deliberately worked herself up to a pitch of hysteria and now she was no longer quite in control of herself. When the door opened at that moment to admit Elizabeth, she was genuinely crying.

'Pippa, Merry, what has been happening? Pippa, stop crying this minute. You'll make yourself ill!'

'I don't care . . . I want to die!' Pippa wept. 'I want to die!'

Elizabeth was on her knees by the weeping girl, her face turned to her brother's with concern.

'Merry, what is she talking about? What has happened?'

203

'He doesn't love me now . . . he doesn't want to marry me. Oh, Liz, I wish I'd died in hospital. I ought never to have believed him when he promised me it made no difference. I can see now that he only said that to make me well . . . '

'Pippa, I swear that isn't true. Liz, tell Pippa the truth . . . that it is only because I'm in love with Charlotte . . . and she with me!'

Elizabeth felt hopelessly torn by conflicting loyalties. She knew how dreadful this scene must be for Merry and yet all her instinct was to protect the weeping girl who was so like a young sister to her.

'Merry, what can have possessed you to tell her *now* . . . when she's ill!' she said reproachfully.

'He wanted to punish me . . . because I got your father to announce our wedding date . . . and Merry hadn't agreed. Oh, Liz, I know it was wrong of me . . . and I'm sorry, truly sorry, but it isn't fair of Merry to torture me like this. It isn't true, is it? He *is* going to marry me? He isn't really in love with . . . with Charlotte?'

Ignoring the appeal on his sister's face, Meridan said desperately:

'I can't lie, Liz . . . it's too late for that.'

Very gently, Liz stroked the younger girl's hair.

'I'm afraid Merry is in earnest, Pippa darling. He is in love with Charlotte!'

'But he just told me he loved me . . . that he always had and always would!' Pippa cried frantically. 'I don't believe he's in love with anyone else . . . it's just a passing attraction. I can see how it happened . . . meeting her when I was ill and he was lonely. And I've not been very good company while I've been getting better. But you'll see . . . both of you . . . I'll be my old self again now. I don't mind if we aren't married in November . . . Merry will want time to get over . . . over this silly little affair. And I'll wait . . . no matter how long.'

It isn't that she hasn't any pride, Elizabeth told herself miserably. It's that she simply can't believe Merry doesn't want her. She truly thinks he still loves her . . . otherwise she could never debase herself like this.

All the same, it was horrible to have to listen to her talking like this . . . must be even more horrible for Merry.

The unbearable situation was brought to an end by the arrival of the doctor. With one worried glance at Pippa's tear-streaked face, he told Meridan to carry her straight upstairs to bed.

'She's quite exhausted!' he said. 'If you've a room for her here it would be far better than for her to be taken home. Can you carry her upstairs, Meridan?'

Obediently, Meridan stooped to gather the girl in his strong arms. Pity and compassion mingled with a strange antipathy to holding her thus closely against him. As she leant nearer him, he lifted his face a little and then, guilty at his inhuman behaviour, clasped her more firmly in his arms.

He did not speak as he carried her upstairs and she lay quietly in his arms. But as he laid her on Liz's bed, she clung a moment to his hands and whispered:

'You didn't mean it, did you, Merry? When I wake up tomorrow, all this will just be a bad dream?'

He would have given anything at that moment to be able to reassure her ... to comfort her. She looked so broken and helpless and ill, lying there on the bright blue eiderdown like a broken doll. But he could not lie. He bent and kissed her lightly on the forehead as any kindly elder brother might do, and quietly left the room.

Ten minutes later, as the library clock chimed two, Liz joined Merry in the library, where he sat with a glass of brandy untouched in his hand.

'She's asleep!' Liz said wearily, sinking into a leather arm-chair, her face showing her own fatigue and concern. 'Fortunately, mother had some luminol tablets, and Doc gave Pippa two. She went out like a light.'

'I suppose you think I've behaved appallingly!' Meridan said thoughtfully. 'But it had to come sometime, Liz. You don't know how difficult it has been for me to go on pretending even so long as this.'

'But why tonight . . . when she was ill anyway?' Liz asked. 'Couldn't it have waited a few more hours . . . until tomorrow?'

'I suppose I should have waited!' Meridan said wearily. 'But I didn't stop to think. Liz, you don't know what happened. Pippa came to me earlier this evening asking me if we couldn't fix a date for our wedding and announce it to the party . . . to give it an extra flip, I suppose. I refused, pleading work at the office or something. Then she went to Father and next thing, he'd made that announcement. You can imagine how I felt . . . and how Charlotte must have felt.'

'No, I didn't know that!' Liz said, wondering what could have possessed

Pippa to do such a thing; some silly caprice no doubt, made innocently enough, but calculated to bring Merry to a point where he felt he must act.

'Charlotte went out with Peter Barnes; she was pretty shocked, I think. When I found her, he was trying to make love to her. How I dislike that man, Liz! But I suppose it isn't fair to blame him entirely. After all, he didn't know about Charlotte and . . . and me. Anyway, there was a scene and I realized then that it couldn't go on. It wasn't fair to anyone, Charlotte most of all. I determined at all costs to talk to Pippa tonight. I *had* to, Liz.'

Elizabeth reached for a cigarette and bent forward as Meridan held out his lighter. Her eyes looked into his face searchingly.

'Merry, you are quite sure . . . really sure about Charlotte? It would be so awful if you were doing all this for . . . for a passing fancy.'

'Liz, I love her!' Merry said sharply. 'It . . . it isn't just that she has been inaccessible? I mean, because you've felt you weren't free that freedom suddenly became doubly important?'

'I love Charlotte with my whole heart!' Merry said vehemently. 'And even if she went away and I never saw her again, I could not marry Pippa, fond as I am of her. I know now what love means, Liz. No matter what happens, I couldn't marry Pippa!'

'Yet you thought once you did love her!'

'Yes, I know! But not this way; not as I now know love can be. I still love Pippa much the same way as I love you, Liz. That just isn't the right way for marriage.'

'I don't know how you're going to make Pippa see it!' Liz said anxiously. 'She simply doesn't believe it, Merry. The last thing she said to me was that tomorrow it would all be all right; that you couldn't have meant it; that she *knew* you still cared for her!'

'Charlotte can't possibly stay on here now!' Meridan said thoughtfully. 'I'd like to drive her back to London tomorrow morning, before Pippa is up and about.'

'But, Merry, you can't just walk out on her . . . on Pippa, I mean. You'll have to be here to face her in the morning.'

'I'm not running away!' Meridan said frankly. 'I'll take Charlotte home in the morning and I'll be back tomorrow afternoon. You can explain to Pippa what I'm doing and why. I'll talk to her when I get back . . . when she's calmer. Maybe she'll accept that I'm in deadly earnest then and put an end to this. Try to make her understand!'

'And shall I tell Mother and Father what has happened?' Liz asked. 'And John?'

'If you think it advisable!' Meridan said. 'I've no doubt they'll all take a very poor view of me . . . but I can't help it, Liz. I've got to stand by Charlotte. Surely you see that?'

Elizabeth tried hard to see herself in Meridan's shoes . . . engaged to someone else and loving John. But then it was so much easier for a girl to break off her engagement. It was an ordinary thing for a girl to do and no ugly implications were attached to such action. Yet when a man tried to do the same . . . even the law of the country permitted breach of promise action and he was generally condemned by everyone for jilting the girl. It hardly seemed fair!

'Poor old Merry!' she said, affectionately pushing a hand through his hair. 'I think you'd better go to bed now. Try to get some sleep . . . you look ghastly!'

'And feel it!' Meridan said, getting to his feet and following Liz from the room. 'I'm terribly sorry, Liz . . . to be bringing you into this. It can't be easy for you . . . especially once John knows. If you'd rather stay out of it . . . well, I'll understand.'

'But I can't keep out of it. You're my brother, Merry, and I want to help you, but Pippa is John's sister and my friend too. I'm as much in this as you are!'

'I'm sorry!' Meridan said again. 'But maybe now it'll all be over soon.'

He would have felt even more anxious, were that possible, had he known what a long time this situation had yet to continue . . . how much they would all suffer for it . . . and how ultimately the final penalty would have to be paid by him alone.

8

When Charlotte woke next morning, it was to find a note on the early-morning tea-tray brought in by the maid. It was from Meridan and read:

Darling,
I want to take you home this morning. Could you give out after breakfast that you've had a phone call to say your mother isn't well. I'll drive you in my car and explain then.
Meridan.

As there was nothing she wanted so much as to leave this house, Charlotte quickly packed her things so that she would be ready as soon as Meridan wished to leave. Briefly she explained to Bess what had happened last night and the real reason she supposed Meridan was taking her home.

Fortunately, only Meridan was down to breakfast when the gong sounded . . . everyone else was late and he was able to tell her briefly that he had finally told Pippa; that as she had not taken it too well and was still in the house, he thought it better for all of them if Charlotte went home.

During the long drive through the country and the deserted Sunday London streets, he gave her a fuller account of what had happened, trying to make light of Phillipa's desperate appeals and her refusal to accept what he had told her. But Charlotte was not entirely deceived.

'She doesn't want to release you, Meridan!' she stated when he had finished his story.

'I'm sure she will, when she realizes I'm serious!' Meridan said, his hands gripping the wheel, his face white and strained. 'Naturally, she found it difficult to credit what had happened. After all, I'd given her no cause to believe until now that I had any interest in

. . . in anyone else.'

Charlotte looked down at her gloved hands, her expression deeply disturbed and unhappy.

'Suppose she will not let you go?'

'But that's nonsense!' Meridan said sharply. 'I'm not married to Phillipa.'

They drove in silence for a few miles. Then Charlotte said:

'I can't go on seeing you, Meridan . . . not now! I just can't bear any more of this.'

'Darling!' For a moment, his hand left the wheel and gripped hers tightly. 'I know it's been horrible for you . . . and I understand how you feel. But it'll all be over soon. Then I'll come for you.'

'Meridan!'

She struggled to find expression for the words that had to be said.

'Meridan, I can't feel happy about it . . . now less than ever. It was bad enough when we had to deceive her . . . but if she really loves you . . . really is going to make herself ill if she loses you, then surely what we are doing is wrong? We *can't* be happy . . . either of us . . . knowing she is wretched and miserable and alone.'

'She won't be alone!' Meridan said sharply, trying not to recognize similar fears in his own heart. 'She'll have Mother and Father and her own parents and John and Liz. They'll all be sympathetic and understanding.'

'I . . . I suppose so. I wish . . . I wish I didn't feel so guilty!'

'Guilty? Because you love me?' Meridan's cry was wrung from his heart.

'Other people have loved and denied their love for the sake of what they believed to be right!' Charlotte said quietly.

'Charlotte! You can't honestly tell me you believe it would be right for me to marry Pippa . . . loving *you*, knowing you love me?'

'I'm not sure. I know it sounds an absurd sacrifice and yet . . . ' She broke off, unable to express the strange feeling inside her.

'Charlotte, tell me honestly, do you doubt my love for you? Yours for me?'

'No, no I don't!' That at least she could say with sincerity.

'Then how can you doubt that we should be married to one another?'

'It doesn't always follow . . . people in love have had to part before now . . . because their sense of duty was more important to them.'

'Charlotte, darling, what are you trying to tell me? That I have a duty to Pippa?'

'In a way!' Charlotte said. 'Oh, Meridan, I don't know. Perhaps I'm just tired and depressed and I'm being illogical and stupid. It's just because I keep thinking that if we hadn't met, Phillipa would be happy now . . . instead of ill and miserable!'

'Darling, that's madness . . . to think that way. We have met . . . and I believe that sooner or later we would have done so anyway. How much worse all this would have been if I'd already been married to her!'

Of course, he was right, Charlotte told herself. And when she really put it to herself that she would never see Meridan again if she denied her own great love for him, the mere thought was almost unbearable. He had become so painfully dear to her ... so absolutely necessary to her. She might not have found much happiness with him and yet she knew she would find no happiness in a world without him.

'And suppose Phillipa feels that way, too!' she thought. 'How much more so since Meridan has been part of her life ever since she was a child!'

If she could only forget Phillipa ... forget that Meridan had ever asked her to marry him, how simple and wonderful and perfect her love and Meridan's could have been.

She clung to him in desperate need of his strength and reassurance as he parted from her just inside the door of her house. Her mother and aunt must be out walking for the house was empty and they were quite alone for their leave-taking.

Feverishly, Meridan was kissing her eyes, her lips, crushing her body against his own as if he could not bear to let her go.

'I love you, I love you, I love you!' he said, over and over again until the sound had no meaning in her ears but became an answering cry in her own heart.

Their need of one another . . . the spiritual need of comfort and love and reassurance was translated in the ever-growing physical need that mounted with every moment in his arms. A great lethargy seemed to take hold of Charlotte's mind and body, and she knew that she was rapidly losing control of her senses. Right and wrong no longer had meaning . . . only this was right . . . this deep-felt longing in every fibre of her being for Meridan's closeness . . . for merging into his being . . . becoming one with him for all time.

It was Meridan who released her

. . . so suddenly that she almost fell backwards away from him, her breath coming in quick gasps, her whole body trembling.

'No, Charlotte, no!' he whispered hoarsely although there was no one to hear his voice but her. 'Not this way. I'm going now . . . but I'll come back for you . . . as soon as I can . . . and we'll be married immediately.'

As she put out her hand to him in a gesture of complete submission, he did not take it but moved away from her, only his face belying the movement, and his voice, full of tenderness as he said:

'I dare not touch you again, my darling. I'm going now . . . before it's too late.'

She understood what he was saying to her . . . knowing full well her own weakness, greater even than his. He wished to protect her as much from herself as from him.

'Good-bye, darling!'

She stood perfectly still, watching

him go, desperately wanting to run after him, to hold him, to prevent his leaving her. It was only by exerting an iron will that she kept still and silent. Then, as she heard the door of the car slam behind him, the engine start and disappear slowly into the distance, did she relax her statue-like position, and covering her face with her hands, break into a storm of tears.

* * *

Ever since he had been a small boy, Meridan had got along well with his mother. There seemed to have existed a special bond of understanding between them despite the fact that Mrs. Avebury always had a nanny or governess to look after the children. But he had known all his life that he could knock on his mother's bedroom door and be welcomed by her to come in and tell her his boyish problems, listen to her sympathy or advice and go away comforted.

He had a sincere affection and admiration for the dainty little woman who so, surprisingly, had given birth to him. Now, from his six foot of height, he looked down on her almost as if she were his child, so tiny and young-looking was she despite her grey hair. But for once, the bond of understanding between them seemed to have failed them both. Immediately upon his return from London, Meridan had gone to see her . . . before he saw Pippa again. She was resting on her bed following luncheon which Meridan had missed. She had insisted on ordering a cold meal to be sent up on a tray for him, but he was not hungry and, after toying with the food, had pushed the tray from him. His mother watched him anxiously.

'You know, darling, you really should eat properly. A man of your size needs food. We'll be having you ill next.'

'How . . . how is Pippa?' Meridan has asked, busying himself over the lighting of a cigarette in order to avoid his mother's eyes.

'Rested . . . but still not well enough to get up!' she told him. 'Look, Merry, Liz told me everything this morning. I simply can't understand you! No wonder poor darling Pippa is so stunned!'

Meridan drew in his breath sharply.

'It's really perfectly simple, Mother. I've fallen in love with Charlotte and she with me. That's all there is to it. Under the circumstances, I can't possibly marry Pippa . . . and I must make her see that.'

'It really has nothing to do with her operation? I could understand you wanting children and be unwilling to give them up.'

Meridan gave his mother a quizzical glance. Strange that his mother should take so opposite a view. Had this really been the reason for his wishing to break his engagement to Pippa, he would never in a hundred years have done so.

'No!' he said adamantly. 'It has nothing whatever to do with it. If I still loved Pippa . . . or had ever loved her as

I now understand love to mean, I would want to marry her as much as ever.'

'I gather Pippa is convinced Charlotte is only an excuse. Are you quite sure that, subconsciously, this isn't your real reason for breaking with her?'

'No, no, *no*!' Meridan said violently. 'Can't you understand, Mother . . . I'm in love with Charlotte, really in love.'

His mother gave a sigh that clearly showed Meridan the state of her mind . . . worried, disbelieving, disappointed.

'Look, Mother, you have to believe what I'm saying. I met Charlotte at Angela Peters's wedding rehearsal. I fell in love with her then. Since, we've met many times and every time I see her, I am more sure than ever that I love her. You couldn't want me to marry Pippa feeling as I do for some other girl?'

'But you thought you were in love with Pippa!' his mother argued reasonably. 'How are you so certain you are right this time?'

'I had never really given 'love' a thought!' Meridan said simply. 'I've always been fond of Pippa . . . and after Liz and John got engaged, well, it occurred to me that it might be nice for Pippa and I to marry in due course, too. I'd simply no idea of what loving meant . . . loving the way I love Charlotte.'

'Love!' Mrs. Avebury echoed. 'It's a much-debated word, Merry, and I'm not at all sure you aren't confusing it with attraction. I know men do get these overwhelming passions for women . . . but surely a lifelong association with Pippa . . . your fondness for her and your shared interests and backgrounds make the feeling you have for her much nearer real love?'

'You are trying to persuade yourself that I am not genuinely in love with Charlotte because you want me to marry Pippa. Well, I can't, Mother. Charlotte is my life now. I know it's only a comparatively short while since we met. But you don't know her as I do.'

'I thought she seemed a very nice girl!' his mother replied easily. The description seemed to Meridan so inadequate for the girl who meant so much to him that for a moment, Meridan almost smiled.

'Perhaps she does seem ordinary to you . . . but not to me!' he said. 'She is everything I've ever imagined a woman should be . . . sweet, innocent, loving, generous, thoughtful, intelligent.'

'And Pippa is not?'

Meridan sighed.

'Yes, I suppose she has many of those qualities, too. I suppose many people would consider Pippa to be prettier, too. But, Mother, surely you can understand? After all, you must have been as much in love with Father when you married him?'

Mrs. Avebury shot her son a swift look and then surprised him greatly by saying:

'As a matter of fact, I was not. I'd wished desperately at the time to marry a young medical student of whom my parents strongly disapproved. He had no money and would have been quite unable to support me at all, let alone in the manner to which I'd been brought up. Meanwhile your father had asked me to marry him and although for two years I refused to allow my parents to persuade me to do so, I eventually gave in. And Merry, I've never been sorry. I was not cut out for life as the wife of a struggling young doctor, living in poverty. I would have been a handicap to him and I'm quite sure the love we believed so important at the time would soon have faded. As it was, I grew fond of your father quite quickly. He was always devoted to me and in time, I grew to love him. Our marriage has been an ideally happy one for us both. So you see, it isn't always the passionate love that endures or makes a marriage a success.'

Meridan was silent . . . digesting this surprising story he had never guessed at before. Although he never doubted its authenticity, he knew that it was not really relevant. For one thing, his mother had been very young at the time

. . . only nineteen when she had married his father, and therefore still a girl when she had believed herself in love with the medical student. She could not really have loved him . . . not as *he* loved Charlotte . . . or she would have waited until she was of age and married him despite her parents' disapproval; despite the poverty and hard work she would have had to expect. Love took no account of such things.

'I cannot see that your story proves very much,' he said gently. 'After all, it is I who will be supporting Charlotte, and while she may not have been used to quite so much money as there always has been in our family . . . or Pippa's, she would nevertheless be perfectly at ease as my wife. We have a great deal in common, a love of good music, of dancing, of the theatre; a preference for country life rather than a town existence; we both like animals and children; we both enjoy the simple, quiet life. I am absolutely certain that we are perfectly suited . . . in every way.'

'No two people could be more perfectly matched than you and Pippa!'

'Mother!' Meridan said sharply. 'I just don't love her!'

His mother gave him a quick, worried glance. It was unlike Merry to be so adamant, so stubborn. He had always been an adaptable child, easy-going and open to suggestion. He had seemed to derive his own happiness from other people's enjoyment and was, in her view, one of the easiest people in the world to get along with. Now he was suddenly showing quite a different character. What she had not realized was that people of Meridan's temperament could be easy-going until something really mattered to them, and then become far more stubborn and immovable than their opposites.

She, herself, had not disliked Charlotte . . . at least, not until she recognized her as the cause of breaking up what seemed to her to be the perfect match. Even then she could find no particular fault with the girl and had to admit that Liz had said she was perfectly sweet and would make Merry a good wife.

But she could not give up the idea of Pippa as a daughter-in-law so easily. The girl had been part of their family life for so long that there would have been no difficulty or trouble in having her as a daughter-in-law and she knew that with Pippa as his wife, Merry would not be lost to her. If he married Charlotte, things might be very different. The girl might want to live elsewhere ... certainly she would not want to live in the same neighbourhood as Pippa! And there would be difficulties for Liz and John, too ... not to speak of poor Pippa's feelings in the matter.

'I never thought you could be hard, Merry,' she said into the silence. 'How can you hurt Pippa like this?'

Meridan's face was suddenly white and drawn.

'Surely you realize that it's the most dreadful thing I've ever had to do? But

I had to do it, Mother . . . you must see that. I couldn't marry her under false pretences. She would have been no happier than I would be.'

'Well, I don't know about that, Merry. For one thing, she doesn't believe you've ceased to care for her.'

'I haven't 'ceased to care for her'!' Meridan broke in angrily. 'I'll always be fond of Pippa. I just can't love her the way I know now a man should love his wife.'

'But that comes after marriage, Merry dear!'

It seemed suddenly hopeless to Meridan. How could he make his mother understand his feelings for Charlotte? If not her co-operation, at least he had expected understanding from her. He knew suddenly in his heart that his mother didn't want to understand . . . that she wanted him to marry Pippa despite his love for Charlotte.

No longer able to bear a continuation of the conversation he excused himself, saying he must go and talk to Pippa. It was an interview he dreaded but nevertheless knew he must endure. Pippa must be made to see that he had meant every word he said last night . . . that it was all over between them and that he would never be dissuaded from marrying Charlotte.

9

Liz met her brother outside Pippa's door . . . or rather her own bedroom door where Pippa had been taken last night and still lay in bed. Hastily, she drew her brother farther along the landing and said:

'Merry, dear, I'm afraid it isn't going to be easy! Mother was in with Pippa for an hour this morning . . . after I'd told her what had happened. Mother took the worst possible line. She kept telling Pippa she was sure you didn't mean it; that it would all blow over and that if she just was patient, it would come right in the end.'

'Oh, no!' Meridan said frantically. 'Couldn't you stop her, Liz?'

'I tried!' Elizabeth said. 'After Mother had gone, I told Pippa I was sure you did mean it and that I'd known for some weeks that you wanted to marry

Charlotte. But Pippa just wouldn't listen. She said Mother knew you better than anyone and that she believed her advice to be best. She would ask nothing of you . . . but wait patiently for you to get over this silly affair and come to your senses again! I'm sorry, Merry.'

'This is an absurd situation!' Meridan said, almost angry now. 'Much as I've thought about what would happen when it came to breaking off the engagement, this attitude of Pippa's certainly never occurred to me. I expected her to be upset, yes! But to refuse to take it seriously . . . well, how can I deal with it Liz?'

'I don't know what to advise!' Elizabeth said anxiously. 'I suppose she's bound to see reason in time if you just go on sticking to your guns. Incidentally, John rang up this morning to inquire after Pippa and I thought it best to tell him what was afoot. Pippa would have told him anyway and I presume now Mother knows, it isn't exactly a secret any longer!'

Meridan bit his lip.

'I suppose it's too much to hope to keep it quiet. Anyway, there isn't much point since everyone will have to know sooner or later that I've jilted Pippa. I've no doubt that's the line they'll take. John, too?'

Elizabeth looked at her brother unhappily.

'Well, he was a bit shaken, Merry. You can see his point of view . . . Pippa ill and she is his sister. But he did say it was your affair and you must work things out your own way. I think he means to keep out of it, as much for my sake as anyone else's.'

Meridan gave a deep sigh.

'I'd better go in and talk to Pippa. Maybe I can make her understand. She's better, Liz? No high temperatures or anything?'

'No! She seems perfectly all right . . . just tired. Doc came just before lunch and said she could get up if she felt like it, but she said she'd rather stay quiet and rest.'

It had occurred to Elizabeth that Pippa was not making things very easy for either herself or Merry. Had she been in Pippa's shoes and John had asked for his freedom, she'd have wanted to get away from his house . . . and him, as quickly as she could. Certainly, her pride would never have let her question John as to his feelings, however much she doubted he had ceased to love her.

But the old loyalty to Pippa . . . her deep affection for her, overcame this moment of distaste for the way she was behaving and pity became once more uppermost. She had been ill, Liz excused her, and tears came easily when you were not very fit. Moreover this must have been a pretty bad shock to her . . . on top of the shock of her illness.

'Be gentle with her, Merry!' she said, as her brother moved towards the door.

It was an unnecessary warning for it was outside Meridan's nature to be unkind to anyone, far less to a young girl he believed to be ill and of whom he was so fond. As with Elizabeth, his pity was uppermost when he went into the room and looked down at the girl lying so still and quiet in the large bed. The large hazel-green eyes opened as he approached her and she held out a hand to him which he took at once, sitting down on the chair beside her.

'Merry, darling! How lovely to see you. Liz told me you'd be coming in this afternoon. She said you were taking Charlotte back to London this morning.'

'Yes!' Meridan said quietly. 'I'm terribly sorry to have been the cause of so much worry and trouble, Pippa. Can you bring yourself to forgive me?'

The green eyes widened and unperceived by Meridan, the pretty mouth hardened a little.

'What is there to forgive, Merry? As I told your mother this morning, it was quite right of you to tell me that you believed you were in love with . . . with Charlotte; no matter how much it might hurt me, you were right to be honest. But then that's so like you,

Merry. You couldn't deceive anyone for long and I'd probably have guessed anyway, knowing you so well.'

Meridan looked at her hopefully.

'Then you do understand?'

Pippa drew a long sigh.

'Yes, of course I do! I can see so well how it happened. You were alone and Charlotte came along and you were roped into a party together. She's very pretty and I can quite see how you were attracted to her. Then when you heard what had happened to me in hospital, you subconsciously turned away from me towards the girl who could give you what you wanted from life . . .'

'Pippa, that is not true! Whatever else you believe you must understand that your operation had nothing whatever to do with it. I give you my solemn word of honour!'

'Oh, I know you don't *think* so,' Pippa broke in quickly. 'But deep down in your subconscious, you felt that way. After all, what other reason had I given you to stop loving me?'

Meridan almost groaned in his desire to make her see the truth. Yet how difficult it was to explain!

'Pippa, I swear most solemnly that my feelings towards you have not changed . . . not one bit. It's just that after I'd met Charlotte, I realized that what I'd felt for you . . . what I'm sure you felt for me . . . was a different kind of love. We'd known each other so long that we all but drifted into our engagement. But I realized that it wasn't the right kind of love . . . for marriage.'

'But, Merry, how can you say that? Surely what we feel for one another is the lasting, true kind of love? What you feel for Charlotte is just . . . well, to use your mother's words . . . physical attraction!'

'Pippa!' His voice was harder now and quite adamant as he said:

'I'm in love with Charlotte . . . really in love. I want to marry her, Pippa, as soon as you'll set me free.'

The girl had not expected him to be so blunt. She had no doubt at all in her own mind as to Meridan's sincerity. She knew that she had lost him . . . at least, lost his love. But she would not give him up! That much she had decided beyond all doubt as she lay on her bed waiting for him to come back from London. Meridan was hers . . . and he had no right to be interested in anyone else but her! She had always adored him and in her own, rather shallow selfish way, she did love him. But not enough to want his happiness at the cost of her own. It did not therefore take her long to deceive herself into believing what she wished to believe . . . that Meridan's feelings for Charlotte were temporary and on a lower plane than his feelings for her. Believing this, then she could convince herself that she was doing the right thing to refuse to let him go.

It did not escape Phillipa's thoughts that if Meridan chose he could just walk out on her and marry Charlotte. But somehow she did not think he would do that. She had only to go on wearing his ring to keep him tied to her. As to her pride . . . well, it was a small price to pay for what she wanted. Meridan's mother was on her side . . . if not Liz. Her own family would certainly back her up for they all approved of Merry as a husband and would be deeply distressed if the engagement were broken. John, too, would be loyal to her . . . although he was almost as much a brother to Meridan as to her. But John was not very clever and she had always been able to twist him round to her way of thinking. Merry, too, in the past. But it seemed as if she had lost her power now. He had told her quite brutally that it was Charlotte he wanted to marry. What more could she do?

Pippa adopted the only course that came to mind. She burst into a storm of tears. As she had hoped, Merry was immediately contrite. His voice softened instantly as he begged her to stop, to keep calm, not to make herself ill again.

'What is there to get well for if you

don't want me any more!' she sobbed. 'I'm useless now as a woman ... I know it ... I don't even want to get well ... I'd rather die!'

Even as she sobbed out the last sentence, her own dramatic words gave her an idea. Merry would never dare leave her if he really believed she would do herself some injury. He had always protected her ... taken the blame for her in their childhood pranks, been the one to see that she did not come to any harm.

Meridan felt his heart sink into a quite hopeless depression. How right Elizabeth had been when she had said that Pippa would be bound to think he was deserting her because of her inability to bear him children! The fact that she had met Charlotte ... that he had sworn to Pippa that he wanted his freedom to marry Charlotte ... she still believed that the other reason was primarily responsible. And he could not walk out and leave her with that thought in mind. Her words 'I'm useless now as a woman' . . . smote his heart with pity and all his resolve to be firm with Pippa melted.

'You mustn't talk like that, Pippa, please! Everyone at the party last night was saying how pretty you were . . . how lucky a fellow I was. You're very young and you're bound to have many proposals. Once I'm out of the way, there'll be suitors swarming all over the house.'

'I don't want anyone but you . . . only you, Merry!'

'Pippa, dear, believe me that is just the way you feel now. One day you'll wake up as I have done and realize that we weren't really meant for one another. You'll be far more in love with some other chap than you ever dreamed of being with me.'

'No!' she cried, her face turned away from him on the pillow. 'No! I'd rather be dead than live the rest of my life as a lonely old spinster . . . and if you don't marry me, no one will. I'll never marry anyone else.'

Without warning to him, she suddenly

sprang out of bed, Liz's diaphanous nylon nightdress swirling about her slim figure. Before Meridan understood what she was doing, she had reached the dressing-table and grabbed the bottle of sleeping-tablets left there from last night. She knew exactly what she was doing . . . had clearly heard Doc tell Liz that two pills would send her off to sleep right away but on no account to give more than three as they were highly dangerous.

As Meridan stood up, his face filled with consternation, she quickly swallowed three of the pills. Then, smiling at him across the room, she said calmly:

'There . . . now you'll be free of me, Merry . . . and I won't have to worry about anything ever again!'

Appalled, Meridan realized suddenly what she had done. He had no idea of what had been in the bottle . . . or how many tablets Pippa had taken. But her words left him in no doubt as to her intention.

'You fool . . . you silly little fool!' he cried, beside himself with anxiety as he rushed to her and swiftly carried her back to bed.

Her eyes were still open and she smiled up at him, feigning a sleepiness she was far from feeling yet!

'Stay with me, Merry. Don't leave me now!'

But he tore out of the room, calling for Liz who came running up the stairs two at a time.

'For God's sake, phone the doctor quickly!' Meridan gasped out. 'Pippa's taken some of those pills that were on the dressing table . . . she's tried to kill herself!'

For a moment, Elizabeth was badly frightened. But even as she turned to rush back downstairs to the phone, she remembered that the bottle of luminol tablets had been very nearly empty last night. Pippa could not have taken very many of them.

But she wasted no time telling Meridan so in case she had been mistaken, but ran to the phone. When she got back Meridan was sitting beside

Pippa's bed, chafing her hands, his own face white as chalk, his voice desperate as he said:

'Oughtn't we to try to keep her awake? Oh, my God, Liz, I never thought she'd do anything like this . . . how could she?'

'Calm down, Merry!' Liz said with a firmness she was far from feeling but felt necessary since Merry was so distraught. 'I don't think there were more than three or four tablets in the bottle. She can't possibly have done any serious damage. Doc said he'd be round in ten minutes and to give her hot coffee meanwhile. I told Annie to make some instantly and bring it up.'

Pippa lay quite still, feigning the sleep that had still not overcome her. She wondered just how long it would be before the pills began to work. Surely if she had taken three instead of two, she would go to sleep more quickly than she had last night! The last thing she wanted was to be awake when Doc came. She listened to the voices in the room, triumphantly hearing the panic in Meridan's tone; and equally gratefully hearing the reassurance in Liz's. It would really have been awful if she had overdone it. The last thing in the world she intended was to kill herself.

'I'll never forgive myself . . . never!' Meridan was saying. 'I'd no idea she would feel all this so deeply. Even now I cannot bring myself to believe she . . . she preferred death to . . . to . . . '

'I'm quite sure she did not!' Liz broke in quickly. No matter how upset Pippa might have been . . . and she had been surprisingly well and cheerful before Meridan had gone in to see her . . . it really was out of the question that she should try to kill herself. It was not in Pippa's nature.

Yet at the back of Liz's mind, an unhappy suspicion remained. Pippa had been very depressed since she came out of hospital. Her gaiety at the party could have been a transient thing. It was just possible that her illness had left her sufficiently depressed for this double shock to temporarily derange her mind. But no! Pippa would never have the courage to try to kill herself. It took courage . . . a great deal of it. Pippa had always held back from danger. When she and John and Merry had been up on the topmost branch of their favourite climbing tree, Pippa had waved to them from below, only too happy to accept Merry's word for it that it was far too difficult for her to attempt! She remembered, too, the night Pippa's appendix had suddenly flared up. She, Liz, had been dining with them and had helped put Pippa to bed while they waited for the doctor to come. Pippa had been more frightened than bothered by the pain. She had cried over and over again:

'What will they do to me, Liz? I don't want to be operated on. I might die under the anaesthetic! I don't want to die!'

But then, argued the other half of Liz's mind, Pippa had still been happy then; she had not known Merry would want so soon to break their engagement. She had everything to live for . . . *then*.

A swift glance at her brother's face warned Liz that he, at any rate, had about reached the end of his tether.

'Go down and see if the doctor's car is coming up the drive!' she suggested kindly in order to get him out of the room.

'I can't leave her!' Merry whispered, indicating the tight grip Pippa's hand had on his. 'She asked me to stay, Liz. I can't leave her now!'

'Nonsense!' Liz said sharply. 'She's asleep so she won't know. Go on downstairs, Merry. I'll give her the coffee when it comes!'

But the tray of coffee and the doctor arrived simultaneously and there was, after all, no need to force the liquid down the girl's throat. Merry had been sent out of the room and Liz briefly told the doctor what had happened.

'I'm *sure* there weren't more than four pills in the bottle!' she ended. 'But you expressly said last night not to let her have more than three.'

The kindly old family physician breathed a sigh of relief.

'Well, if you're *absolutely* certain, Liz, we've no need to worry. Those were half-grain tablets and two grains isn't an overdose. We needn't even use the stomach pump on her. She'll probably sleep the clock round but that's all to the good. Come to think of it, I recall asking you last night how many pills there were altogether and you said 'six'!'

'That's right!' Elizabeth confirmed. 'So she can't have had more than four . . . and look, Doc, here's one on the carpet . . . it must have dropped from her hand. That means she's only had three!'

'Then we can leave her to sleep it off. Now, I suggest we go somewhere else where we can explain more fully exactly what has happened. I'd like Meridan to be there, too!'

'We'll go to the schoolroom!' Liz said

thoughtfully. 'We won't be interrupted there and no one else knows . . . yet. I'll get Annie to bring up some more coffee . . . I expect you could do with some, and I know Merry could. He's had a bit of a shock!'

So indeed, had Liz. Sitting in the old chintz-covered window-seat, listening to Meridan recount the whole unhappy story, she felt washed out and desperately tired. Only her sympathy for her brother, who looked near breaking-point, kept her from giving way to the trembling of her hands.

'So there's the whole truth and nothing but the truth!' Meridan finished off with a wry attempt at a smile. 'I feel terribly guilty, Doc, but what else could I have done?'

'Nothing!' the doctor said thoughtfully. 'Old as I am, I don't hold with the old-fashioned obligatory marriages. And you're really under no obligation to marry Pippa if you don't wish to. Even if she were going to have a baby by you . . . which, poor child, is impossible for her . . . I'd still say you were right not to marry her unless you loved her.'

Meridan gave a deep sigh.

'You've no idea how much comfort it is to hear you say that. All the same, I'm not so certain as I was. Suppose Pippa had . . . had . . . ' he could not bring himself to say the words. 'Well, I'd have blamed myself all my life.'

'Well, she hasn't been successful this time. Frankly, I'm extremely surprised to hear she made such an attempt. I brought her into the world and I've known her all her life. I'd never have believed her capable of this.'

'That's how I feel, Doc!' Liz broke in. 'But the alternative isn't very . . . well, palatable, is it? I mean, it infers that she only took those pills to frighten Merry. Surely Pippa wouldn't stoop so low!'

'When you have lived as long as I have, Liz, you'll realize that human nature can make people do very odd things . . . not always very nice things, either. But for everyone's sake, I think we'll treat this as if it had never happened. We don't want it spread around the neighbourhood, do we? In fact I dare say you'd prefer to keep it even from your parents. I ought, of course, to tell Mr. and Mrs. Bates. Pippa is a minor and they are responsible for her. I don't see how I can avoid my duty to them.'

Meridan bit his lip.

'I wish they hadn't got to know, but I can see that you must tell them!' he said at last.

'What about you pushing off for a while, Meridan?' the doctor suggested kindly. He felt extremely sorry for the boy.

'No!' Meridan said sharply. 'I won't have Pippa's family saying I've run away. I'll have to go back on Monday to the office, but I'll stay here tonight. In any case, Pippa may ask for me when she . . . she wakes up.'

The older man looked at Meridan quizzically.

'It's not really my business to discuss your private affairs, my boy, but I think it's time you got things straight in your own mind. If you're breaking with Pippa, it ought to be a clean break. You're quite sure you aren't still in love with the girl?'

'No!' The word came without doubt from Meridan's lips. There could never be any question of his loving Pippa again. Yet he could not walk out on her now . . . not after what had happened. It could so easily happen again. He said so to the Doc.

'We still don't know if she meant it in the first instance, Meridan. In any case, kindness or pity . . . call it what you will . . . isn't always the best way. If you're still around tomorrow, Pippa may well think you're changing your mind. My advice to you is to go . . . and marry the other girl as soon as possible. But, of course, it's really your affair and you must make up your own mind!'

Every instinct in Meridan's body cried out to him to go. It was the easy way . . . the way he wanted for himself and Charlotte. He would not have to face Pippa again . . . to have to discuss the affair with his mother . . . to face the criticism that must surely come from Pippa's family. He could walk out now . . . drive to London and as soon as possible, marry Charlotte by special licence and go abroad . . . forget everything that had happened in the past and live only in the present.

But his rigid sense of duty warred with his instinct and prevented his feet taking him along the road his heart desired. Much later, he was to remember Doc's advice and wish with all his heart that he had taken it. But now he could only see that it was the act of a coward to go. He would not leave until he could be sure that Pippa was all right. Meanwhile, she lay now genuinely in a deep sleep, unaware as yet that she had won the first round.

10

Charlotte had finally confided in her mother. It had really been unavoidable since she had come back from a walk with Aunt Ethel to find Charlotte alone in the house in tears. She had been put to bed and cosseted, and all the time the tears had run down her cheeks . . . tears that were mostly from tiredness and strain.

Gradually, her mother had persuaded her to talk. The older woman was seriously perturbed by what she heard. She had only guessed that Charlotte's love for Meridan Avebury was not running an easy road and now she had to fight against her own instinct in advising her daughter. Above all, Charlotte's happiness came first, and even although the prospect of the lonely years she believed must face her if Charlotte married now appalled her, she spoke only for Charlotte's happiness when she said:

'I truly believe you should not see him again . . . until he is free, darling! Then marry him by all means if you are sure he loves you . . . and that you love him.'

'That is all I am sure of . . . that we love one another!' Charlotte said unhappily. 'At least, I don't doubt Meridan's love for me when we are together! Yet for a time . . . down there in his home, it seemed to me that he belonged really to *her* . . . to Pippa. Maybe it was just the way she behaved . . . and everyone else believing they were soon to be married. Oh, I don't know, Mummy! I just felt it was wrong of me ever to come between them.'

'Then all the more reason to refuse to see Meridan again until he is free to ask you to marry him!' Mrs. Matthews said firmly. 'I know it won't be easy meanwhile, but you've got to give him a chance to see things dispassionately. While he is with you he naturally believes you alone matter to him. But if you are right and he has some feeling left for this other girl, then he should have every opportunity of discovering just what matters most to him. If he should go back to her . . . well, you will know you have done the right thing. If eventually he comes for you, then your conscience can be quite clear; the choice will have been of his own free will.'

In her heart, Charlotte agreed. And when that night Meridan telephoned her to tell her of the day's dreadful event, she knew quite certainly that she must stay out of his life. When he asked if he might call in on Monday night to talk things over with her, she refused immediately.

'Don't question me now, Meridan. If you're going to be in London, I'll write and explain. No, darling, nothing has changed . . . yes, I still love you!'

She wrote that letter long into the night, explaining her feelings to him and reassuring him again of her love.

After it was signed and sealed, she felt a little better although Meridan's news had shaken her badly and Pippa's small heart-shaped face haunted her dreams.

It haunted Meridan's dreams, too. In the morning, he woke exhausted and wondered how he could face a day at the office. Yet he must go up if only to collect Charlotte's letter!

He guessed fairly correctly at its contents and knew that she was right. But he had never before felt so deep a need of her . . . so great a longing to feel the comfort of her arms about him and her soft cheek warm against his own. For him, Charlotte meant peace . . . peace of mind and spirit, and he knew that peace of body would come, too, when she belonged completely to him.

Meanwhile, Pippa still slept and after a quick word with Liz and a hurried breakfast, Meridan left for town promising to return late that evening.

The day was one of extreme difficulty for Liz. She herself had undertaken to 'nurse' Pippa and when the young girl woke, she wept continuously and hysterically every time Liz tried to extract from her the truth of what she had meant to do. There was no reasoning with her and even Liz began to lose patience. Then, later in the morning, Pippa's parents arrived and inevitably let the cat out of the bag to her own mother and father who were equally appalled. They said some harsh words about Meridan and only the fact that they were her future-in-laws prevented her defending her brother and telling them what the doctor had said. As it was, she refused to discuss the matter with them beyond telling them that Meridan was coming back that evening and would prefer to give them his point of view himself.

The rest of the day they spent alone with Phillipa who quickly made capital out of their ready sympathy and distress. Her conversation ran continually on the same lines:

'Please, help me to hold Merry. I

know he doesn't really love this other girl . . . I shan't want to live if he leaves me! I'll do it again . . . only I'll do it properly next time!'

It was wretchedly painful for her parents to listen to her, and neither had the heart to say what was at the back of both their minds . . . that if Meridan had really changed his mind and wanted to marry some other girl, nothing they could say or do would alter things.

Phillipa's father, perhaps alone of her near family and friends, had some true inkling as to her real nature. An observant man who had for many years been the local magistrate, with every occasion to judge his fellow human beings, he knew that his young daughter was both spoilt and selfish; that as the much-wanted daughter, born so many years after John, it had been inevitable that she should be protected and petted and her every whim satisfied. He had thoroughly approved of the four children playing together and being so much one family, for he hoped that Pippa would learn that she could not always have her own way if she mixed with others and learned to share. But busy as he was so large a part of the day, he could not know that John, Meridan and Elizabeth all gave way to Pippa, the boys because they were older and took a protective view towards her, Elizabeth because she was naturally unselfish and in any case, felt Pippa to be the weakest physically of the four of them and as well as a year younger than herself.

It was clear to Pippa's harassed father now that this was the first occasion in his daughter's life when she had had to forgo what she desired. He would have given her anything within his power to remedy matters but unfortunately he realized that here there was nothing he or his money could do. That his adored daughter should actually have tried to take an overdose of sleeping pills . . . no matter for what reason, shocked him deeply and gave him a feeling of estrangement from her. He had a rigid sense of right and wrong and he believed his daughter to have been very wrong in her action, even while he felt desperately concerned at her reasons.

He tried to remind himself that she was still ill and depressed after her operation, the outcome of which had no doubt affected her more deeply than he or his wife had realized. When they had themselves been asked to sign their consent to the operation, they had felt as if they were ruining her future happiness themselves although there had been no alternative were her life to be saved. But Pippa herself, when she was well enough to be told, had taken the news comparatively calmly, saying that she had no particular desire for children and if Merry did not mind, she certainly did not.

Could she have been merely putting forward a brave front? Or had she only begun to mind now Meridan had admitted he no longer wanted to marry her? And was this Meridan's real reason, or did he seriously love this other girl?

'Daddy, please speak to Merry. Maybe he'll tell you the truth . . . one man to another. He told me himself he hadn't changed in his feelings towards me. How can I reconcile that with his statement that he wants to marry someone else?'

Taken out of the context, Meridan's statement did in fact sound illogical and unreasonable to the extreme. All he had meant, of course, was that he had recognized his feelings for Pippa to have been those of a genuine affection whereas in Charlotte, he had discovered the real meaning of love. It had been quite clear to Pippa but she had not chosen to understand him.

'Darling Pippa, if Merry really does want to marry this girl, would it not be better to give way now . . . without fuss?' Mrs. Bates was asking. 'I'm sure you would soon meet someone else . . . someone much more worthy of your love. You know, darling, Daddy and I have often said that you have never had a real chance to meet other men because Meridan was always at your side. Everyone in the county took your engagement for granted and for that reason, no other young men have ever come near you.'

'That isn't true, Mummy. I've met hundreds of eligible young men at dances and hunt balls and riding and so on. I've just never been interested in any of them. I never will be . . . not in a hundred years. I love Merry. Can't you understand?'

'But you wouldn't still want him, knowing he loved someone else?' her father stated rather than asked the question.

'If he'll only marry me, I won't ask anything more of him. I know he doesn't love Charlotte . . . I know it! In time he'll turn back to me. His own mother said so and she knows him better than anyone.'

It was one of the few really genuine remarks Pippa had made. She really believed that if only Meridan could be dissuaded from taking any drastic steps now, he would in time turn back to her . . . start loving her again. Every action she had so far made and would go on making, was with this end in view. Such was her vanity that she could not believe Meridan might prefer the quiet, nondescript Charlotte to her! It was relevant to Phillipa's judgment of others that she put appearances in such an important place. It did not occur to her that Charlotte might have qualities she did not possess . . . a finer character, a more lovable disposition. For no one had ever told Pippa the truth about herself . . . that she was small-minded, shallow, spoilt, selfish; that her action last night had been vindictive and cruel and quite unforgivable. Had Meridan even guessed at her real nature, he would have left her side years ago. As it was, she had always been gay, amusing, appealing, very feminine and charming as was her wont when things went right for her. There had been no occasion until now in her nineteen years for her mettle to be tested . . . or for the other side of her nature to appear uppermost.

Her parents tried hard now to persuade her to go home with them. They naturally felt they could keep a better eye on her there and, as they pointed out, it was hardly fair to inflict the Aveburys with an invalid to nurse.

But Pippa had no intention of going. For one thing she knew Meridan would be home that evening. For a second, she felt that her position was much stronger while she remained in the care of *his* family. She told her mother and father that she did not feel well enough to undertake even the three-mile journey by car and they had not the heart to argue the point. In fact, she did not look well, despite or perhaps because of the drugged sleep. There were shadows beneath the tear-rimmed eyes and the pupils were enormous.

The week-end visitors having left on the Sunday afternoon after being informed of Pippa's illness, the spare rooms were empty and Mrs. Avebury immediately suggested Pippa's parents should stay overnight. But they felt this unnecessary as well as a little embarrassing for Meridan, so they left shortly after tea, having secured Mrs. Avebury's promise that Meridan would call over for a talk with them after dinner that night.

The dinner gong had already sounded by the time Meridan returned from town in his car. He was worn out and near the point of physical and mental exhaustion. He dreaded what he knew must be waiting for him when he got home and even once nearly turned his car on the road to drive back to town. But that inner stubbornness to see a thing through, held him to his course. He would make certain that Phillipa was recovering, explain matters to her family and to his own, and then he would go . . . back to London, a free man. Nothing should keep him longer from Charlotte, whose letter was lying in his breast pocket against his heart. He knew that she, too, could endure no more of this uncertainty and while he had no doubt at all that she would wait indefinitely for him to settle matters his own way, he had no intention of making her wait any longer than one more day.

A sudden whim decided him to turn into the drive of Pippa's house as he passed it on his way to his own home. He would probably be late for dinner but he felt he could not sit down at his own table until he had seen Pippa's mother and father.

It was Mr. Bates who elected to see Meridan, explaining that his wife did not feel well and had gone to lie down. He took Meridan to his study and as he poured him a stiff whisky, tried not to notice how tired and ill the boy looked. His job was to protect Phillipa first and foremost. He would have felt a good deal happier had he not such a respect and liking for Meridan, equal only to that he felt for his own son.

'Look here, my boy!' he said, coming

straight to the point. 'My wife and I have heard the whole story today so you can speak out frankly on all counts. I've no doubt that is why you have come to see me?'

'Yes, sir!'

Meridan, in his turn, wished that he liked Pippa's father less and that he had not to make the kindly man of whom he was so fond, feel disappointed in him.

'Your sister refused to discuss the matter with us ... quite rightly, of course, for it's yours and Phillipa's affair only. I don't want to press you to do anything against your will, Meridan, and yet at the same time, I have to ask you, are you perfectly sure that you know your own mind?'

'Yes, I'm quite sure ... at least that I'm in love with Charlotte!' Meridan said, his utter weariness reducing him to an admission, by omission, that he had not realized himself. But Phillipa's father was quick to pick him up.

'Then you are not happy in your

271

mind about . . . well, about a break with Pippa?'

'How could I be happy about it?' Meridan asked wretchedly. 'To hurt someone you have known and loved so long is a terrible thing to have to do. And I never realized until . . . until yesterday . . . quite how much it meant to her.'

Seeing the look of surprise on the older man's face, he explained:

'By that I mean I never knew Phillipa felt things quite so . . . so deeply. After all, sir, we did rather drift into this engagement. When I knew I had to break it up, I was very much concerned for Phillipa's feelings, especially as I was afraid she might connect my change of heart with . . . with that operation. But I never believed that . . . that I, personally, meant so very much to her. I really thought that she'd get over it and find someone else. Don't you think she would, sir, given a little time?'

The older man stirred uncomfortably in his chair.

'How can one answer for another's

feelings? Frankly, my boy, my wife and I were horrified by what . . . what Pippa tried to do. I would never have believed her capable of such a thing . . . but it showed, of course, the true state of her feelings. Allowing that she might be as much in love with you as you are with this . . . this other girl, can you say that you'd get over *her* in time?'

'No!' Meridan thought instantly. 'I could never forget Charlotte . . . never stop loving her, needing her, wanting her . . . not to the end of my days.' His silence was the answer Mr. Bates waited for.

The older man sighed deeply.

'I cannot ask you to act against your own beliefs, Meridan,' he said at last. 'If you feel it to be doing the right thing to break with Phillipa and marry Miss Matthews, then I cannot and would not stop you. But I would ask you to be as gentle as you can with Pippa. If you could only give her a little time to get used to the idea. I do agree with my wife that the sudden shock of hearing you no longer wished to marry her may well have been responsible for . . . for what she did . . . tried to do!'

'How can I give her time?' Meridan asked. 'It seems to me that the kindest thing I can do is to go . . . and quickly, so that she can get used to the fact rather than the idea. To be quite frank, I'd hoped to leave home tomorrow and not come back until after I was married . . . and Phillipa had quite got over it all.'

'Tomorrow?' Mr. Bates echoed. 'But, Meridan, suppose she tried again? I think it unlikely but she might. You know, it was quite clear from her conversation today that she does not believe in her heart you mean to leave her . . . or that you've stopped loving her. If you go now . . . she'll have to believe it and then I dare not think what will happen!'

'I cannot be responsible for her!' The words sprang to Meridan's lips but remained there unuttered. After all, were not all human beings responsible for one another in a way, more especially when they laid claim to your affection. However much he might feel that it was unfair, he would nevertheless always feel guilty if Pippa did not find happiness after he had left her.

Yet what alternative was there? If he remained, Pippa would begin to hope again ... to expect that he was weakening in his resolve. Charlotte, too, might have the same thoughts. Charlotte! Her letter burned against him and he recalled suddenly a phrase she had written to him:

Unless you can be quite, quite sure that you would be doing the right thing to break with Phillipa, then for my sake as much as for yours and hers, I beg you not to leave her. If it is just a question of time, you know I will wait, no matter how long it might be for. And, darling, if you come to feel that you should marry her after all, then I shall understand ... '

When he had read those words, he had taken them to mean only a declaration of her great love for him. Now he wondered if she, too, was trying to persuade him that it would be wrong to rush a decision, not because she doubted herself, but because she doubted the way his duty lay. Yet how could he be said to be 'rushing a decision'? He had had weeks, months, to think of little else and he had never doubted from the day he first met Charlotte, that it was her and not Pippa he wished to marry. Only Pippa's illness had prevented him acting on that knowledge long ago. As to duty . . . well, Doc himself had said that he believed it wrong for a man to marry a girl he did not love, no matter what was at stake.

Why then did he hesitate? Because Charlotte asked him to think it over? Because Pippa's father had asked the same thing? Because his mother had advised him to wait? Because Pippa herself had begged him to do so? Was the whole world in league against the instincts of his heart?

Desperately, he said:

'Suppose I were to marry Pippa after all? Do you think she could ever be happy with me after what has happened? Could you yourself ever feel happy in your mind, knowing how I feel?'

'I don't know, Meridan! I suppose it could work out since Pippa is certainly convinced that what you feel for this other girl is only a passing attraction. I don't doubt your sincerity myself, but it is possible that given a little time and being as fond of Pippa as you are, you might yourself find happiness. The kind of love you speak of doesn't always bring happiness to a marriage. Real affection and unselfishness are what count most, and shared interests. They are the things which add up over the years.'

His mother had said almost the same thing. The pile-up of evidence in favour of his leaving Charlotte was almost frightening. Could he after all be wrong? Could his feelings for Charlotte lessen with time? Could he learn to love Pippa again? Not as he loved Charlotte, but with that different kind of affection that the older generation seemed to think so important?

'I just don't know!' The words were spoken aloud and caused the older man to look at him seriously.

'If you are not sure, then I beg of you not to act hastily, Meridan!' he said. 'Why not give it a few weeks? Tell Pippa you want time to think it over and that you'll give her your final decision at the end of a specified period of time. If she has any sense she will not press you or try to over-persuade you. I'll see to that myself. Just carry on as if all this had never happened and see how you feel. If you are of the same mind at the end of say, one month from now, then I shall be entirely with you in your decision to break the engagement. It must come easier for Pippa to accept it then, since she will have had time to prepare herself for the possible decision that you will leave her. Moreover, she will be fit and well again by then and better able to stand up to the disappointment. Could you not agree to this, my boy? For all our sakes?'

One month ... a month more of having to face Pippa's anxious, pleading eyes, if not actually to hear her voice asking him not to leave her! A month while his parents, and hers, waited and watched to see what he was going to do. A month in which he would not see Charlotte ...

Yet, if it would make things easier for everyone else ... make everyone happier, what could there be to prevent his agreement. Four weeks were not so long ... and he could go to Charlotte at the end of it with a clear conscience and everyone's blessing. Moreover, there would be no fear of Pippa doing herself some harm since her father believed she would accept the fact more readily then.

'All right!' he said, feeling that he was

being a traitor to himself if not to Charlotte; that he was taking the easy way. 'A month from now I'll come to see you again, sir, and meanwhile, I do ask you not to hold out any hope that I'll change my mind . . . nor to give Pippa any false hopes either. If I go through with this, it must be on that understanding.'

'Very well, and thanks, my boy!'

As he showed Meridan to the door, he felt a slight easing of his mind. A lot could happen in a month and if Pippa were sensible and did not try to force his hand, she might yet win Meridan back to her side. It was up to her now; he had done all he could for her, all he felt to be right. Further than that he could not and would not go. Meridan could come to no harm by holding off his decision a few weeks longer, nor would the girl he professed to love. And Pippa stood to win back her happiness.

After saying an affectionate good-bye to Meridan, he went upstairs to tell the good news to his wife.

As he was getting into his car, Meridan saw John coming across the drive towards him. He felt unable to deal with another discussion on the subject of Pippa yet he knew he must have a word with John, his closest and dearest friend. He had not seen him to speak to since the night of the party and he knew John would be expecting an explanation.

He waited till the other man came up to him.

'Just been down to the stables!' John said, sitting himself next to the driver's seat and pulling out a cigarette-case. 'Didn't expect to see you here. Is Pippa home?'

'No! I've been talking to your father!' Meridan said. At least there had been nothing but friendliness in John's voice. 'John, I want to tell you . . .'

'I think it's better not to talk too much about these things!' John broke in quickly. 'I know most of it anyway . . . and it seems to me it is none of my business. I know you'd never do anything underhand or . . . or even unkind, unless it was necessary. Let's leave it like that, shall we?'

'That's very decent of you, John. Thanks! As a matter of fact, I've just agreed to leave things as they are for a month . . . so there won't be any more . . . unpleasantness, at least for a while.'

'That's good news anyway!' John commented quietly. 'Must be nearly dinner-time . . . hadn't you better be getting home?'

They smiled briefly at one another and then John climbed out of the car and Meridan drove slowly home.

It was only a few miles' distance, yet already Pippa's mother had been on the phone to her, and by the time Meridan had parked the car and gone into the house, the girl was up and dressed, and had surprised everyone by announcing she was going down to dinner. Meridan was most surprised of all . . . and not a little disturbed. He had hoped at least to avoid seeing Pippa for a little while.

Instead, she greeted him with a

charming little gesture as he came into the hall. Neither his parents nor Elizabeth were about.

'Merry! How late you are! We were all getting anxious about you.'

He did not try to kiss her but stood in silence, unable to reconcile his last sight of her, white and heavily drugged, lying like a broken doll in Liz's bed, with this fresh, pretty girl in a cherry wool dinner gown of Liz's, eyes bright and cheeks aglow.

'Father just phoned me and told me you'd been to see him,' Pippa went on, sensing Meridan's surprise. 'I hoped you might get home before the others came down. I wanted to apologize, Merry . . . for what I did. I'm terribly ashamed!'

He was extremely embarrassed and quickly told her that he thought it would be best if they all forgot about it. Pippa readily agreed. Then, aware of his new shyness of her, she tactfully suggested he had better hurry if he wished to change before the second gong sounded for dinner.

At the meal, which proved an ordeal for Meridan, so tired was he, it was his mother and Pippa who kept the conversation going. Pippa's laugh rang out many times, surprising Liz almost as much as it surprised Meridan. Pippa had, of course, told her of Meridan's agreement with her father, and Liz had not been too happy about it. She felt Merry might have been forced into this against his better judgment. Glad as she was for Pippa's sake, she could not be happy for Meridan. She noted anxiously how ill and tired and terribly depressed he looked. No wonder, considering the strain he had been under. And it must continue for another four weeks!

Pippa's good spirits never flagged during or after the meal. She behaved as she might have done before her illness, vivaciously, charming to everyone, referring every now and again to Merry's opinion, pretending not to notice that his attention was elsewhere.

Knowing her brother as well as she did, Liz guessed at his state of mind and as soon as coffee had been served in the drawing-room, she said:

'You look terribly tired, Merry! Why don't you push off and have an early night?'

She pretended not to notice Pippa's angry glance as Merry quickly took his opportunity and made his escape. Nor to notice the sudden silence that fell on the room after he had gone. Pippa no longer chatted gaily and the bright sparkle in her eyes vanished as did the pretty mouth turn down in a disconsolate pout.

'You look a little tired, too, Pippa!' Liz said thoughtfully. 'Don't you think you've been up long enough for today?'

'But I don't want to go back to that room all by myself!' Pippa cried petulantly. 'I hate being alone. And I'm tired of being ill and in bed.'

It was on the tip of Liz's tongue to say that she should not have made herself ill again, but she remained quiet, surprised by this sudden antipathy to the girl she had known so long and loved as a sister. Now, suddenly, she was seeing a different side to Pippa and she could not yet bring herself to accept what she saw. Nor would she admit that she had come to believe these last few hours that Pippa had never really intended an injury to herself at all . . . that she had only wished to frighten Merry into staying.

Well, she had succeeded, at least for a while. Liz could almost feel more sorry for her than for Merry who looked so wretched, guessing that four weeks could not stop him loving Charlotte, and therefore knowing that Pippa must lose him in the end. Conscious of her own change of feeling towards the girl, Liz said quickly:

'I'll come up and sit with you, Pippa. John's not coming over this evening so I can stay with you till you want to sleep.'

But Pippa did not want to sleep for a long while . . . She wanted to talk . . . about herself and Meridan and the future. Again and again she tried to elicit some word from Liz that would give her backing for her own wishful thinking . . . that Merry was already doubting his feelings for this other girl. She asked Liz endless questions about Charlotte . . . and appeared to ignore Liz's refusal to say anything derogatory about her.

'Father thinks that if I play my hand carefully, I'll win him back!' she said at last unguardedly. Liz stiffened.

'Pippa, this is not a game. Meridan's happiness as well as your own and Charlotte's is at stake. It is not a matter of 'playing your hand'. It's a matter of what is best for all three of you.'

Pippa's eyes clouded with tears.

'Oh, Liz, you've turned against me! You don't want Merry to marry me any more!'

'That isn't the point!' Liz said quickly. 'Of course I want you to be happy . . . but not at Merry's expense, Pippa. I cannot believe you would want him to be unhappy yourself!'

'Well, of course not!' Pippa said quickly. 'And I've already told him I'm terribly ashamed of myself for having worried him as I did. But as to being unhappy with me . . . well, you know he always was perfectly happy with me before that girl came along. I don't see why it shouldn't be the same once she has gone out of his life.'

'Is she going out of his life?' Liz asked.

But Pippa gave only a vague negative gesture of her head, unwilling to tell this new, unsympathetic Liz her plan to write to Charlotte, asking her to let Merry go.

But her letter to Charlotte remained unanswered and Pippa could derive no satisfaction that it had served any purpose, except to distress Charlotte. She tried in the succeeding days to get Charlotte on the phone but always some other woman, her mother, answered, saying briefly that Charlotte was not at home.

Pippa was left very much to her own devices during the week. John spent long hours at the stables, Liz came over from time to time, but Merry was working at the office and it was really only Merry she wished to see. She might have worried that Merry was seeing Charlotte in town were it not for the fact that her father had told her of Merry's promise not to see Charlotte until the month was up. One week-end had gone by during which she was constantly with Merry, either at her house or his. But although he was as kind and considerate to her as ever, he had somehow contrived never to be alone with her. Whether he had arranged beforehand with Liz not to leave him alone, or whether it was accidental, Pippa could not be sure. But she felt fairly certain that Merry had arranged it. He avoided any intimate contact with her, freeing his arm as soon as he could decently do so if she had linked her own through his; pecking her cheek or forehead when she lifted her face artlessly to his when they were meeting or saying good-bye.

Angry and frustrated, Pippa decided

to take some action. Charlotte might refuse to answer her letters or the phone, but she could not very well refuse to see her if she, Pippa, were to arrive on the doorstep.

Her mother, of course, might refuse to let her in. Pippa's mind, searching for an alternative, lit on the office where Charlotte worked. She could not remember the name of the firm but it was a comparatively simple matter to elicit the detail from an unsuspecting Liz.

On the Sunday night, Pippa announced her intention of going to London to do some shopping. Meridan could drive her up on Monday morning and she would come back by train. This would mean at least an hour or two alone with Merry, too.

Liz immediately offered to accompany her but Pippa insisted she preferred to go alone.

That night, Pippa wrote in her diary:

They all think it's just an excuse to be alone with Merry . . . no one suspects I'm going to see Charlotte. I don't know what I'll say to her but somehow or other I'm going to get Merry back. I've only three weeks left and I'm not going to stand by weakly doing nothing . . . he's mine and Charlotte shall not have him, no matter how he feels about her.

She wrote a few more lines, then locked the diary away in the secret drawer of her desk and with a light heart, carefully selected the clothes she would wear next day.

11

'Merry, do you realize it will soon be Christmas! I expect the shops are full of Christmas things already, don't you?'

'Christmas!' Meridan thought. 'But this year, for the first time in my life, I shall not spend Christmas with the family. I shall be with Charlotte.'

He had not written to or heard from Charlotte for the ten days since he had seen her, but every morning, on his arrival at the office, he had telephoned to the nearby florist to send her a dozen flowers. Sometimes they were roses, sometimes carnations, chrysanthemums; once a bunch of Spring flowers which he had felt sure she would like. He sent no note with them, content that she was well aware from whom they came and the message intended by them . . . that he thought of her constantly and still loved her. By Christmas, they would be together again.

'I suppose we'll have the usual houseful of friends!' Phillipa chatted on happily. 'Can't we think of something really original for this year's party, Merry? Do you remember how we enjoyed those amateur theatricals, with everyone having to do something to entertain everyone else?'

He had not the heart to remind her that he would not be there . . . yet at the same time, he wondered how she could possibly have put the possibility from her mind. He knew that he ought to disillusion her at once but before he could speak, she had said:

'In case I do any Christmas shopping, Merry, what would you like as your present from me? And have you any idea what Liz wants? Something for her trousseau I expect. You know she and John have decided definitely on a Spring wedding. It should be lovely with the village church full of Spring flowers . . .'

'She is waiting for me to suggest that we have a Spring wedding, too!' Meridan thought with sudden appalled concern. 'Surely she can't suppose that because I agreed to wait a month that I have changed my mind!'

Yet he could not just say, brutally: 'You know I'll be married to Charlotte by then!' or: 'You haven't forgotten that I don't want to marry you now!'

And Pippa gave him no opening during the journey to town, taking care that her remarks were driving home the fact that she believed he would marry her eventually . . . that he would be home for Christmas . . . that Charlotte did not even exist!

She allowed him to drop her in Oxford Street, parting from him with a gay smile and a wave of her hand. She felt she had not wasted the journey, and now she had an even more important job on hand . . . to see Charlotte.

It was still not quite ten o'clock so she filled in the next two hours shopping. Among her purchases was a

294

very expensive silver cigarette-case which she left to be inscribed:

To darling Merry from Pippa, with love.

Then she made her way by taxi to the City and as it was now just on half past twelve, she told the driver to wait while she went up the dusty stairs to the solicitor's office where Charlotte worked.

As she had expected, the typists were already preparing to leave for their lunch. Charlotte, she was told, was in with Mr. Everwell, taking dictation. Pippa said she would wait.

When Charlotte came out from her employer's room, she did not at first recognize Pippa. The expensive fur coat and fur-tipped tiny hat made her look older and more sophisticated than Charlotte recalled. She imagined for one moment that this must be some client for Mr. Everwell. Then, as she walked over to her, Pippa turned her head and Charlotte knew who it was. The colour rushed into her cheeks, then slowly receded, leaving her deathly pale.

The typists were still in the room and conscious of their attentive eyes and ears, Charlotte could find no excuse for refusing Phillipa's invitation to lunch. Had she been prepared, she would have refused . . . said she had a previous engagement . . . anything. But Phillipa had taken her completely by surprise and no ready excuse sprang to her lips.

'I have a taxi waiting outside,' Pippa said with her sweet smile. 'And I've booked a table at the Caprice . . . they always give you a good lunch there!'

Unhappily, Charlotte put on the serviceable black coat she always wore to the office, knowing that beside Pippa's expensive elegance, she looked drab and work-a-day. As she led the way down the steep dark stairs, she sought frantically for a reason for Phillipa's visit. It could have only one reason, of course . . . Meridan, and he was the last person in the world she wanted to discuss with Phillipa. Did Meridan know she was here? Had something happened? *Why had Pippa come?*

Pride forbade her asking for a reason and she sat in silence in the taxi as it took them to Arlington Street and the smart restaurant Pippa had chosen for lunch. As Pippa had hoped, its very elegance put Charlotte at a disadvantage as much as did her immaculate appearance.

The head waiter showed them to a corner table and Pippa took her time ordering her meal. Charlotte had no appetite but was forced to order something. She chose at random, not caring about her food.

Then Pippa said quietly:

'I expect you have guessed why I wanted to see you?'

'I . . . I suppose . . . about . . . Meridan?'

How pretty Pippa was, with those fair curls and green eyes and beautifully shaped face. How right she looked in this particular setting. Charlotte's admiration was quite sincere.

'Naturally! He doesn't know I've

come, of course. But it became obvious to me that we ought to meet. After all, both our futures are at stake, aren't they? That's why I tried to reach you on the telephone.'

'I'm sorry!' Charlotte said. 'I felt it might be better if we . . . well, it really is up to Meridan to . . . ' she broke off unable to express herself as she wished.

Pippa hid a triumphant little smile. So Charlotte had no intention of putting up a fight. She was ready to accept Meridan's decision, whatever it might be. Quickly, she changed her strategy to take a different line from the one she had intended. She had imagined she would have to plead with Charlotte to let Merry go! Instead, all she must do was indicate that Merry regretted having led Charlotte to believe he meant to marry her; that he wanted to marry her, Pippa. Then Charlotte would step out of the picture . . .

'I've hoped to spare Merry any more worry!' she said smoothly. 'You know, he's been feeling pretty awful about all this . . . and I didn't want him upset if it could be avoided. He's been so wonderful to me it seemed the least I could do for him.'

'What . . . what exactly are you trying to say?'

'Well, only that I felt sure if we could meet and talk this over we could agree on what would make for Merry's happiness. That's my only concern and I'm sure it's yours, too. I've never doubted that you loved him whatever anyone else has said.'

Two women, sitting talking, trying to decide what was best for the man they both loved! It struck Charlotte as being extraordinary, even while she realized that Pippa was being very straight-forward and sensible. She herself had never wished to rival anyone for Meridan's happiness. That was the only thing in the world that mattered to her.

'You see, Charlotte, I have known Merry so much longer than you. I know how impulsive he can be . . . and how kind. He can't bear to hurt anyone. I can quite understand how it all happened. He was lonely and you came along. Then there was my operation . . . and, well, I believe Merry really did think he'd be happier married to you. Naturally, it was a ghastly shock to me when he told me and for a while . . . well, life just didn't seem worth living. But gradually I was made to realize . . . by his parents and mine, that I was being silly to give up hope. People like Merry don't just put on and off a deep affection like you'd put on a coat. His feelings for me were really deep-rooted and nothing could change them underneath. This last week, I've seen the family were right. Deep down inside, Merry still wants to marry me. That's why I'm here. Had I reached any other conclusion, I'd have come to you today and said: 'Merry loves you, Charlotte . . . I won't fight you for him . . . his happiness is the only thing that counts!''

There was no escaping Phillipa's meaning now. What she just said was perfectly clear to Charlotte. Merry really loved Phillipa . . . had never stopped loving her. Yet, if that were true, why did he send all those wonderful flowers . . . tokens, surely, of his love for *her*! Or had they been merely a kind of peace offering, a preparation for what he had not yet dared to tell her?

'If . . . if you are right, I . . . I won't stand in your way!' Charlotte said at last.

Phillipa hid a little smile of triumph. This was to be far easier than she had anticipated.

'Unfortunately, it's rather difficult for you . . . I see that!' she said thoughtfully. 'Merry is such a kind person he just can't bring himself to hurt anyone. But of course, you know that already, don't you . . . because of how long it took him to tell me about *you*! And even when he has told you, how can he be happy knowing you still care for him? That's what worries me. It'll be on his conscience all his life that he has ruined *your* life!'

'Meridan knows that I want only his happiness! I've told him so.'

'Yes, but how *can* he be happy knowing you are still in love with him? There's only one way you can release him from that feeling of guilt, Charlotte . . . to let him think there's someone else. Or at least to convince him that *you* no longer care!'

The arrival of the waiter with their first course prevented Charlotte from giving the reply that had sprung to her lips . . . that never, never could she lie to Meridan about her feelings for him. But by the time the waiter had left them alone, she had seen the selfishness of such thoughts. If she could believe Phillipa, and surely no living human being could lie about so important a point? then to continue to allow Meridan to believe she loved him was to put a chain round his neck . . . invisible but binding. She would be doing the same as Phillipa had done! Yet this last fact escaped her, for although she knew from Meridan that Phillipa had tried to take an overdose of sleeping tablets, Charlotte sincerely believed that the younger girl had acted on some terrible impulse brought on by shock and illness and with no intention of revealing to Meridan how tragic the loss of his love would be for her.

Nonetheless, she was not yet convinced that Meridan loved Phillipa. She believed that Phillipa thought he did . . . yet what would she say if she knew about the flowers? And how could Meridan have changed so completely in so short a while? It was not two weeks since he had held her in his arms, vowing his love for her and, she knew without doubt, utterly sincere.

Could he really have changed his mind so quickly, so easily? Was it possible that he was regretting his 'affair' with her, wishing to be back where he was, engaged to Phillipa? Had his family and Phillipa's really so much influence over a man of his age and character?

Somehow it did not seem in the least

possible and yet the strict honesty of Charlotte's thinking, forced her to admit to herself that he had once changed in shorter time from loving Phillipa to being in love with her!

Was Meridan really weak at heart? Unstable in his emotions? Had she misjudged the sincerity of his feelings . . . putting more into them because she had so desperately wanted to believe he loved her? Had her own love for him blinded her to the real Meridan?

These questions tortured her with a horrible new uncertainty from which there was no escape.

'Did you know he had been sending me flowers every day?'

The question was wrung from her lips and momentarily shook Phillipa. She believed there had been no communication between them. Quickly, she covered up her surprise in a non-committal nod of her head.

'Flowers are very often sent as a kind of sop to one's conscience, aren't they? I know Meridan feels he has behaved very badly towards you . . . although he never intended to deceive you. He genuinely believed he was in love with you, Charlotte. So you must not blame him too much'.

'But people don't fall in and out of love so quickly!' Charlotte almost whispered the words.

'I know!' Phillipa agreed smoothly. 'That's exactly what I said to Meridan . . . what everyone has explained to him. Of course, he knows now that he wasn't really in love at all. It is sometimes a great deal easier to see things . . . people . . . more clearly against your own family background.'

The implication was unmistakable and here Charlotte could not doubt Phillipa's inference to be correct, so conscious had she been that she did not 'belong' in Meridan's home

. . . that beside Phillipa, she was poor and even shabby and out of her depth. Even the certainty that she could have made Meridan a good wife, entertained for him, run his home, coped with servants, lived up to his standards, could not be argued against the knowledge that Pippa could do and be all these things a great deal better! She had only to glance down at her drab, serviceable black coat and compare it with Phillipa's luxurious furs . . .

Bitter now, she said harshly:

'Couldn't Meridan have told me all this himself?'

'He'll never tell you!' Phillipa said, truthfully. 'That's why I felt I should come to see you, Charlotte. He'll never be the one to make the break . . . I know that and I think you do, too. It'll have to come from you.'

There was no questioning the sincerity in Phillipa's voice now for she was speaking the truth. Charlotte knew it and did not question it. It only confirmed what she had believed in her heart for so long . . . that she should step out of the picture and leave Meridan to Pippa . . . to whom he really belonged. She had always felt that way . . . from the moment she knew he was engaged to someone else. She had never felt anything but guilty at coming between two people who, until then, had been in love. Only Meridan's insistence that it would be more wrong for him to marry a girl he no longer cared for, had allowed her to continue the association, for she agreed that a marriage without love could bring happiness to no one.

But Phillipa had changed all that now. She had told Charlotte frankly that Meridan did still care for her ... that were he free of Charlotte's love, he would settle down and be happy in their old relationship. It was all Charlotte needed to be sure of for her pride to rush to the fore ... a pride that forbade arguments, pleading, further questions; a pride that for the moment at least, held back the bitter, salt tears.

'All right! I'll write to him tonight ... tell him I've been thinking things over and that I have discovered that I don't really love him ... that it has all been a ghastly mistake!'

Phillipa drew in her breath sharply . . . trying to hide the triumph in her eyes. She had won . . . *won*!. It had been so much easier than she had dared to hope it would be. Except for the flowers there had been no difficult moment even. Now it would be only a question of time before Merry turned his affections back to her!

'Believe me, I'm very sorry . . . ' she said kindly. 'I never did doubt that you loved him but had I done so, I would know now that your love is the real, unselfish kind. I admire you, Charlotte!' But the words this time were lies. Secretly, she despised Charlotte for not putting up a fight . . . for not hanging on to what she wanted . . . for not behaving as she, herself, had done! Charlotte did not deserve a man like Merry! Nor could she love him so much if she could give him up so easily!

It was not long before Phillipa had convinced herself that she really had acted for Meridan's good as well as her own; that Charlotte had never really loved him at all and that he was well rid of her.

She noticed that the food lay untouched on Charlotte's plate and said:

'You look very pale. Are you not feeling well?'

Quickly, Charlotte grabbed at this excuse.

'If you would excuse me, I think I'd better go now. I'm not feeling very well and I'd like to go back to the office to finish off one or two things and then go home.'

Phillipa stood up.

'But of course. I quite understand. Don't worry about the bill . . . I'll pay for the lunch.'

Awkwardly, Charlotte held out her hand.

'Good-bye then! And I . . . I hope you'll be very happy with Meridan . . . that you'll both be happy . . . now.'

Pride kept her head high as she made her way through the crowded room and out of the restaurant. Pride alone kept the tears back as she took a bus . . . not to the office . . . but back to her own home. Once there, she asked her mother to phone the office to tell Mr. Everwell she was not well, and refusing further explanations, ran upstairs to her room. She knew her mother would not follow her . . . that she could be alone at last and give way to the terrible sense of loss and despair.

But now that she could permit herself the luxury of tears, they would not come. Dry-eyed, she lay on her bed, thinking, remembering every word Phillipa had said; then reaching back to the times she had spent with Meridan and her own great happiness with him.

'He did love me . . . *he did*!' cried her heart, but already her mind had accepted Phillipa's lies so entirely that unconsciously she had put Meridan's love for her in the past. No man could have shown such tenderness, such gentleness, such a wonderful understanding had he not cared! Yet how was she, who had never been in love before, to judge the depth of Meridan's feelings? Maybe they had been prompted by something quite else than love . . . true love such as she felt for him. Maybe he had been lonely, as Phillipa said, and had found her, Charlotte, attractive. Passion had certainly always run close to the surface whenever they were near one another and she knew that he had desired her physically . . . even as she had desired to give herself to him. But for her, it had been only a small part of the whole . . . a part of the great need for Meridan and her wish to give him all he needed from her, too.

'Meridan, Meridan!' she whispered, her hands clenched in terrible pain at her sides. 'Am I never to see you again? Never to feel your arms round me? To hear your lovely deep slow voice saying: 'I love you, Charlotte . . . you belong to me!''

Yes, whatever *he* might feel, she would belong to him always. No matter how long she might live, there would never be another man in her life. She would be like Aunt Ethel who had lost her only love in the First World War and who had never wanted anyone else . . .

Slowly, Charlotte climbed off her bed and went to the desk beneath the window. She knew that if she did not write the letter soon, she might weaken in her resolve to do what she now felt sure to be right. She took up her pen and, biting her lip, calmly wrote her address. Then:

Dear Meridan, (not darling, not dearest, not Meridan, my love! Yet dear had its significance, too, for how very, very dear he was to her. The fact that he had ceased to love her . . . perhaps never really loved her, could not alter her love for him!)

This is to thank you very much for all the lovely flowers you have been sending me. But I would be glad if you would stop doing so. You see, I have had plenty of time these last two weeks to think things over . . . something that was impossible for me to do clearly while I was still seeing you. I have come to realize these last few days that I had no right to come between you and Phillipa ... not because of your engagement to her, but because what I believed I felt for you I know now was not really love.

I am afraid you will think very badly of me for deceiving you, but please believe me, I did think I was in love. My only excuse is that I had no yard-stick against which I could measure my feelings for you and at the time I truly believed it was the real thing.

Please try to forgive me and believe me whan I say that I wish you and Phillipa every happiness in the future. For all our sakes, it would be best if we did not meet again, and there is no need for you to write to me. I hope you will understand and forgive me.

Charlotte.

How easily the words had flown from her pen ... words that were each of them painful lies. Yet, re-reading what she had written, they had a strange ring of sincerity. Meridan would not doubt she meant them for he would be only relieved to think them true. They would give him the freedom he desired and there would be no more worry or indecision for him. Or for her!

'Meridan!'

Now, at last the tears came, choking sobs that were torn from the depth of her being. Desolation swept through her, leaving her chilled and shaking as if she were physically cold.

So her mother found her when she brought up a tea-tray. Aghast, she stared at her daughter's face and knew that something terrible had happened. Guessing it had to do with Meridan, she waited until Charlotte was sufficiently controlled to speak.

'You can . . . read . . . the letter I've written him!' the girl said.

Her mother turned back to her, the letter in her hand, a question on her face.

'But, darling? Is this true?'

Slowly, Charlotte shook her head.

'I love him, Mummy. I shall always love him. But he isn't any longer in love with me.'

Then her mother's arms were round her, but there was no comfort for Charlotte even in this warm, loving embrace.

12

Meridan sat with his sister in the schoolroom, an envelope in his hand which was shaking. The letter had been waiting on the hall table since the afternoon post had arrived and he had only just returned from town to find it there.

Immediately he had read it, he called to Elizabeth who was changing for dinner. Giving her no time to put on her dress, he insisted she follow him to the schoolroom where there was no chance of their being interrupted. Mrs. Avebury frequently wandered into her daughter's bedroom and Meridan needed to see Liz alone.

He held out the letter and watched Liz's face as she read it. As he had suspected, her expression revealed only surprise.

'But I don't understand, Merry! How

can she have changed her mind so quickly. I'd have sworn she was as much in love with you as any girl could be!'

'So would I!' Meridan said flatly. 'Yet she speaks of 'a yardstick' for measuring love. Liz, does that mean she has met someone else?'

'Oh, nonsense!' Liz said, a frown on her forehead. 'Even if she had, it's only a couple of weeks since you saw her, so it must have been since then. You don't fall out of love and in love with someone else as quickly as all that!'

'I fell in love with Charlotte at first sight!' her brother reminded her.

'I know!' Liz argued. 'But both you and Charlotte were, to put it bluntly, fancy-free at the time. You didn't know it until then but you obviously weren't in love with Pippa . . . and there was no one in Charlotte's life, either. You met . . . and it happened. But I refuse to believe she's found someone else. No, Merry, there's something else behind this.'

'But what?' Meridan asked desperately. 'It's such a short time since I got this . . . ' he reached in his breast pocket and brought out Charlotte's earlier letter to him.

'. . . I love you, Meridan, with my whole heart, and I'll wait for as long as you feel necessary. I want you to be absolutely sure about Phillipa for all our sakes . . . never doubt my love for you. It is the only thing of which I am perfectly and completely sure . . . '

'Something must have happened!' Liz commented again when Meridan stopped reading. 'Maybe she is just doing this with some mistaken idea of making things easier for you!'

'But how? Why?' Meridan asked. 'She knows I only agreed to stay on here another month . . . that I have never had any intention of going back to Phillipa . . . of continuing our engagement. She knows I love her. How could this . . . ' he indicated the letter Liz still held in her hand . . . 'do anything but confuse the issue still further?'

Elizabeth felt extremely unhappy. An idea had crossed her mind, but one that was so horrible, she hardly dared admit it even to herself. Yet she had to consider it. It was Pippa! This last twenty-four hours, Pippa had been a constant visitor in their house. This had not been unusual in itself, but her remarks, as she shadowed Elizabeth from room to room, had certainly puzzled the elder girl. She had talked, of course, continuously of Merry . . . despite the fact that Liz had told her outright that she did not feel she should discuss her brother or the affair with Pippa. But the remarks had not been what she had expected . . . a repetition of her erstwhile pleas to Elizabeth to reassure her that Merry did still care! On the contrary, they had been of an entirely different nature.

'I've chosen a cigarette-case for Merry for Christmas, Liz, because you know he lost his old one. It's being inscribed. We were talking on the way up to London about the Christmas party this year. It's our turn to have lunch in our house and dinner in yours, but as you have just had a dance, maybe it would be best to change around. I don't really mind but I do think we should try to have something different this year. Merry and I thought we might have some amateur dramatics . . . you know, Liz . . . as we used to do when we were children . . .'

Always, Merry and I . . . always plans for the future without one single doubt as to whether Merry would be there or not! Liz had come to the conclusion with a degree of pity, that poor Pippa was trying to talk herself into believing something which was far from being a fact; that by saying such things, she could make them come true.

Now, suddenly, she found a different explanation. Pippa's attitude had changed completely since that day in London. Therefore it was not only possible but quite probable, that something had happened on that day to give her cause to believe Merry had changed his mind again.

Unhappily, she questioned Merry as

to whether he had inadvertently given Pippa cause for fresh hope when he drove her up to town.

'But quite definitely not!' Merry said adamantly, not following Liz's train of thought and therefore not understanding what her question inferred. 'I'm sure of that, Liz. Pippa did all the talking . . . I don't think I said more than an occasional 'yes' or 'no'!'

'Then it wasn't that!' Liz said, relieved. Then a further idea hit her with painful suddenness.

'You didn't lunch with her, Merry?'

'No! It was never even suggested I should!'

'Then whom did she lunch with?' Liz asked flatly. 'She told me she went to the Caprice. I assumed it was with you. But she was hardly likely to eat there by herself . . . '

Now there was no avoiding the suspicion that lay behind Liz's remarks and Meridan was quick to see it.

'Charlotte!'

'Oh, no!' Elizabeth cried, hating to

think it could be true. 'Surely Pippa would not stoop to . . . to . . . '

She broke off, frightened by the expression on her brother's face.

'If I find Pippa has been seeing Charlotte . . . telling her a lot of lies . . . that'll be the end of everything . . . for always!'

'Merry, calm down. I don't think for a moment it could be true . . . and you mustn't rush off in a stew like that and accuse her of something you can't prove!'

'But I'll find out the truth!' Meridan said violently. 'My God, Elizabeth, I'm beginning to wonder if any of us really know Pippa at all.'

'Merry, let me ask her. You can't talk to her in that frame of mind.'

'Can't I?' Meridan asked roughly. 'Well, we'll see. I promise I won't accuse her of anything . . . just ask her. If I find she is responsible for this letter of Charlotte's I'm leaving this house tonight! Is Pippa here?'

Elizabeth shook her head, her face taut with worry.

'No! She and John are coming to

coffee after dinner. Merry what are you going to do? Please don't rush over to their house now! You'll be late for dinner and I'll have to find some story to tell Mother and Father. Besides, it makes such an issue of it if . . . if it isn't true!'

Meridan paused. Liz was, of course, right. He must not pre-judge Pippa . . . and yet in his mind, he was sure that somehow she was responsible. Maybe it would be better to wait till he had cooled down a little.

'All right!' he said. 'But I insist on seeing Pippa myself . . . alone . . . as soon as she arrives.'

Dinner was a painful meal for both brother and sister. Elizabeth, as well as her brother, was somehow sure that Phillipa was behind this strange letter from Charlotte. It was almost worse for Elizabeth, thinking ahead to what must happen if it were true. Meridan would certainly walk out of the house and finish with Pippa for good and all. It would be left to her to make the explanations, cope with Pippa and try to keep her peace with John.

Suddenly, Elizabeth knew that come what may, she and John must be married soon ... get away from their respective homes and families and live only for each other. She would tell him how she felt tonight and she was sure that he would understand and agree. Dear John! He might not be very glamorous or exciting but he was nevertheless just what she wanted, cool, steady, unemotional and very much in love with her.

Her nerves were strung up to such a pitch that she started physically when the front-door bell rang. Meridan immediately got to his feet and went out of the room. Liz guessed that he intended to waylay Pippa in the hall.

She heard their voices, Merry's low and inaudible, Pippa's high-pitched and gay, then John came in by himself.

'Meridan wanted Pippa in the schoolroom for something!' he murmured as he kissed Elizabeth's cheek. But there was no chance for him to ask Elizabeth what was up since Mr. and Mrs. Avebury were both telling him to sit down by the fire and get warm.

Phillipa followed Meridan upstairs without a qualm in her mind. On the contrary, she was full of confidence. Merry must have got Charlotte's letter and now he wanted to tell her, Pippa, that their engagement was still on. She turned to face him, a smile on her lips, as he closed the door behind him.

'Pippa, I want to ask you something and I want the truth. Did you lunch with Charlotte yesterday?'

The smile remained fixed on her face but a little of her confidence departed at Merry's strange, harsh tone. She had, of course, expected that she might be asked with whom she lunched and had resolved to say it was Angela Peters. Now she was nonplussed by Meridan's question. How had he known it was Charlotte? Had he spoken to Charlotte? Had her plan somehow misfired?

Anxiously, she risked another lie.

'Well, yes, as a matter of fact I did,

Merry. I didn't want to upset you but Charlotte phoned me and asked me to meet her . . . said she had something important to tell me.'

'And what was it?' Meridan asked brutally. 'That she had changed her mind and didn't love me any more?'

'Why, Merry, how did you guess . . . ?' her voice trailed away at the expression in his eyes. They were cold as steel.

'Then you would have no objection if I telephoned Charlotte's home now . . . just to confirm what you say?'

Phillipa's pretty face crumpled into painful anxiety she could not conceal.

'Oh, but Merry, surely there is no need to do that? You know I wouldn't lie to you . . . and anyway, she said she was writing to you herself to tell you she didn't love you any more. You can't do any good by phoning her, Merry . . . *please!*'

'*What did you say to her, Pippa? I want to know!*'

Pippa was really frightened now. Never in her life had she heard just such a whip-lash of a tone in Merry's voice.

Quickly, all too readily, she dissolved into tears.

'I didn't mean any harm, Merry . . . really, I didn't. I knew she couldn't love you as much as I did . . . and I was right wasn't I? She would never have agreed to give you up so easily if she really cared . . . ' Her voice trailed off into a choked sob as she realized the slip of her tongue had finally revealed to Merry what had happened between her and Charlotte. She gazed up at him from tear-brimmed eyes but saw no softening in his face, only a hard stare that was almost hatred.

'Merry . . . I'll put it right again . . . I promise I will. Only don't leave me . . . I love you . . . please, Merry . . . *please!*'

He was sickened by her abjection and by the knowledge that she could stoop so low to achieve her own ends . . . Pippa, his dear, childhood friend, his first sweetheart, the girl he had intended once to make his wife. He saw her now for what she was . . . utterly selfish, egotistical, egocentric. His anger gave way to a sudden pity for her . . . a pity this time without surrender but nevertheless it was there, just as any respect he might have had for her was as surely gone for ever.

'This finishes everything, Pippa. I'm sorry if I have been the cause of making you unhappy . . . but there is no point in pretending that it can go on. I'm in love with Charlotte and I intend to marry her. It'll probably be easier for all of us if you and I don't see each other again for a while. I hope next time we meet we can be friends again. Good-bye, Pippa.'

'Merry!'

He steeled himself against her voice and, turning from her, went swiftly down the stairs. The sound of her feet running after him, her voice repeatedly calling his name, followed him to the hall. Liz, too, must have heard, for she and John came hurrying out of the drawing-room. As he reached for his coat, he saw them . . . John taking

Pippa forcibly by the arms holding her from running to him.

Liz said in an undertone:

'Where are you going, Merry? You can't possibly drive up to town now!'

'I must!' Meridan said sharply. 'It's all over, Liz. I have to get away.'

She looked at him anxiously.

'Please, Merry, not till tomorrow morning. You're in no fit state to drive now. To please me, wait till morning. You've no need to see Pippa again. Go straight to your room now.'

Sudden, unutterable weariness took hold of him. Liz was right. He was completely done in. To drive forty miles in the dark now was asking for some wretched accident.

Without looking at Pippa, sobbing in John's arms, without even a good-night to Liz, he turned and went slowly up the stairs.

'I'll take Pippa home!' John said quickly, but Pippa twisted from his arms and flung herself at Liz.

'Don't turn me out, Liz. Let me stay

here tonight. I don't want to go home. I can't face Mother and Father's questions if I go home. Please, Liz, *please!*'

'All right, Pippa!' Elizabeth said wearily. 'You'd better go to bed now. I'll come up with you.'

But she stayed behind a moment longer to tell John she thought it would be a good idea for him to stay, too, and take Pippa home first thing in the morning.

'You don't think she'll try . . . to do anything awful again?' John asked anxiously.

Elizabeth shook her head.

'I'll stay with her till she's asleep. Don't worry, darling, if you can help it.'

John took her quickly in his arms.

'I'd like to take you away from all this now,' he said with unusual passion. 'Promise me you won't let this come between us, Liz?'

'Never, never,' she vowed, and broke quickly away from him to go to the unhappy girl upstairs.

No one slept well that night. Mr. and

Mrs. Avebury had been told by Liz what had happened, and felt powerless to do anything. The young people must, after all, manage their own lives. But not even John's cautious admission that he believed Merry's decision to go to be best in the end, made them feel happier about the situation.

Neither John nor Liz slept well, either, and were downstairs breakfasting even before Meridan who had not slept at all. He looked into the dining-room to say good-bye and both were appalled by the fatigue in his face.

'Look after her, Liz!' he said, and then hurried out through the front door.

He knew now a frantic haste to get away. From inside the house, he heard the sound of Pippa's voice calling him, and he knew a sudden angry dislike of her lack of pride. Even now she was calling to him not to go. He had wanted to remember her as she was . . . not as he had last night discovered her to be.

His car was in the garage, and he

hurriedly backed it out and swung round into the drive. It seemed an eternity since he had turned in here late last night, yet it was barely twelve hours ago. He accelerated and gathered speed along the curving drive that ran between two rows of high rhododendron bushes to the iron gates a hundred yards away. Anxious though he was to be on his way, he was driving slowly because of an early-morning fog. But still he did not see the dark shadow that sprang towards him from behind one of the tall bushes. He knew only a sudden impression of something moving to the side of the car, then felt a faint thud and heard the scream before he jammed on his brakes and stalled the car into a stop.

Afterwards, when he had time to remember, he could not understand why he had failed at that moment to realize that it might be Pippa. But at the time, he knew only a sickening certainty that he had run over or knocked into some stranger lurking in the drive.

Even when Liz came towards him as he stepped out of the car to walk back the few yards to where the accident had happened, he still did not suspect anything of the tragedy that awaited him. Liz flung herself at him, the tears streaming down her face.

'Merry, what have you done! She's dying . . . Oh, God!'

'Liz! Who?'

Even the curtness of his question could not reach through Liz's panic, and it was not until he came upon Pippa, her head pillowed against John's arm as he knelt beside her in the wet grass, did he at last realize whom he had hit.

Horror-struck, he gazed down at the inert form.

John looked up and his voice was painfully controlled as he said:

'We lost hold of her, Meridan. She pulled away from us and rushed off up the drive while you were getting the car out. We wasted a few precious moments wondering if we should stop you before we saw her disappearing up this way towards the rhododendron bushes. I tried to catch her up . . . but I was just too late . . . I saw her, Merry . . . saw her run full-tilt into your car!'

Meridan knelt quickly in the grass beside him, his hand searching for Pippa's heart. There was still a faint beat.

'Quickly!' he said. 'We must get her back to the house . . . phone for the doctor.'

But it was too late. By the time Doctor Nivan arrived, Phillipa was dead.

★ ★ ★

'No, Doc, I'm sure she wasn't trying to kill herself. I think she was hoping to stop Meridan's car . . . that was all. He didn't even see her till it was too late.'

Meridan gave John a grateful glance. On top of the ghastly shock of Pippa's death had come the almost worse shock of realizing maybe she had intended it.

But John's voice had a blessed certainty about it.

'I'll have to notify the police . . . it's unavoidable. But in view of what happened the other night, I thought it best to find out first whether it was accident or . . . or . . . '

'Or suicide?' Meridan finished for him.

Doc nodded, his face sympathetic. This was a pretty horrible state of affairs . . . more especially for Meridan. He must be feeling responsible in so many ways.

'Perhaps I'd better tell you exactly what happened last night!' Meridan said quietly. He glanced at John and Liz. 'You've all a right to know.'

Briefly, factually, he gave an account of what had passed between himself and Pippa. Then Liz took up the story, her face white, her hand tightly holding to John's.

'She was not so much hysterical as . . . as determined, when she ran downstairs this morning,' she told the old doctor, carefully choosing her words.

'She kept calling Merry to stop and then turning to us . . . to John and me . . . to say: 'I'll not let him go . . . I won't, I won't!' It was when Merry was getting the car out of the garage that she suddenly broke away from us and started to run. We were both hesitating, wondering whether to go after her or stop Merry. Then John started running up the drive and I followed.'

'I tore after her . . . ' John took up the story. 'But I was a second or two too late . . . I just saw her run out at the car, her hand lifted as if she were going to wave to Meridan to stop. That's why I'm so sure it wasn't . . . wasn't intentional. It was just one arm, Doc . . . and she was waving it up and down . . . '

'I never saw a thing!' Meridan broke in desperately. 'It was pretty foggy and I must have been almost past her before I saw something moving through the far side of the windscreen. Then there was a slight bump and . . . and a scream . . . '

He suddenly buried his head in his

hands as if he was hearing that scream again.

'I can't see that you were in any way to blame!' Doc said firmly, his hand touching Meridan's shoulder. 'She died of heart failure, you know . . . due no doubt to the shock of being flung backwards. In fact, she was very little hurt by the fall. Well, I'd better ring the police unless someone else has done it?'

No one had thought of it. Liz, John and Meridan had sat in appalled silence outside the bedroom door where they had carried her. Doc had come within five minutes and not long after, Pippa's parents. They were still in the room with their daughter when Doc came out to tell the others that Pippa was dead. Mr. and Mrs. Avebury were sitting alone in stunned silence in the drawing-room, still praying that the accident was not so serious as the children had supposed. They would have to be told, too.

'I'll tell Mother and Father!' Liz said, suddenly calmed. The sight of Meridan's distress had brought her back her control.

She had forgotten herself.

'I'd better go in to my parents!' John said quietly. But first he put a hand on Meridan's shoulder as the Doc had done and said:

'Don't blame yourself, Meridan. I'll always be sure it was an accident and I saw the whole thing. You couldn't have acted any differently, you know. After what Pippa had done, I'd have behaved exactly as you did.'

It was some small measure of comfort to Meridan to have the brother of the girl he had killed absolve him from all blame. Yet the same appalled feeling of guilt still held him in sway.

It was unfortunate that Meridan, sitting alone now outside the bedroom door, should have had to be faced with the accusations of Pippa's parents in his present state of shock.

Mrs. Bates was sobbing hysterically, and seeing Meridan, she cried:

'You killed her! You killed her . . . my little girl!'

'Mother!' John's voice was sharp but

it was too late to prevent the damage that was done by those few words. Nor was it made better by Mr. Bates saying:

'You'll never forgive yourself for this, my boy, and nor will I!'

In a less emotional moment, neither he nor his wife would have spoken as they did. Later, each was to become as convinced as their son, John, that Meridan was in no way to blame, and that Pippa had had no intention of killing herself. But the shock and consequent agony of their sudden loss could only be eased at the time by those cruel, thoughtless remarks; remarks which were to have more reaching results than they could have supposed. Unguardedly, they repeated them later to the police officer who arrived to take down notes and so were inadvertently the cause of starting up the all too ready suspicions of the law. It could all have been hushed up! True an inquest would have been necessary in any event, but neither Pippa's nor Meridan's private lives need have been made public as they were, nor need there ever have been any doubt as to the fact that it was accident and not suicide.

It was the last thing in the world that Mr. and Mrs. Bates could have wanted, but it was too late to retract their first statements and the damage was done.

13

Charlotte sat in the back of the court, her eyes never leaving Meridan's face. He did not know she was here but Liz . . . dear, kind Liz . . . had come to see her yesterday, the day after the accident and begged her to stand by Meridan.

'He'll need you so badly now, Charlotte.'

She needed no further request to do what in any case her heart demanded of her. But she could not go to Meridan's home, and he was remaining there until after the inquest and funeral.

Liz had agreed that it might be best for Charlotte not to get in touch with Meridan until then. It was possible that any request from Charlotte to see him might only tax him further . . . and Liz feared that if he had much more worry, he would be in no state to give account of himself in court.

Charlotte was horrified now by the sight of Meridan's face. He looked at least ten years older, deathly white and with new lines about his mouth and eyes that she had never seen before. Her hands clenched at her sides as her longing to go to him became almost unbearable. But the jury was now being sworn in and her attention was momentarily directed away from the man she loved as she studied the faces of the men and women who were to decide on the circumstances attending Pippa's death.

There were two women on the jury of seven . . . ordinary, not very smart women who might have been house-wives. They both wore wedding-rings. Surely they would understand . . . sympathize! Yet maybe their sympathies would be with Pippa.

The Coroner drew her attention now as he gave his opening speech. She followed his words carefully but there was nothing he said at first she did not already know. Then he addressed the jury again:

'You have been asked to attend this

inquest for the purpose of ascertaining whether this unfortunate girl's death was the result of an accident . . . or self-intended. Witnesses will be asked to tell you what they know of the circumstances leading up to the accident. I shall then sum up the evidence and you will be asked to give your verdict . . . '

Charlotte felt momentarily sick. Surely they did not really believe Pippa had meant to kill herself? Liz had said that John had seen the accident and that Pippa's obvious intention had been to stop the car. How could they think it was suicide? Then she remembered the overdose of sleeping tablets, and for a moment her courage failed. The police officer was called as first witness to give his account of what had occurred at Meridan's house when he was first called there. He was followed by Doctor Nivan who now stood in the witness-box.

'You signed the death certificate of the deceased and ascertained that she died of heart failure brought on by shock?'

'That is correct!'

'Were there any other injuries?'

'Slight bruising of the left temple and on various parts of the left limbs. That is all.'

'Compatible with the deceased having come in contact with and been knocked over by a motor vehicle?'

'Exactly!'

'Now will you tell the court what, in your view, was the state of health of the deceased prior to her death?'

'I should say she was in very good health. Some months ago she had an operation for appendectomy which was subsequently followed by an operation for partial hysterectomy. She was discharged from hospital last August, made an excellent convalescence and in my view, a complete recovery.'

'You saw your patient fairly regularly and must have had plenty of opportunity for forming an opinion of her state of mind?'

'Yes! I would say she was completely normal . . . in so far as any of us can be called normal.'

There was a faint stir of laughter in court but it quickly petered out as the Coroner said:

'How then do you account for the circumstances which led up to your being called in to attend to the deceased on the fifteenth of October? On that date, so I believe, she took an overdose of sleeping tablets.'

For a moment, the old doctor looked uncomfortable, although he had been prepared for such a question.

'That is correct. I would prefer, however, to call it a large dose of luminol rather than an overdose. I am quite sure in my own mind that there was no intention at the time of Miss Bates attempting to take her life. In my view she was upset and merely wished to ensure a good, long sleep.'

'Thank you, Doctor. I now call Mrs. Bates.'

Charlotte nearly failed to recognize the white-haired woman who in a barely audible voice, was taking the oath. Her eyes were swollen and red from incessant weeping, and her face drawn with grief. How different she looked from the smart, gay woman who had attended Meridan's and Liz's party that Saturday night!

'Please sit down if you would prefer, Mrs. Bates. We all understand that this must be very distressing for you. Now, would you tell me in your own words what happened on October fifteenth?'

'Well, I wasn't there when it happened . . . when she took the pills, I mean. I ought never to have left her alone. She was upset the night before and I should have stayed with her . . . or insisted she come home . . . '

'Can you tell the court why your daughter was upset?'

For a moment, Mrs. Bates turned to glance at Meridan in the court below the witness-box. There was an expression almost of apology on her face. Then she said in a quavering voice:

'Well, her fiancé, Mr. Avebury that is, had just suggested they break off their engagement. Pippa . . . my daughter, was very shocked and upset. That's why she stayed overnight in their house. You see, she had fainted only a short while before he told her.'

The quavering voice faltered and there was a murmur of sympathy through the court as she raised a handkerchief to her eyes.

'Do you feel able to continue, Mrs. Bates?'

The Coroner's voice was kind and sympathetic.

'Y . . . yes! Well, I didn't know the cause at the time. There was a party in progress and I thought my daughter had been overdoing things. I didn't realize what had happened until the doctor telephoned me next afternoon to tell me about . . . about the sleeping pills.'

'Can you remember the doctor's words to you on the telephone?'

'Well, not exactly, but they were to the effect that my daughter had taken too many sleeping pills . . . I don't think he used the word overdose!'

'Yet that was the impression you had?'

'I . . . I suppose so! But I could not believe she . . . she meant herself any harm . . . I'm sure she did not!'

'Thank you! Thank you!' Charlotte thought with a sigh of relief.

'I see! And you had no reason to change your mind?'

'Must I answer that?'

'It is preferable that you should do so.'

There was a moment of silence during which Charlotte waited in an agony which she knew was Meridan's at the same instant.

'Well, when I went round to see her, she did . . . she did say that she wished she . . . that that had been her intention . . . '

There was a stir throughout the court to be followed by instant quiet as the Coroner said:

'In your statement to Police Officer Jones, you said that you believed your daughter had tried to run in front of

Mr. Meridan's car?'

The words were very faint but clearly audible as the poor woman nodded her head:

'Yes, I did! But I was not myself . . . I wasn't thinking clearly. I know now that it wasn't so. I'm sure it wasn't so!'

'Thank you, Mrs. Bates. You may stand down now.'

Pippa's father was called next and he confirmed his wife's evidence, reiterating that despite their statements neither of them really believed Pippa had intended to take an overdose of luminol, nor when they knew the facts, that she had tried to run under the car. Before leaving the witness-box, he looked down at Meridan's bowed head and said clearly:

'My wife and I would like Mr. Avebury to know that we don't blame him in any way . . . *in any way at all!*'

Charlotte glanced again at the jury. Surely they were impressed by the evidence of Mr. Bates, himself a man of law. But there was no expression on their faces except of interest in the next witness.

'You are Mr. John Bates, brother of the deceased?'

'Yes, sir!'

'Can you tell us anything further about your sister's state of mind prior to the accident?'

'No, I'm afraid not. I was not in her confidence. I knew only what Elizabeth . . . Miss Avebury had told me . . . that her brother wished to end the engagement and that my sister was naturally very upset. I found it very difficult to believe that Pippa meant to . . . to do herself any harm by those sleeping pills. She was not the type.'

'And on October fifteenth?'

John repeated what he had already told the doctor and police officer. He, too, ended his evidence with a public statement to Meridan that he personally did not blame him in any way for what had happened. Then he stood down.

Elizabeth should have been the next

witness but she had refused from the first to go into the box. Her position if she were to do so would have been quite impossible. On the one hand she had her loyalty to and wish to help Merry. On the other, she still loved John and intended marrying him. She could not blacken Pippa's name . . . more especially now she was dead, by giving her view of what Pippa had been trying to do when she took too many pills . . . to frighten Merry into submission!

She was therefore represented by the family solicitor and was not in court, having obtained a certificate from Doctor Nivan to say she was not well enough to attend.

There was, therefore, little to add to what was already known.

Meridan's solicitor then stood up and said that he would like to call Meridan to the box and question him for the benefit of the jury.

Meridan! Charlotte's eyes followed him as he walked the few steps to the witness-box, took the oath in his slow, husky voice, and turned to face his questioner. If she could only have stood this ordeal for him, how willingly she would have done so!

'It is true that you had asked the deceased to release you from your engagement to her?'

'That is correct!'

'Had you, in fact, wished to do so some time ago?'

'Yes, when she was in hospital.'

'And you refrained from saying anything at a time when she was not well? You waited until you felt she was fit enough to bear with the disappointment?'

'Yes!'

'You were there in the room when she took the sleeping pills?'

'Yes!'

'Were you surprised?'

'Yes, very! You see, she seemed unable to appreciate that I had . . . had stopped loving her. She kept repeating that she did not believe it was true I was in love with someone else, although

I had told her this was the case.'

'And since she could not believe you meant to leave her, there was therefore no reason why she should wish to kill herself!'

Meridan nodded.

'What happened subsequently?'

'I decided not to take any action for another month, so that she should have time to get used to the idea of my going. I thought, perhaps, that she would see for herself in that time that it would be best for everyone if I went away.'

'But you did not wait that month. Why?'

'I learned that . . . that Phillipa had tried to come between me and the girl I hoped to marry when I was free to do so.'

'I don't wish to press you for details which must be painful for you. I think it will suffice to ask you if it was for this reason that on the evening of October fifteenth you told the deceased finally that you were going?'

'That is correct!'

'You were, in point of fact, leaving the house when the accident occurred?'

'Yes!'

'Will you tell the court what happened as far as you were concerned after you left the house?'

'Poor Meridan! Poor darling!' Charlotte thought as she listened to his slow voice repeating those few ghastly moments he had endured as he drove away from the house.

'I thought at first I had knocked over some stranger lurking in the bushes . . . it never once occurred to me it might be . . . Phillipa. Then my sister ran out to me and she told me what had happened.'

'Thank you, Mr. Avebury. One last question, in your opinion, was Miss Bates trying to run under your car?'

'I don't know! I've thought about it so much but I can't believe she meant to kill herself. And why, if she had so intended, should she have chosen this particular way?'

The Coroner then questioned Meridan.

'Can you please give us some indication as to the speed at which you were driving when the accident occurred?'

'About twenty-five miles an hour.'

'Was the visibility good?'

'No, sir; it was foggy.'

'Have you ever had a driving conviction or your licence endorsed?'

'I have never had an accident of any kind and I have held a licence for fourteen years.'

No further witnesses were called. The Coroner's summing up was brief, but Charlotte, sensitive as to how it must affect Meridan, was uncomfortably aware that the verdict was still in doubt.

'You have heard all the evidence and have these facts now to consider. It has been satisfactorily proved that the deceased met her death by coming into contact with a car, driven at moderate, but not dangerous speed, by Mr. Avebury. There is no question of Mr. Avebury having been driving dangerously, or without due care. The deceased ran out from behind a large rhododendron bush and on the evidence of her brother, Mr. John Bates, there can have been only the barest hope of Mr. Avebury seeing her in time to avoid her. You have therefore to consider the state of mind of the deceased prior to her death. It has been stated by all the witnesses that in their view, it seems unlikely that the deceased intended to commit suicide by taking an overdose of sleeping pills. Nevertheless, she did take more than the prescribed dose of these pills and on the evidence of Mrs. Bates, her mother, says she had intended to kill herself. Not long afterwards, she met her death by running into a car. While it was not the case on the previous occasion, there is no doubt that at this time she was fully aware that her fiancé had finally broken off the engagement, thereby providing her with a possible motive for wishing to end her life. It is for you to decide whether on this occasion she did, in fact, intend so to do.

'While considering this, you must

bear in mind a remark made by the last witness. If the deceased intended to kill herself, what made her choose this particularly unfortunate method? She might have found other, perhaps less painful, ways, such as she may have tried before. Whether she did in fact try to commit suicide and in the latter case succeed, is for you to decide.

'As to your verdict, I must direct you that there being no evidence at all that the deceased was of unsound mind, there are three alternatives open to you, verdict by misadventure, meaning by accident, if you consider that she was merely attempting to halt the car . . . the only eye-witness, her brother, stating this to be so; a verdict of *felo de se*, that is, suicide; if you feel there is insufficient evidence to support either verdict, you may say so, in which case an open verdict will be declared. You may now retire to consider your verdict. Meanwhile, the court is adjourned.'

Charlotte felt badly in need of some fresh air, but unfortunately, the rain was pouring down steadily into the streets as if in keeping with the morbidness of the proceedings. Hesitantly, she went back inside the big buildings, anxious at all costs to avoid running into either Meridan's or Pippa's family.

Meridan did not know she was here. Liz had promised not to tell him. If she could avoid being seen by him then she would never tell him that she had been a witness of the misery and pain that was so clearly his at this moment. True, he did not love Pippa. But nearly twenty years of friendship could not be quite undone even in those few moments when he had told Liz anger had made him hate her. Maybe that was why he felt so particularly guilty . . . because his last moments with Pippa should have been spent in anger.

Would he ever be able to forget that ghastly night? Could anything . . . anyone . . . erase the horror and futility and guilt? Would her own presence serve as a reminder rather than as a comfort to him?

Liz had been so adamant that Meridan needed her . . . that she must be firm now and stand by him whatever he said or did.

'Don't you see, Charlotte, that he may feel he *cannot* ask you to marry him now? That it wouldn't be fair to couple your name with that of a man whose private life has been dragged through the courts? Even supposing they exonerate him completely from all blame and give a verdict of misadventure, he is still going to feel responsible.'

Charlotte did not voice her immediate thoughts . . . that she, too, would always share that guilt with Meridan . . . equally with him. All that he had done had been for love of her and she would do only what was for his ultimate happiness.

She found now that she had wandered into a corridor she did not recognize. Hastily, she inquired of a passing policewoman the way back to the court-room.

'I'm afraid you won't be able to go in

now. The jury have given their verdict and I expect the Coroner is giving judgment. If you care to sit down and wait here a moment, I'll try to find out what has happened!' She added these words at sight of Charlotte's sudden extreme pallor.

So Charlotte did not hear the foreman of the jury say to the Coroner:

'We feel that there is insufficient evidence to make it possible for us to decide on the state of mind of the deceased prior to her death. We feel therefore that an open verdict is the only one we can give under these circumstances.'

It was only a matter of minutes before the Coroner, in agreement with the jury, pronounced an open verdict and put an end, for the time being anyway, to the proceedings.

'But . . . but that means . . . there'll be another inquest?' Charlotte asked the young policewoman who came back to tell her that the court had now been cleared.

'Not necessarily! Only if fresh evidence comes to light.' She gave an anxious look at Charlotte's white face and said: 'The canteen is open if you would care for a cup of tea?'

Charlotte shook her head. Slowly, she got to her feet and started back the way she had come. It was still pouring with rain but this time she did not notice it as she walked heedlessly along the shining pavements towards the railway station. So lost in thought was she that she did not notice the car slowing down behind her, nor see Meridan, without mac or coat, running to catch her up. Then she heard his voice calling her name and she swung round to face him.

'Charlotte! I was sure it was you! Darling, what are you doing here? You're soaked through. Come quickly and get into the car!'

Too surprised to argue . . . and with no wish to do so now that the sight of his face had brought back all the great pain and longing and need of him which she had kept so strictly under control, she followed him back to the car. With rain-wet faces white and stark in the sombre light of the November day, they looked into one another's eyes.

'Oh, Charlotte!' Meridan said on a deep sigh.

Had it not been for the public place in which he had halted the car on sight of her, he would have taken her in his arms. Now, he hurriedly restarted the car and drove out of the town. As soon as they were in the comparative privacy of the country road, he stopped once more and this time they turned to one another at the same moment.

There were tears on Charlotte's cheeks, tears that mingled with the rain, just as happiness surged through her to ease the misery of these last hours. She clung to him, her need of him equal only to his for her. Then, inevitably, they drew apart to talk.

'You shouldn't have come, dearest. Liz had no right to suggest it!' Meridan said when Charlotte had explained how she came to be there.

'But I wanted to go, Meridan. I couldn't have stayed home wondering . . . '

Meridan's face was suddenly bitter.

'Is it any better to have heard the final result? An open verdict, Charlotte . . . that means they will continue with their inquiries into Pippa's state of mind . . . they could hold a further inquest if they chose and say it was suicide!'

'Meridan, don't. None of those who really knew Pippa believed she meant to do it. Her own parents exonerated you. We must try to forget that there ever was a possibility that she meant herself any harm. It's our only chance.'

Meridan's face was suddenly drawn with pain.

'Our only chance? Charlotte, surely you realize that I cannot possibly marry you now!'

Purposefully, she misunderstood him.

'You mean, it is true you don't love me any more?'

'Charlotte!' He drew her against him

with such intensity of emotion that instinctively, her hand went to his face, her own deep feeling of tenderness calming him as no touch of her lips could have done.

'Then if you love me, Meridan, we shall be married. It would be impossible to consider that all this . . . this tragedy . . . had happened for nothing.'

'But Charlotte, don't you see? Everyone will point you out as 'the other woman' in the case? You'll come in for as much horrid publicity and eye-staring as I have done! Do you think I would let you go through that? Already we've had all the daily newspapers offering fantastic sums of money for sole rights to print the inside story!' His voice was bitter with disgust. 'They ring up . . . call even . . . and yesterday we caught one journalist trying to worm out of the gardener *your* name.'

'They've got a job to do!' Charlotte said gently. 'And anyway, darling, I don't mind. Nothing matters except that we should be together.'

'Then you believe there is still some chance of happiness for us?'

'Happiness?' Charlotte spoke thoughtfully. 'I don't know, dearest. But I do know that my life would be utterly meaningless without you. I learned that after . . . after I'd written to you . . . when I began to believe that you didn't love me. I'd rather be unhappy with you, Meridan, than go on living without you.'

'You should not tempt me, Charlotte! In my heart I know I have no right to ask you to be my wife.'

'Meridan, you have done no wrong! None of this is your fault . . . not even if she had meant to kill herself. No one blames you and you *must* stop blaming yourself. In time people will forget all about it and perhaps so can we. We have our whole lives ahead of us, Meridan. Surely you can't mean to throw them both away?'

'It . . . it won't be easy!'

'No, darling, I don't suppose it will. But whatever happens, we love each other and no one . . . nothing can destroy that love!'

But the moments which should have been so happy . . . when two lovers agree to join their lives together and wait to receive the congratulations of the world . . . were sadly different for them. There could be no joyful drive to Meridan's home to tell the news to his family. For the time being, at least, they must keep it to themselves. And because Charlotte would not be welcome by Meridan's parents at such a time . . . because John might be there to see Liz, he could do nothing but drive her to the station to go back to London alone.

He could not even tell her he would see her later for he must stay at least until the funeral was over.

Their love for one another might be complete and perfect and right in the eyes of God. But it could not yet be presented to the eyes of the world.

'I'll come as soon as I can, my dearest!' Meridan promised as he kissed her for the last time . . . a desperate kiss that held no real happiness for either of them. Only when Charlotte was there, held against his heart, could he shut his mind to the memory of Pippa, her crumpled figure lying on the wet grass.

14

It was Charlotte's wedding day ... a bright but sunless February morning, with grey clouds blowing across the smoky London sky. She had woken earlier with a wretched sense of premonition, due, she was sure, to the long conversation with her mother that had lasted well into the previous night. Her dreams had been hazy ... of a nightmarish quality and now her head ached and her eyes felt heavy and tired.

'Poor Mummy!' Charlotte thought. 'If she could only forget ... '

But Mrs. Matthews had continued to strive right up to the last to dissuade Charlotte from this marriage. Not because she disliked Meridan ... not because she must inevitably be losing her daughter, her only child ... but because she could not feel that Charlotte's happiness was safe in

Meridan's keeping.

Useless for Charlotte to say again and again:

'But Mummy, he loves me . . . and I love him. That is all that matters!'

Her mother was convinced that it was not!

'You may think you don't care what other people say. But you will, Charlotte . . . after a time. It'll begin to worry you that Meridan's parents have asked him not to take you to his home. And you'll mind if his friends look at you strangely and you'll know what they are thinking. Why, you can't even have a nice church wedding the way we'd always planned!'

It might not have upset Charlotte so deeply if she had not somewhere deep in her heart, felt that her mother was right!

It was upsetting to realize that her future mother- and father-in-law could not see their way to welcoming her to their home; that they had asked to be excused from attending Meridan's wedding; that they considered him very callous to be marrying so soon after the tragedy of Pippa's death.

Yet against all this she had weighed Meridan's need of her. He had spent every moment not actually working, in her company, as if he could not bear to let her from his sight. His love-making had had a desperate undertone that worried and disturbed her. It was almost as if he were a man going blind and she his only means of sight. He looked terribly ill and his nerves were so on edge that she had had to be more than careful as to what she said to him. The slightest form of criticism or argument, even if only meant in fun, was sufficient to have him stiffen up immediately and offer to free her from her promise to marry him if that was what she desired!

Against this loss of self-confidence, what mattered her own petty disappointments? In time, his family would come round. Liz was already a constant visitor and had grown as close to her as any friend could do. And Liz had sworn that it was only a matter of time.

'Mother and Father aren't young any more and they need a bit longer to get over the shock. It isn't just the fact of Pippa's dying; it was Merry having to face that horrible court inquest. And, of course, their friendship with Pippa's parents is naturally rather strained. But they'll get over it, Charlotte. They have nothing at all against you personally.'

Liz would be at the registry office today . . . the only one of Meridan's family or friends. And to see Charlotte married, only her mother and her Aunt Ethel, who was coming to live with her when Charlotte left, and Bess.

Bess was now engaged to be married to Peter Barnes. Neither girl had been very happy about the other's engagement; Bess for the same reasons her mother held; Charlotte because she still could not bring herself to like Peter. She did not believe that he was in love with Bess and had a horrible suspicion that he was only marrying her for her money. On the one occasion when she and Meridan had dined in town with the other couple, Peter had stared at her in a way that made her very uncomfortable, remembering as he forced her to do, the night of the party, and how he had tried to make a play for her. But she tried for Bess's sake to like him better and Meridan seemed to have no objections to him, despite the fact that he had nearly knocked him down! Peter was to be his best man today.

Charlotte was almost angry with her mother when she had brought up a breakfast-tray to her daughter, her eyes red and filled with tears.

'Do try to pull yourself together, Mummy! Anyone would think you were going to a funeral! Couldn't you try to be happy on my wedding day . . . for my sake?'

'You . . . you don't look very happy yourself, Charlotte!' her mother had countered tearfully but with spirit. 'There's still time to call it off if you wish . . . '

But Charlotte had cut her short and, leaving her tray untouched, had flung out of the bedroom to have her bath.

A phone call from Meridan . . . just to tell her how much he loved her, brought some of the colour back to her cheeks, and a return of happiness to her heart.

When at last she stood beside him in the bleak, rather shabby office where they were to be made man and wife, she felt beyond anything else, an overwhelming desire to make Meridan happy. She refused to notice the dreary surroundings, to hear the disinterested voice of the registrar gabbling through the brief ceremony or the sound of her mother's tears behind her. Her hand was in Meridan's and this brief contact was more than sufficient to make her forget everything but how much she loved him.

As Meridan put the thin gold band on her finger, she felt her heart jolt. What did a church wedding, a white gown, the bells, the confetti, matter?

This was the only part of the ceremony that had any import . . . the moment of becoming Meridan's wife. Looking into his eyes, she dedicated herself in that moment to him.

'Dear God, let me be a good wife for him!' she prayed. Then the brief ceremony was over and Meridan's lips were touching hers. Liz was hugging her and her mother kissed her and attempted to smile.

Meridan's hand holding hers tightly, Charlotte let herself be led out of the building and into the car, draped somewhat half-heartedly with a single white ribbon from bonnet to door. The others were to follow in another car for the reception at Charlotte's house.

As the chauffeur closed the door on them, Meridan bent his head and kissed her again.

'Charlotte! My wife!'

It did not seem real . . . not to her . . . not at that moment. She knew it was so and yet throughout the short reception, when they cut the simple cake, when Peter Barnes made a speech congratulating them as their health was drunk in champagne, as they opened the few telegrams, she felt as if she were living some dream; that she would wake up and find it was not really true at all.

Even as Liz came upstairs to help her change from the creamy-white jersey wool frock she had chosen for the wedding, into the warm blue matching dress and coat in which she was to 'go away', still she could not believe she was really Meridan's wife.

'Don't look so dazed, Charlotte, or I'll begin to wonder if you've had too much champagne!'

'Oh, Liz! Is it really true?' Charlotte asked.

Liz's face smiled at her with a deep and real affection.

'Yes, dear Charlotte! We are now sisters-in-law and you are Merry's wife. I wish I could tell you how very, very happy I am that it should be so at last!'

'Oh, Elizabeth . . . you really mean that, don't you?'

'Yes, I do, Charlotte. I think Merry is very lucky and that's not just an idle remark. If anyone can make him happy again, it is you!'

They were going to Switzerland for their honeymoon. Their passports and air tickets to Zurich were in Meridan's care. But they were not going today. Meridan had thought she might be too tired to travel after the wedding and had arranged for them to spend their first night together at one of the big London hotels. Then they would catch the plane early next morning. Amongst Charlotte's luggage was a new ski-outfit and only their skis would have to be hired when they arrived at the mountain hotel where, for the first time in her life, she would be initiated into the joys of winter sports.

'There is nothing in the world quite so wonderful as a mountain holiday,' Meridan had said, his face young again in his enthusiasm. 'And February is a perfect time of year. There's still plenty of snow about and yet the sun is hot enough for sun-bathing. There'll be dancing in the evenings and you won't be too tired to join in because the air is like champagne. I know you would love it, darling.'

It was enough for her that *he* wanted her to go, that even the thought of a ski-ing holiday could erase the tired lines around his eyes and bring a smile back to his mouth, an enthusiasm and eagerness to his voice. His happiness was all she needed to ensure her own.

Meridan had had their hotel suite filled with flowers. Their perfume greeted her as the porter unlocked the door and she walked past him into the room. She had forgotten . . . or was not conscious until now, how little money meant to Meridan. This was one of the best hotels in London and the suite was as luxurious as the exotic out-of-season flowers that filled it.

She walked across the thick soft carpet to the table by the window where a huge vase of red and white carnations gave off their heady smell.

She was reminded suddenly of the carnations Meridan had sent her as a similar token of his love. And she had believed for a few days that they were emblems of guilt . . . guilt because he had ceased to love her . . . because Pippa had told her . . .

No! she would not remember Pippa . . . not here . . . not now . . .

'Charlotte!'

They were alone at last and she was a prisoner in his arms. It was almost a year since they had first met, first fallen in love; a year filled with that love and with tragedy and unhappiness; a year which had been leading up to this moment . . . this first real understanding that she was Meridan's wife.

There was only tenderness in his eyes, in the touch of his hands. He seemed to guess instinctively her sudden trembling expectancy that was almost fear.

But she need not have been afraid. Not of him . . . not of his love . . . never of him. It was not just a physical union of their love that they experienced together, but a mental and spiritual union as well. Each was determined only to give . . . to become one with the other in the way God had ordained for those who love.

What she could not have foreseen in the blinding happiness of this first hour alone with him, was that it would be the only one unmarred by a third person . . . by someone whom she had never before disliked but was to grow to hate . . . by Phillipa's ghost. Over and over again she was to force herself to remember this first giving of herself to Meridan's keeping, this first perfect occasion when each bore only the other in mind, and in heart. Despair might have come so much sooner and hope ceased altogether were it not for this one sweet memory.

As it was, she had no knowledge of what was to come. Mercifully, she lay now in Meridan's arms, her cheeks flushed with happiness, her mouth close against his, her eyes closed as she heard his soft, low voice, telling her over and over again how much he loved her. Now at last she could really feel she was his wife! With the deepest tenderness, she traced the lines of his face and gently touched his lips with hers. How much she loved him, too! She had believed herself incapable of greater emotion than she had felt with him in the past. Now she knew that she had barely touched the beginnings of this great love. Her discovery of the man she had married as a lover was a miracle to her ... a miracle of perfection. Part of her joy lay in the knowledge of the peace and the joy she had been able to bring him, too.

'I'm so happy ... so happy!' she whispered, although there was none to hear them. 'I never knew ... never guessed ... that it was possible to feel like this!'

Meridan looked into the beautiful, shining eyes so close to his, and his voice shook a little as he said:

'It is because we love each other,

dearest heart! It should never happen except between people who love as we do.'

For a fleeting second, the thought of Pippa lay in the edge of Charlotte's mind. She could see now why Meridan had been so sure he should not marry her. But only for an instant did she permit it to last. Her arms tightened about Meridan's neck and she drew him closer against her, no longer shy or reticent of her need of him, only surprised that she could feel so deeply with her whole being; that she could have lived till now without knowing what it was she missed. Even when Meridan had held her and kissed her and she had been aware of her longing for something more, she had never guessed that she could feel like this . . .

It was Meridan who reminded her, smiling as he did so, that if they did not hurry they would miss dinner altogether. Hurriedly they bathed and changed and went hand-in-hand from their room to the lift. Neither could know what cruel stroke of Fate awaited them as the lift boy drew back the gates to let them in. It was even a moment or two before Charlotte or Meridan recognized one of the two other occupants of the lift. Only when she felt a sudden tightening of Meridan's grip on her hand, felt the shock ripple through his body, did she look up in surprise.

Then her eyes followed the direction of Meridan's gaze and with a jolt of her heart, she recognized the face of the man opposite them . . . the face of the Coroner who had held the inquest on Pippa's death.

★   ★   ★

Almost as embarrassed as Meridan, the man said quickly:

'It's Mr. Avebury, isn't it? May I present my wife?'

'And mine!' Meridan said.

Then the lift doors were opened and they were all four standing in the brightly lit hall.

'Would you care for a drink before dinner?' the older man asked, and was glad when Meridan quickly refused.

After the young couple had gone, he briefly explained to his wife how he had come to know Meridan.

'Very unfortunate case!' he said. 'Never went any further, of course. The police made some more inquiries but they learned nothing new. There was no other verdict possible, of course. One can't help feeling sorry for the fellow although he doesn't seem to be exactly broken-hearted now!'

'Oh, but my dear, didn't you see . . . there were two or three little pieces of confetti on the floor where his wife was standing. They must be newly-weds!'

Her husband gave a wry smile.

'Should be more women in the police force!' he joked. 'I never noticed!'

'Poor things!' said his wife thoughtfully as she followed him into the lounge. 'It can't have been very nice for them coming face to face with *you*!'

This was a complete understatement

of the disastrous effect the meeting had on Meridan. Anxiously, Charlotte watched the face on which all the youthful lines had disappeared again. For her part, it had been rather an unpleasant shock running into the Coroner like that, but a meeting she could quite soon have forgotten despite its painful reminder of Phillipa . . . *if only Meridan had not been so upset!* He left his food untouched and at last, over coffee, turned to her with an apology, saying:

'I'd have given anything in the world not to have had this happen . . . tonight of all nights!'

Glad that he had at last broached the subject she had not herself liked to bring up, Charlotte said with a quick, warm smile:

'But, darling, it wasn't in the least important. Let's forget about him.'

So easy to suggest and yet apparently so impossible for Meridan to do. Even as he danced with her, she felt that his attention was somewhere else, his glance going continually round the room to see, no doubt, if the Coroner and his wife were there watching him.

Unable to bear it any longer, she suggested they leave the dancing and go back to their rooms. She was in fact terribly tired . . . as much by the emotions of her wedding day as by the strain of these last two hours. She felt instinctively that back in the privacy of their suite, Meridan *must* forget the unfortunate incident in the lift and think once more only of her.

Hitherto, her relationship with Meridan had always been one of deference. It had been her pleasure to accede to his wishes, his moods. She had, therefore, adapted herself to the various facets of his character, gay when he was gay, talkative when he wanted conversation, responsive when he felt the stirrings of that sweet, deep passion for her that had so enthralled her now that she understood and reciprocated.

But tonight, their roles were reversed. It was Charlotte, shy, reticent inexperienced wife though she was, who tried to woo Meridan to forgetfulness in her arms. Meridan would have been inhuman had he not felt his pulses stirring swiftly in answer to the question in her eyes, the appeal of her arms held out to him.

But although Charlotte at last fell into a deep, untroubled sleep, believing as she did that she had put all thought of the past from Meridan's mind, her success was short-lived with the man who lay awake by her side. He could not still the memories that had for so many months now haunted his dreams. Not even the great love and tenderness he felt for the young wife in his arms, could banish the ever-present feeling of remorse and guilt. He knew that he was entirely blameless as far as his driving was concerned. No human being could have seen Pippa running so swiftly from behind the clump of bushes, not unless they had known beforehand that she would be there. But he could so easily have been more gentle, more understanding with her the night before! He had been so terribly angry . . . to the point of hating her. If anyone had forced Pippa to do what she had done, it had been he with his treatment of her.

As clearly as if they were in the room speaking to him now, their eyes hard and accusing, he could hear the voice of Pippa's mother: 'You killed her . . . you killed her . . . ' and Mr. Bates: 'You'll never forgive yourself for this . . . '

Oh, they had taken back those words . . . tried to do their best for him in court, but he knew that in their hearts they held him responsible, just as he did himself. Yet what other course could he have taken? Marriage to Pippa after what she had tried to do would have been a parody of what marriage was meant to be. She had lied to him and deceived him and he could never have trusted her again, never have felt a return of the old affection for her. Even in death, she had not been able to revive his old lifelong fondness for her.

But even while he could never have

married her, had he been less precipitate that night, that morning ... less keyed up with anger and an intense desire to see Charlotte, the whole ghastly accident could have been avoided. Everyone had preached caution to him ... his mother, Pippa's father, even Charlotte herself. All had begged him not to act hastily ... and this was exactly what he had done. Now there was to be no escape from Pippa ... ever. He could not be allowed to forget her ... not even on his wedding day! He had been prepared for the police questioning him after the funeral; three times in all they had come to his flat in town to go over the whole story with him. The Inspector had been polite enough, kind and even sympathetic, but Meridan knew that he was trying to find out if Pippa had really intended her death. His answer had always been the same ... the truth:

'I don't know ... I just don't know!'

He had realized that there might be a further verdict issued in court ... that an open verdict meant only that it was open to fresh evidence and the vital factor still in doubt. That nothing more had happened did nothing to relieve his fears for he would have preferred to face what was coming before his marriage to Charlotte.

But for Charlotte, Meridan felt that these last months would have been even more unendurable. She alone gave him some measure of hope for the future. With her, he could for a time forget his painful thoughts. Her obvious love for him gave him back a little of his lost self-confidence. Her complete trust and belief in his innocence restored a little of his own faith in himself. But nothing . . . no one, had been able to still his conscience. He might have been able to leave Pippa and forget her while she lived, but dead it seemed she was to haunt him forever. Even on Christmas Day he had been appalled to receive the expensive cigarette-case chosen by Phillipa and sent as ordered by her to arrive on December twenty-fifth. The inscription: *'To darling Merry, from*

Pippa with love', was like an accusing voice from the past; and made the festivities a parody of what his first Christmas with Charlotte should have been. He had not told her . . . could not then or now, burden her with his own terrible conscience.

Whatever happens, he had vowed, Charlotte should not suffer for this. But what he did not realize yet was that his own suffering must all too soon become her own.

15

Charlotte sat in the brilliant sunshine, her pen poised above her writing-pad, distracted for a moment from the letter she was writing by the arrival of a gay party of young skiers who had just sat down at the neighbouring table.

How noisy . . . and happy they were! Their bright, lively suntanned faces were aglow with the exercise they had just had and full of the joy of being alive on so wonderful a morning and in such a beautiful place.

It was beautiful! Charlotte, who had never seen mountains in the snow before, had been completely enslaved from her first sight of them. Meridan was right, she had told herself instantly. How could anyone fail to be happy and gloriously content in a place like this!

The hotel, while not being of the expensive tourist class, was nevertheless very comfortable and warm. Theirs was a moderately large room with a large balcony overlooking the ski-slopes outside, where they breakfasted on rolls and honey and hot chocolate in the warm sunshine. The furnishings were simple but adequate and Charlotte instantly felt at home . . . feeling that here for the next two weeks she would be the happiest girl on earth . . . and more in love than any other girl in the world, too!

Meridan looked wonderful in his ski-ing outfit, and it soon became clear to her that he was very adept at the sport and very much the focus of admiration for the party of young Norwegian girls who were just now sitting next to her. There were plenty of attractive young ski-guides to take them out on the slopes and to dance with them in the evenings in the crowded *salon* with its semi-circular carved wooden bar. Nevertheless, they and many other women in the hotel were frequently glancing at Meridan, and

with a certain amount of envy at her!
. . . a fact which had not escaped
Charlotte. She had felt . . . and was so
proud of him.

Around the hotel circled the mountains . . . they must have been about
half-way up for they towered above her
now as she gazed at them, seeming
almost to touch the brilliant blue of the
cloudless sky. Yet far below they spread
out into the tiny valley, already green
with Spring grass and in places with
early Spring flowers. There was a
funicular to take the skiers and hotel
visitors up and down to the hotel and
Charlotte had spent a day with
Meridan in the town, buying little gifts
for her family and friends, hand-carved
wooden ornaments, bright silk scarves,
gaily coloured hand-knitted gloves and
jerseys. Meridan had given her what
had seemed to Charlotte an enormous
sum of money for her personal expendi-
ture and it had been lovely to go round
the shops, choosing what she liked without thought of cost.

Then they had sat together on a little wooden bench outside one of the numerous cafés, sipping the sweet red refreshingly iced drink that most skiers enjoyed so much after the long ski-run down to the valley. It had taken Charlotte almost as long to come down in the funicular as it had Meridan to make the descent on skis.

But this had been one of the happy days . . . one of the first few days after their arrival when they had still wished to spend every second of their time together . . . and had done so. Patiently, Meridan had taken her out on the nursery slopes and started to teach her the joys of ski-ing. He had said she had a natural balance and aptitude and she had felt herself that she was making good progress. She had fallen often into the now hardened snow (there had been no snowfall for some weeks and the many skiers had flattened it almost to ice!) but apart from a few bruises she was not hurt and, laughing, had allowed Meridan to help her up and try again.

Now she tried alone . . . or occasionally attended one of the lessons for beginners given by the hotel ski-guides. Meridan was at this moment out on some ski-run high up in the mountains with three other men, all excellent skiers like himself. He had left with a packed rucksack immediately after breakfast, and because it would take them at least four hours to ascend since there was no ski-lift to the higher points, he was lunching there and would not be back till early afternoon. Virtually she would be alone all day . . . and far from feeling sad, she had welcomed the thought. It was as horrible to admit this fact as to admit the reason for it . . . that in Meridan's company, there was no longer any joy or happiness for her . . . or, as she knew, for him.

What had happened to them? When had this unvoiced separation begun? Unfortunately, Charlotte knew only too well. It had been all a honeymoon should be, perfect in every sense, for those first two days. Then the young Swiss girl had arrived with her mother and father ... the girl whom even Charlotte could not deny, bore such a remarkable resemblance to Pippa!

With a deep sigh of pain and bewilderment, Charlotte looked down again at the letter she was writing to Liz.

To no one else in the world would she have admitted that everything was not perfect. To her mother and Bess her letters had been glowing accounts of the beauty of the place, the comfort of the hotel, the gay evenings dancing and the sun-lit days learning to ski.

But reticent as she was by nature ... especially in such a matter as her personal relationship with the man she had married, Charlotte had felt that she must tell someone ... ask advice. Maybe Liz could advise her what to do!

... I know it all began with this girl! she continued to write. *At first I did not notice her, but I saw that Meridan was looking continually at*

the bar where she was sitting and thinking at first he wanted a drink, I suggested we leave our table and go for one. His face turned completely white and he said 'No!' so rudely that I was amazed. Then I looked back at the bar and I, too, saw the likeness. She had Pippa's fair, curly hair, cut in much the same style; her green eyes and small mouth. Only the nose is different but the general effect, especially at a distance, is uncanny.

Liz, how can Fate be so cruel to us both? This is our honeymoon. There can't be many girls like Pippa . . . or so like her . . . in the world, and yet we have to meet this girl here, just as we had to run into that beastly Coroner in London. I would not have noticed myself . . . at least, I doubt it. Certainly, I should not have worried unduly. But it had an appalling effect on Meridan . . . .

She could not tell even Liz, his sister, of that night, the first they had spent not falling asleep in each other's arms. At first, Meridan had made love to her . . . not gently or with tenderness but with a hard, almost brutal, passion that had frightened her, almost as much as did the moments afterwards, when he had suddenly got out of bed and walked across to the window where a brilliant moon turned the snow-covered hills into a sparkling fairyland. Only the night before she had stood beside him in the circle of his arm, sharing with him the beauty and romance of that night. But tonight, she knew he did not even see the view. Maybe she could have prevented this barrier between them ever coming to fruition if she had gone to him then, stood beside him and made him tell her what was on his mind. But she had lain, silently watching him, feigning sleep; had seen him suddenly bury his face in his hands and heard the hard tortured sounds of a man weeping.

Knowing he would never have given way to what he would call such weakness if he had imagined her to be awake, she had held herself rigid in the warm bed, the palms of her hands cold and wet with sweat, her teeth clenched together as she strove not to go to him. It was one of the most agonizing moments of her life . . . hearing with her own ears this dreadful unhappiness; knowing that she had not, after all, succeeded in making him happy . . . in helping him to forget.

It seemed hours that he stood there, and when at last he came back to bed, he was as cold as ice. His fingers touched her face and now the tenderness was there; but in the touch, too, Charlotte sensed pity. She heard his voice, barely a whisper, saying over and over again:

'What have I done! God forgive me! What have I done!'

Unable to bear it any longer, she pretended he had awoken her and turned to him, putting her warm arms around him in a desperate effort to offer him consolation. But he had only whispered:

'Go back to sleep, darling!' and soon

afterwards turned away from her, gently releasing her arms before he moved.

. . . Next day, he was quiet and seemed to be absorbed in his thoughts. He looked terribly tired and I know he didn't sleep much. I didn't either. The girl was sitting in the sun when we went out after breakfast. I could not help noticing that Meridan picked a chair as far away from her as possible, but in spite of it, his head kept turning towards her.

Oh, Liz, I could have coped, I think, if it had just been Meridan admiring another pretty girl. How much I'd welcome at this moment a good honest feeling of jealousy instead of this despair. I know he cannot forget Phillipa. I know she haunts him, waking or sleeping, and that it is because he blames himself for what she did. How can I make him forget her? He tries so hard not to let me see what is on his mind. If he would only confide in me we could be close again. But when I attempted this, by remarking on the likeness of this girl to Phillipa, he merely gave me a strange look and denied completely that he could see the resemblance. As if to prove it, he made a point of striking up an acquaintance with her father in the bar that night, and we all sat at the same table for at least an hour. It was a kind of crazy 'bravado' and I could do nothing about it.

Every day we seem to grow farther and farther apart. The girl is also a beginner and skis on the same slopes that I do. To make it easier for Meridan, I suggested he go off for some of the more difficult runs and that I'd really get along better with a professional teacher. As soon as he saw I didn't mind his going, he left. I know he was glad to get away from the sight of her.

It occurred to me that we should move to some other hotel, away from *her. But after considering it all one night, I realized that it can't do any good running away. If this is the kind of thing we have to face, then we had better face it now. We have five more days here before we come home. As you know, Meridan is coming to live with us until we find a house or flat. I dread the thought that Mummy will guess something is wrong. She knows me so well and it will not be nearly so easy to pretend to her as it is to Meridan. He believes I am quite happy, and at least I thank God for that. But we are really two strangers living together, Liz . . . not man and wife . . . not close any more as we used to be. I know he is not happy and I just can't think what to do. If you have any ideas at all, Liz, please write and tell me. You know Meridan so well and perhaps there is something you can think of . . . .*

Liz's reply awaited Charlotte when they arrived home. As soon as they had unpacked their suitcases and given her mother and Aunt Ethel their presents, Charlotte left Meridan to show them the snaps he had taken while she retired to the bedroom to tear open the envelope.

Darling Charlotte,

I cannot tell you how distressed I was to read of your unhappiness. What appallingly bad luck you seem to have had. At least it is some consolation to me to know that you go on loving Merry despite his moods. I suppose I should not say this since she is dead, but I could cheerfully do Pippa some serious harm, were it not too late. How can Merry go on feeling he was responsible! I am convinced, as you are, that it was an accident, nothing more, and that the previous time was only to frighten him. But that's no help since Merry doesn't believe it, too.

My dear, I don't know what to suggest. Perhaps after all it would be best to let Merry see that you are not as happy as you have made out. Maybe for your sake . . . and I know how much he loves you . . . he will try to get above this thing and at least try to forget. I think it is wrong to let him brood over it alone and I've no doubt you feel that even if it is painful for him to discuss what is on his mind, it is better than going on as you are.

I do hope matters will improve once you are home. At least there won't be that Swiss girl to remind him. I'll join my prayers to yours that nothing similar comes your way. Can I come and see you both soon? John would like to, too, but perhaps it would be better not . . . for a while anyway. Don't hesitate to confide in me, dear Charlotte, if you feel the need to do so. I would never reveal your letter to another living soul, not even to my John.

All my love meanwhile,
Liz.

But in the comparatively small suburban house where they must temporarily make their home, there was little chance of the privacy they had had until now. Aunt Ethel had Charlotte's old bedroom and the young couple were in the spare room adjoining. Charlotte knew that the walls were far from sound-proof and that any conversation she had with Meridan could be heard without much difficulty from either her mother's or her old room. As to the day-time, her mother or her aunt were always around, and in any event, Meridan had returned to work the day after their arrival home so she barely saw him until the evening meal.

Time hung heavily on her hands. She had given up her job to get married and now she wondered if she should take it up again. Yet even though she should find a similar job, it could only be temporary for every day there were long lists from house agents of flats and houses she must see.

There was little joy in viewing these

possible homes, however, for Meridan seemed incapable of anything but a feigned enthusiasm for those she said she liked. It was as if his mind had completely withdrawn from the future . . . their future . . . and could contemplate only the present, or was it the past?

At last, Charlotte knew she could bear it no longer. By careful planning, she managed to persuade her mother and aunt to go to the cinema. She was therefore alone in the house when Meridan arrived home. It was the first time they had really been alone together since their honeymoon ended, six days ago.

Charlotte had changed into a warm, long, woollen house-coat, for March in England was proving very cold. She had taken exaggerated care with her appearance although she was almost sure that when Meridan came in, he would not notice but give her his now customary kiss on the cheek. This evening, however, she drew her arm through his and led him into the sitting-room.

'A drink first, darling, before you change,' she said with a lightness she was far from feeling. She gave him a whisky-and-soda and then curled up on the rug, one arm resting on his knees, the firelight making a warm glow on her face.

'Busy?' she asked, to break the silence.

He seemed to return from his thoughts with an effort.

'Not very. And you?'

'I saw nothing today I liked as much as the house in Richmond. Do you think we could go over it together at the week-end, darling? I'm sure you'll approve.'

'Of course, if you'd like to!' Meridan answered, but as usual, there was no enthusiasm in his voice.

'Meridan!' He looked up from his glass at the sharpness of her tone, noticing her for the first time. How beautiful she looked with the firelight on her face and hair, the soft shape of her body outlined against the wool coat she wore; beautiful and desirable . . . and she was his wife. Why, then, could he feel nothing but despair in his heart when he looked at her like this? A despair that robbed him of all response . . . all warmth . . . all hope! Luckily, she seemed not to have noticed this strange new feeling he had for her . . . or was it lack of feeling? It was not that he loved her less . . . but differently . . . as he might have loved some treasured *objet d'art*. But he could no longer give any physical expression to this love . . . it was as if all emotion had been frozen out of him. He could not even feel desire for that beautiful body . . . except as a means of forgetfulness and after that one night when he had used her as a means of escape, he had hated himself so bitterly for betraying the sweetness of their earlier unions that he had sworn to himself he would never touch her again unless it could be without any thought of Pippa hidden in the back of his mind.

Because she was gentle and sweet, and as loving as ever towards him, this had not been easy at first. She might be able to forgive him for that night for she could not have guessed how the sight of that Swiss girl, so painfully like Pippa, had affected him. But he could not forgive himself, and now he sought to avoid Charlotte knowing that too great a physical proximity to her might lead him to another betrayal of her love for him . . . his love for her.

Only in her arms could he forget. Every other moment of the day, something, someone, served to remind him of the girl he had killed. He no longer sought to escape from what he believed to be his guilt. And recognizing that he was guilty, he knew that he had had no right to marry Charlotte.

So, in his own twisted thoughts, Meridan was unmaking that marriage as surely as if he had openly asked Charlotte for a divorce. Every instinctive move he made towards her, he checked. Every time he felt himself drawing towards her, needing her presence, the sound of her voice, the touch of her hand, he deliberately walked the other way. It had not been too difficult . . . nor too obvious with Mrs. Matthews and Aunt Ethel around the house. But he knew that Charlotte was anxious to move into a home of their own and that there it would be different. Just as it was different now that they were quite alone together in this firelit room, Charlotte's arm resting on his knee.

'Meridan!' she said again, more sharply, so that he was forced to look into her eyes. He was deeply and painfully shocked to find them full of tears. But he dared not put out a hand to comfort her . . . dared not even question her for fear he might relent completely and take her in his arms.

'Meridan, we can't go on like this. You must tell me what is wrong!'

As if the effort of saying it at last was too much for her, she laid her face against her hands and silently, began to weep. Meridan stared down at the bent, dark head, aghast. He had never realized she was unhappy ... never realized that she had been aware at all of anything wrong. In his company at least, she had always been her gay, cheerful, lively self.

He did not know what to say to her. To tell her outright that he could see no happiness for either of them in the future would be too cruel. Yet that was the truth. While the memory of Phillipa haunted him, he could not accept Charlotte's love ... nor give her his own. The ever-growing feeling of guilt had made him virtually impotent both in mind and body. How could he explain this to his young bride? How to tell her that barely three weeks after their wedding, he knew he ought never to have married her at all!

'Meridan, you have to tell me! Whatever it is, you must say it. It began out there ... in Switzerland ... when we met that girl. I know it upset you to see her but it doesn't explain why you should stop loving me!'

'Charlotte!' His voice was a hoarse cry of denial, wrung from his heart.

'That isn't true. I shall always love you . . . always!'

She held both his hands now, her tear-wet face turned beseechingly up to his.

'Then what is wrong? Why can we not be close to each other any more? You avoid me now, Meridan . . . don't deny it, you do! You cannot be happy near me. Even now you are wishing I would let go of your hands. Isn't it so?'

'Charlotte!'

He pulled her upwards so that she lay now on his lap, her arms entwined about his neck, his face buried in her hair. But he still could not . . . would not talk about Phillipa . . . about the nightmare dreams that made him dread sleep . . . about the terrible conscious-ness of guilt that as clearly haunted his days. He could not ask her to share this burden with him . . . Charlotte, who was innocent of all blame, who still believed him innocent, too!

Hopelessly, Charlotte lay in his arms, knowing that she had failed. This physical nearness to him was only a parody of what she had hoped for. He was still as deeply lost to her as ever . . . lost in his thoughts.

'Meridan, I love you . . . can't you trust me? Can't you share with me . . . your wife . . . whatever it is that is on your mind? I cannot bear to be shut out like this. I would tell you anything . . . anything in the world. Even if you were to tell me now that you had deliberately run Pippa down . . . that you had meant to kill her, I should not love you less. And I would know it wasn't true!'

The last words were Charlotte's undoing. He had been on the point of saying to her:

'But that's what I did, Charlotte, even though I did not mean it . . . I killed her!'

Now he knew it was hopeless. She had said herself that she would not believe it was true. How could she then understand that he felt as guilty as if the verdict had been of death by his hand! Unless she could see for herself that he and he alone was responsible for what had happened, then they could never hope to be close to one another again. And to disillusion her would be the cruellest thing of all. Better to leave her if need be . . . if to continue as they were was making her unhappy.

'There is nothing wrong!' he said at last, his voice filled with weariness, with despair. 'You are being far too imaginative, Charlotte. What should be wrong? I admit I thought that girl was like Pippa . . . but what of it? Did it upset you?'

Quietly, resolutely, Charlotte slipped off his knees and stood up in front of the fire, her back towards him so that he should not see the agony in her eyes.

'It's no good, is it, Meridan? You won't be honest with me! Something has come between us and once we agreed that nothing ever could. Whatever it is, I know it can be removed if

414

only you want to do so . . . *if only you'll tell me what it is*. I *know* it had something to do with that girl . . . that it has to do with Phillipa. Well, she tried hard enough to come between us during her life . . . are you willing to let her succeed now she is dead?'

If the words were brutal and to the point, she did not care. She had to reach him somehow. But he remained silent, unmoving in his chair.

'Meridan, what do you want me to do? To go on pretending that nothing has happened? To go on living as we have done these last two weeks? Is it in this way you want us to choose our first home? Or perhaps you no longer want a home?'

A home . . . a house where he and Charlotte could live in happiness, raise a family . . . a place of comfort and peace where he could forget! How much he wanted it. And yet what hope had they of achieving it this way, as she so truly said.

'I only want you to be happy,

Charlotte. I'm sorry if I haven't been very enthusiastic about the house. I'll come at the week-end to see the Richmond one and, if you like it, we'll buy it as soon as we can.'

'Meridan, I don't want a house . . . I want you!'

But the words were never spoken. At the instant of forming in her mind, her pride suddenly choked them in her throat. She would not plead with him for his love . . . for his confidence. Both would have to come voluntarily, and trust in her, too.

'I'd better go and see about the dinner!' she said stiffly, and without looking at him again, she turned and left the room.

He knew he had hurt her by his silence . . . hurt the one person in the world he loved most dearly. But even as he realized it, he felt even further convinced that to tell her the truth would be to hurt her more. It had become so exaggerated in his mind that it was just as if he were to himself some criminal who had to conceal his guilt or be damned for ever; not because of the consequences but because there would be none. Charlotte would protest his innocence to him as much as to herself. There was still some faint chance that he could lay Pippa's ghost in time, but if he ever admitted to Charlotte that it was there, Pippa would come between them for ever and there would be no hope. Whatever the cost to Charlotte now, he *had* to fight this alone.

'Dear God,' he prayed silently. 'Help me to forget!'

16

Meridan's mother and father were away, and because of it, Elizabeth had insisted that her brother and Charlotte should come for the week-end. She would brook no refusal although several times, Meridan had tried to get out of it on some pretext or other.

'It's quite ridiculous, Merry!' she told him firmly. 'It is your home and even if Mother and Father were going to be there, there is nothing whatever to prevent you coming down if you please . . . and Charlotte, too. I could understand Charlotte feeling it might be a little awkward if Mother and Father were there. After all, they have never made her very welcome as a daughter-in-law despite the priceless tea-set they gave her for your wedding! But Charlotte has already said she'd like to come so there is no reason for you to refuse!'

Charlotte felt a bitter relief in Liz's bluntness. It was a week since she had had that rift with Meridan and they had exchanged only the barest civilities since then. If anything, the barrier between them was higher than ever and she had appealed once more to Liz for help. Liz had immediately taken matters in hand and over the threesome lunch-party in town, she was stating her case to her brother.

'I feel it is hardly fair to John . . . ' Meridan began, but his sister interrupted him.

'That's nonsense, too. John told me to tell you he'd be delighted to see you both. So that's that, Merry. I'll expect you both Friday night after Merry finishes work!'

They had driven down in silence . . . a journey of misery for Charlotte, who could not see how all this would end. Meridan looked ill and she knew that she, herself, did not look too well. There was, of course, a reason for her state of health. She was nearly convinced that she was going to have a child. But the thought gave her no pleasure. She could not see that it would make any difference to her relationship with Meridan and that mattered far more to her than anything else in the world. Nor did she wish him to become suddenly solicitous and tender towards her as he might well do if he guessed she was pregnant. It would be too bitter a pill for her to swallow that he could still show her some feeling merely because she was to be the mother of his child!

She told Liz, however, choosing a moment after dinner when Meridan and John were playing billiards and they were alone.

Liz looked at Charlotte compassionately. She could understand her wish to keep her condition from Meridan under the circumstances. But she would not be able to do so indefinitely. It seemed tragic that the love between her brother and his wife . . . a love she believed to be perhaps deeper and even more enveloping than her own great fondness for John . . . could have come to this point. She had no doubt at all that they still loved each other. Or that this was somehow Merry's fault. Yet if Charlotte could not get the truth from him, how could she, his sister? Maybe the thought of a child would make a difference, yet that was not the difference Charlotte wanted. Nor, under the circumstances, would she!

In fact, Elizabeth was worried that she, herself, was in the same condition. They had told no one, but she and John had been secretly married a week after Pippa's funeral. It had been John who had wanted so much to do this. He had felt, not unreasonably, that with this new rift between their two families, somehow they might be parted. In deference to public feeling in the district, it would be at least six months before they could have a church wedding, and it would be bound to revive a lot of talk locally about the tragic death of John's sister when they did so.

Sharing his feeling to some extent,

Elizabeth had agreed. There was no reason why she and John should let Pippa come between them and she was secretly pleased that John was suddenly so determined to marry her. It was proof that his love for her had not suffered in any way. At the same time, they were both all too well aware of what their parents would feel. The tragedy had naturally separated them, although they had been lifelong friends. They had, therefore, each given their family a false address for staying away a long week-end, and they had been quietly married in London, before spending two precious days alone together . . . all they had for their honeymoon. Then they had come home and resumed their normal lives which, fortunately, included a great deal of time spent together.

There was really no reason now, after so long, why they should not admit to their marriage except that each knew their parents would be upset at having been deceived. It had been their intention to say nothing of the earlier registry office wedding and to have a second church wedding. But if she were, in fact, going to have a baby, this could no longer be done.

On a sudden impulse, Elizabeth told Charlotte the whole story. Charlotte was surprised and delighted and insisted that Meridan be allowed to know, too, although both girls agreed to say nothing about their expected babies for the time being.

'If only everything were right between you and Merry, what fun this would be!' Liz said wistfully. 'Our children would be born about the same time and it would be much nicer going through the next few months with someone else to share the experience.'

Charlotte's face clouded again. There was no joy for her in the thought of a coming child . . . and as Liz so truly said, it could have been such a wonderful time!

'I know I should not say this to you for Pippa was your friend and I know you loved her,' she said, unable to repress the words any longer. 'But, Liz, I can't help feeling she never once thought of Meridan's happiness! That she was selfish and cruel. Even in the manner of her death, she has spoilt things for him although I suppose she cannot be blamed for that. Now we shall never know if she meant to do it and Meridan will go on blaming himself for ever. Our marriage can have no hope of success while he feels as he does.'

Liz said nothing. Every word Charlotte had spoken was painfully true. Suddenly, she jumped to her feet, her eyes bright with inspiration.

'Charlotte, I've just remembered something . . . something that could be important. I can't think why I never remembered it before. Charlotte . . . ' she grasped the other girl's hand and stared excitedly into her questioning face . . . 'Pippa's diary. It might tell us something . . . something important. We always kept diaries as children, ever since we could write. Every year at first and then we gave each other five-year diaries with little locks and keys. When we were children, we always used to let each other read what we'd said in them, but that suddenly stopped ... I remember it was after Pippa came out of hospital. She used to lie on the couch in the schoolroom scribbling and when I asked her what it was about, she wouldn't tell me. I didn't think much about it at the time although I must have thought it unusual for Pippa to be so reticent with me, or that moment would not have remained in the back of my mind. I can see her now, shutting the book and turning the key and saying:

'Diaries are private thoughts, Liz, and it's high time we stopped looking at one another's!'

'Then it must have been something ... very personal she was writing!' Charlotte said. 'But, Liz, even if you know where her diary is, we can't look at it now ... now she is dead!'

'I can!' Liz said. 'I can, *and I'm going to, Charlotte*. If it has nothing whatever to do with you and Meridan, then I'll never reveal to another living soul what is in there. But if on the other hand . . . ' she broke off, her forehead wrinkled in concentration.

'I'm trying to remember what happened . . . that last week. Yes, Charlotte . . . she did . . . she had the diary here in this house. I remember going in to say good night to her the very night before the accident . . . and she was scribbling in it then. It must be somewhere in this house. I'm going to find it, Charlotte . . . now!'

Without waiting for Charlotte's opinion, Liz ran from the room and up the stairs. It seemed extraordinary to her now, that no one had thought of this before. The police had asked each of them if they knew of any last letter Pippa might have written . . . but they had never considered the possibility of a diary, and nor, apparently, had anyone else.

Feverishly, she searched through the empty drawers of the spare room, now covered in dust-sheets, where Pippa had spent her last night. At first, she thought her search was going to be fruitless. The room was quite empty. Then, as she was about to leave, downcast with disappointment, she remembered their childhood practice of slipping their diaries down between the headboard and the mattress last thing at night. She ran to the bed and pulled back the dust-sheet, her hand searching and at last finding . . . a small square object. She pulled it out and one glance told her she had what she wanted . . . Pippa's blue leather diary.

The maids who cleaned the room would not have discovered it for the mattress had a spring interior and was not meant to be turned. The padding of the quilted headboard would have kept the little book firmly lodged in its hiding-place, even when the bed was moved. She had found it! But there was no key. That, she knew, would be on a little gold chain round Pippa's neck . . . where she kept her own.

With her lips set firmly together, Liz felt for her own key. There was just a chance, since their diaries, apart from the colours, were identical, that the key of hers would open Pippa's too. With trembling fingers, she tried, and the book fell open, revealing the large childish scrawl. For a moment, the words blurred before Elizabeth's eyes ... that well-recognized writing bringing Pippa back from the past as clearly as if she had been a ghost standing here in the empty room.

Liz hesitated a moment longer. How could she do this to Pippa ... to her dear childhood friend? It was a kind of betrayal, and of a particularly nasty kind since Pippa had so expressly told her she did not wish Liz to know what she had written. She had loved Pippa ... loved her with an almost maternal feeling, for Pippa had always seemed so much younger than herself ... someone who needed to be taken care of and championed and consoled when things went wrong. They had all tried to protect Pippa from the unpleasant factors of life ... she, Merry, John.

Perhaps the three of them had been responsible for the fact that Pippa had never really grown up. Her behaviour those last weeks had been so much that of a spoilt child . . .

Then Liz remembered what had brought her here in search of the diary . . . not Pippa who was dead, but Merry, her brother, and his wife, Charlotte. For their sake, she must look . . . and for the baby, too, if there was to be one as Charlotte supposed.

'I'm sorry, Pippa!' she whispered the words aloud. Then, slowly, she turned the pages of the little book.

★ ★ ★

Pippa's diary:

The hospital, June 18th.

Today Mummy told me they had removed part of my inside. Can't say I feel much different . . . in fact, I feel a lot better. She seemed very upset about it so I suppose it is fairly serious. Fortunately it won't make any difference to my being happily married although I shan't be able to have any children. Well, I don't much care about that . . . I've never liked babies and they're an awful tie and responsibility even if you have got a Nanny.

Mummy seems to think Merry will mind though I can't see why. He shouldn't care if I don't. I think it is silly to make such an issue of it . . . I've no intention of telling him I don't want to marry him now. I've always wanted to marry him and I'm jolly well going to. He'll make just the kind of husband I want . . . he's rich and kind and always lets me have my own way. I shall be able to do exactly as I please when I'm married to Merry and he'll be happy because he doesn't ask much of life . . . just to see everyone else having a good time.

Nurse says Merry can come to see

me tomorrow. I bet he arrives with armfuls of flowers. All my nurses are anxious to see him and I shall feel jolly proud when he walks in . . . he's so distinguished looking . . . not like old John. But Liz seems to think John perfect . . . I suppose I don't because he's my brother.

Gosh, I'm getting bored lying here. Roll on tomorrow.

Hospital, June 19th.

Mummy had another 'jaw' at me this morning. She says I must tell Merry. I can't believe he'll really mind. He never said he wanted children. Mummy seems sure he won't let it make any difference so that's all right . . . all the same, I don't want to take any chances. I'll wear my new bed-jacket and tie my hair with that pink ribbon this afternoon when he comes. I think I know just the way to handle this.

Later. Well, it all went according to plan. I didn't actually have to offer Merry his ring back. I just cried a little when I told him about the op. and he was all sympathy and love. All the same, I couldn't get him to agree to an early wedding. I wonder why. I don't really mind much myself when we are married but it would seem a good idea to make sure he won't let me down. It's funny but I sensed a kind of difference in him. He was sweeter than ever to me. I suppose he feels sorry for me now.

All the nurses thought him very handsome. He didn't look his best . . . rather tired, but I expect he has been worrying about me.

Liz is coming to see me tomorrow so I'll get all the gossip from home. It's an awful bore not being able to ride for six months or so. The more I think about it, the better the idea seems for Merry and me to get married and fill in the time when I can't do anything much with our honeymoon. *It'll be something to do . . . especially as we're sure to go abroad. Of course, Merry won't be able to do any sports of any kind . . . not if he's looking after me, but that's not my fault. Anyway, he'll be busy enough looking after me. Mummy says I'll need a lot of care when I leave this place. She says I nearly died, so I suppose I have been pretty ill. Everyone has been worried to death about me.*

P.S. I rather liked that new young doctor who came this morning . . . the one with the curly hair. Nurse said all the girls are after him. I hope he comes again tomorrow.

Hospital, June 22nd.

I've been too fed up to write in my diary these last two days. For one thing, Liz has refused to back me up about getting married when I'm out of here. She agrees all the time with

433

Merry who says it's best to wait till I'm really well. I don't think it's fair. They, none of them, seem to mind what I want, and I'm the one who's been ill. Merry is pretty gloomy company. I don't know what's the matter with him. He says he's just overworked and tired. He brought me some nice chocolates, though. I expect I'll be able to talk him round in time.

The other thing that's annoyed me is young Dr. Andrews. He came again the day before yesterday and although he's only just left medical school, it seems he's engaged, so he's not interested in me, except as a 'case'! It'll be a blow to all the nurses ... they don't know because it's a secret but I might tell my nice nurse, just to put her on her guard. Dr. Andrews will be furious if he finds out but it won't worry me ... I'll be out of here by then. Of course, I'm not really interested in him although he is jolly nice looking, but it would have passed the time a bit to have had a flirtation and it couldn't have done anyone any harm. He might have fallen desperately in love with me, I suppose, but he'd have got over it. Oh, well, only another two weeks to go and I can go home.

Home, July 22nd.

It's ages and ages since I wrote this diary. There really wasn't anything to say anyway. I was pretty bored in hospital but it's even worse now I'm home. I only see Merry at the weekends, and from Monday to Friday I'm so bored I could scream. Doc says I'm perfectly well enough to get up and be on my feet. But what's the use. At least when I lie here on this sofa, people do come and see me, even if it's only Liz and John and Mummy and Daddy. If I let them know I could amuse myself, they'd all go off and leave me. I know Liz

435

and John have been aching to get off to the stables several times but don't like to leave me by myself. It really isn't fair.

Merry is being beastly, too . . . oh, I don't mean beastly to me . . . he brings me flowers and sweets and runs round doing things for me and all that. But he won't even discuss our getting married. Anyone would think he was a doctor the way he talks about it being important for me to get well first! I told him yesterday I thought he was trying to get out of it because of my op. and he looked so remorseful I'm pretty sure it isn't that! All the same, he isn't the same as he used to be. When he thinks no one is looking, his face is terribly gloomy. John says he probably has a lot of business worries. Liz says I ought to stop worrying him about when we'll get married. It's all very well for her . . . she knows John will marry her whenever she says the word.

Home, September.

We're going to have a party
. . . Merry and Liz are filling the
house for the week-end and there'll
be a dance on Saturday night. It'll be
just like old times. I'm going to get a
really beautiful dress to wear, something kind of bridal. And I'm going
to show Merry that I'm perfectly well
again and then he can't put off our
wedding any longer. I can see now
that I've been stupid to go on
pretending I'm an invalid. I've really
never felt better and I shall be the
gayest person at the dance. Merry
won't be able to refuse me. I really
don't know what is the matter with
him . . . he seems not to like it when
I try to snuggle up to him and make
him tell me how much he loves me.
I'm beginning to wonder if he does. I
wonder if he's met some other girl
in town. Maybe he's got fed up with
me because I've been so scratchy all
these weeks instead of the gay me he

used to know. It's quite possible he has found someone gayer ... I wonder if that's it. Anyway, I'll soon put a stop to that. No one else is going to get him ... he's mine!

Friday night.

I'm all dressed for the party and in a few moments I'm going downstairs ... I hope to catch Merry by himself. I'm almost sure I'm right ... about the other girl. When she came this afternoon, I had a strange feeling about her ... I think it was the way she wouldn't look at Merry ... or the way she looked at me. I'm pretty sure she loves him ... she turned away when I put my arm through his and showed her he was mine! I don't know how Merry feels about her, but I don't care ... tonight, somehow, I'm going to get him to fix our wedding date. At least that girl isn't much to compete with ... I admit she is pretty but that old Harris tweed coat and skirt she was wearing looked positively shabby compared with my Hartnell green tweed dress. She obviously hasn't any money . . . she's just someone's typist in the City. I'm sure whatever she wears tonight she won't begin to look as lovely as I do. I hope when I write again in this diary, it will be to say Merry has agreed a date at last. I'll fix it somehow.

Sunday morning.

I have just woken up with a ghastly headache . . . it must have been those sleeping pills they gave me last night. What a terrible mess I've made of everything. Everything went wrong right from the beginning. I pretended not to notice when Merry mistook me for Charlotte . . . it seemed the only thing to do. I didn't want to give him a chance to tell me how he felt about her. Oh, it became quite clear that he's in love with her . . . and she loves him. But I'll never give him up. I don't think she'll put up much of a fight for him . . . she seems to know he's mine. But I never imagined Merry would act as he did. I suppose I forced him into it by having his father make that announcement at supper, but it seemed worth taking a chance. I never thought for a moment that Merry would be so angry. Even pretending to faint didn't soften him. When he told me about Charlotte I just went on pretending I didn't believe he meant it. And I won't believe it. He can't just walk off with her and leave me. Anyway, she can't really mean so much to him . . . they've only known each other a short while and besides, Merry is engaged to me. I won't be thrown over like this. I'll think of some way to keep him. He'll soon forget her. It isn't fair of him to upset me like this . . . it isn't fair.

Monday afternoon.

I think I've won! Everyone is on my side now. Last night I really frightened them. When I saw Merry meant to leave me, I decided to pretend to kill myself. The sleeping pills they gave me the night before were on the dressing-table and I knew exactly how many I could take without harming myself. They all thought I meant to kill myself . . . Merry, Liz, even Doc. After this, Merry won't dare go for fear I'll try again. And if necessary, I would, though next time, I'll find some other way. They're all wrong if they think I want to die! They won't get rid of me so easily. I'm going to keep Merry whatever I have to do. I'm sorry to upset Mother and Father and John. But Liz is on Merry's side, I know that. She seems to think he could be happy with Charlotte. Well, even if he could he's not going to get the chance. Why should she have him?

Mother and Father will do everything they can to persuade Merry to stand by me. And I think Merry's mother will, too. She's always wanted him to marry me. She knows I'd make him a good wife . . . far better than that other girl could. Merry will see it for himself in time. I'm just going to pretend she doesn't exist. It'll be just as his mother says . . . it'll all come right in the end.

Wednesday.

I think my plan is working fairly well. Merry comes home every night and I can usually get Liz to ask me over with John for the evening or else Merry comes here. I think he has stopped seeing Charlotte. Mother hovers over me like an anxious hen . . . poor darling really believes I wanted to kill myself. I'm sorry she is so worried but I dare not tell her the truth. I've got to have her help. In a

442

way, I'm sorry for Merry, too, but he'll find out I'm doing the best thing for him in the end. I don't believe he'd be happy with her even if he does love her. I've got far more to give him than she has. I'm just pretending everything is the same as usual. Father says Merry is giving it a month so I've got to win by then.

Sunday night.

It hasn't been much of a week-end. I could almost laugh at their glum faces except I don't think I'm getting much further with Merry. He avoids any physical contact with me . . . I suppose he's thinking of her. Well, I've hit on the perfect plan. Tomorrow I'm going back to town with Merry and I'm going to see Charlotte. They all think it's just an excuse to be alone with Merry . . . no one suspects I'm going to see Charlotte. I don't know what I'll say to her but somehow or other I'm going to get Merry back. I've only three weeks left and I'm not going to stand by weakly doing nothing . . . he's mine and Charlotte shall not have him, no matter how he feels about her. Somehow I'll make her see Merry doesn't really love her. Once she's thrown him over, he'll come back to me. I'm sure I can make her give him up. She knows he is mine just as much as I do. We'll see.

Monday night.

Success! I never thought it would be so easy. She has actually promised to write and tell him she doesn't love him any more. I never thought she'd believe me so easily but maybe she doesn't really love him all that much . . . or believe he loves her. She didn't eat any lunch and looked pretty upset, but it is her turn to suffer after all the trouble she has caused me. Anyway, *it's all over now and it will only be a question of time before Merry finds out it is me he loved all along. Merry should get her letter tomorrow or the next night. I must somehow contrive to be at his house. Liz will ask me round if I give her a hint . . . not why I want to come, of course, or she would be horrified . . . but that I'd like to be there. She doesn't like saying 'no' to me any more then Merry does.*

Tuesday night.

It's been awful . . . awful. Merry got her letter but he didn't believe she meant it . . . he guessed it was something I had planned and he was absolutely furious. I'm really frightened now . . . I think he means to go. He's never hated me before but there was hate in his face tonight. I tried to worm out of it . . . tears, threats to kill myself . . . everything, but nothing seemed to move him.

Oh, I'm afraid he'll go to her now. There must be some way I can stop him. Liz put me here in the spare room for the night because I was hysterical so if I get up early enough in the morning, I might see Merry before he goes. I've begged and begged Liz to make him come and see me but she says there is no use trying any more . . . his mind is made up and tomorrow he is going . . . for good. I won't let it happen. I'll find some way to stop him. I've all night to think of something. Perhaps I could try to kill myself but there are no pills here now. If I throw myself out of the window, I might really hurt myself and I don't want to do that. Perhaps there is no need. In the morning, Merry will be calmer, less angry with me, and I'll be able to talk him round. The trouble is the whole family will be at breakfast and I may not get a chance to see him alone. Perhaps I could stay in bed and then slip out when he goes to the garage and waylay him up the drive. Yes, that is the thing to do. He can't just drive right past me. I'll stand in the middle of the drive and he'll have to stop. It isn't too late. I'll make him give me another chance. He'll see things differently tomorrow ... he'll see that I only said what I did to Charlotte for his sake, and then in time I can make him see that she can't love him, to give him up without a fight.

I'd better go to sleep now or I might not wake in time. What a good thing they have a breakfast gong. No one can sleep through that.

There were no more entries in Pippa's diary ... for she had carried out her last plan. But like the others she had contrived to get her own way, it had misfired. Liz and John had stopped her in the hall and when she escaped from them, she was just too late. Instead of running ahead of Meridan, she had reached the turn in the drive as he did and had run out against the side of the car. She could not have known that she would stumble and fall against the car . . . could not have realized that Merry wouldn't even see her. Mercifully, she died still believing that she could get what she wanted.

She left behind a record of her feelings . . . feelings which were a revelation of her true character. Never once had she considered anyone's happiness but her own. Never once had she stopped to consider the wishes of the man she professed to love, and never once in all those closely, childishly scrawled outpourings, had she spoken of her love for anyone but herself.

Liz put down the diary and no longer tried to stop the tears that were running down her cheeks.

17

When Elizabeth had recovered her composure, she sat down on the bed and tried to consider what she should do. Show the diary itself to Meridan, of course. But to Charlotte? To John? To their parents? Somehow she could not bear the thought of so many eyes reading the outpourings of that spoilt, shallow heart. None of them had ever begun to guess at the girl beneath the bright vivacious exterior . . . the real character of the girl who had died. It had come as a shock to Liz, who had had, perhaps, some small inkling. But to Mr. and Mrs. Blake, her parents, it would be a terrible revelation.

Slowly, the book in her hands, Liz walked downstairs. Charlotte had perhaps suffered more than anyone by Pippa's behaviour. Let her decide what to do.

Charlotte took one look at the book in Elizabeth's hand and at the white, strained face, and waited with every nerve in her body for her sister-in-law to speak. She knew that her future depended now on what Liz had discovered. If Pippa had indeed intended to take her life, then there could be no hope for herself and Meridan, no future happiness for their child.

'You'd better read it!' Liz said.

Quickly, Charlotte shook her head.

'No! I've no right to see it . . . *her* private thoughts!' she said. 'Just tell me, Liz, please!'

Briefly, Liz described the part of the diary she had read, not sparing Pippa in the telling. When she had finished, she looked into Charlotte's face and saw only relief . . . and compassion there.

'Poor Pippa!' Charlotte said at last.

Liz was suddenly stung out of her own mood of sentiment. Charlotte's goodness of heart, even at a moment like this, made her feel aware again of the damage Pippa might have done.

'She had no thought of Merry!' she said harshly. 'Not once on all those pages did she write of her own love for him . . . only her wish to make him marry her. I don't think she did love him, Charlotte . . . not as we understand the word, anyway. I think she just resented the thought of giving him up to someone else . . . to you! Why, even in hospital, she was trying to attract the attention of that young doctor. Had he not been already engaged to someone else, who knows that she might have been the one to give Merry back his ring of her own accord!'

Charlotte could find nothing to say. For the first time, she was appreciating what this would mean to Meridan . . . it would be as much to him as a reprieve to a condemned man . . . for that was how he seemed to her now, a man walking in the shadow of death. If Pippa's diary showed, as Liz said, that she had never really loved him at all, then he could never again feel the slightest emotion of guilt towards her;

never again feel in any way responsible for her death.

The phrase Liz had quoted repeated itself over and over again in Charlotte's mind:

'They're all wrong if they think I want to die!'

Pippa had never meant to kill herself for love of Meridan . . . only to frighten him into giving her her own way. And she had so nearly succeeded . . . even nearer in death than in life.

'I'm going to show the diary to Merry now!' Liz was saying. 'It'll be up to him to decide what to do next. Maybe the police ought to see it. It would certainly have affected the verdict at the inquest and he may want to clear himself entirely. At the same time, I can't bear to think what Mr. and Mrs. Bates will feel, either when they read the diary or if Pippa's thoughts are revealed in court. John will suffer, too.'

'Must they know?' Charlotte asked. 'Can't we pretend we never found it? No one but you and I know.'

'Y . . . yes, I suppose we could destroy it!' Liz said thoughtfully. 'Though I'm sure it's a criminal offence to destroy evidence. There has been no further inquest demanded, so perhaps it would be the kindest thing to do. But on the other hand, Merry has a right to clear his name. He'll have to decide.'

But it was to Charlotte that Meridan came when he had read and in his turn, been horrified, by the pages in Pippa's little book. But stunned though he was, he had no false illusions left about the girl whom he had once thought to marry. Now he knew that some deep inward instinct had revealed to him the true quality of Charlotte's love just as surely as the true nature of Pippa's so-called affection for him. His instinct had tried to guide him correctly and only a sense of duty and loyalty had ever made him hesitate in what he felt was the right thing to do.

Very tenderly, he sat beside Charlotte in the quiet privacy of the room, his arms about her shoulders.

'It is for you to decide what we should do with this!' he said. 'I know I have made you suffer terribly these last weeks, Charlotte . . . but I could not help it. I felt I had done the wrong thing by you in marrying you. And every day that passed, it became more difficult for me to touch you . . . feeling as I did. Every waking and sleeping thought was haunted by Pippa's memory and my hopeless feeling of guilt towards you both. I felt . . . unclean, Charlotte . . . unworthy of you . . . of your love. You have so much to forgive!'

'Meridan!' She clung to him, the tears streaming down her face as she assured him again and again that nothing she had endured could compare in her view with what he must had been through. 'There's nothing . . . nothing to forgive!'

'Only Pippa!' Meridan said quietly. 'And I suppose if you can forgive her, I can, too. She has, after all, paid fully with her death. Yet you have the right to take this farther, Charlotte, although Liz tells me you were the one to suggest

we pretend we have never seen this . . . '
He touched the diary as if it might burn
his hands. 'This is typical of your gener-
osity, darling, yet I can't permit you to
suffer any more for Pippa's sake. With
this evidence, my name can be completely cleared in court, and no one can
ever point at you as the wife of the man
who might have been responsible for
another girl's death.'

'But, Meridan, I don't care what
other people think or say. *I've never
cared.* All I've ever wanted is that you
should be happy. And, in any case, my
darling, I don't think anyone has ever
considered you responsible in any way.
Everyone exonerated you . . . even
Pippa's parents. The unspoken accusations have been only in your own mind.'

'Perhaps . . . perhaps that's true!'
Meridan said thoughtfully. 'All the
same, I believe Pippa's parents still feel
in their hearts that I was to blame.'

'Then, dearest, clear your name if
you wish. But don't you feel that it
might be easier for them, who loved her

so much, to be able to go on blaming you, if indeed they do? It would be so terrible for them to learn what their daughter was really like!'

'Yes!' Meridan said quietly. 'I've no wish to drag Pippa's name through the court again for my own sake and certainly not if it will cause her parents any pain. I'm free now, Charlotte . . . free in my own mind. And now I know she never meant herself any harm, I shall never feel guilty again.'

'Then let's destroy this!' Charlotte said, taking the book gently from Meridan's hands. 'They were her private thoughts, Meridan, not meant for others to see. Let's burn them now . . . here . . . in the fire, so no one can ever find them. I'm sure we're doing the best thing for Pippa's parents . . . and for John, too. Liz told you they were married? It would make things very hard for them if Pippa's death became public gossip again. Let's burn it, Meridan, please!'

Slowly, Meridan took the book from

her hands and threw it into the fire. When the last page had burnt to ash, he turned with a faint smile and said:

'Now I can be prosecuted for destroying Queen's evidence. You'll have to keep this a secret for ever, Charlotte, or I'll end up in court again!'

'I can keep a secret!' Charlotte said softly. 'As a matter of fact, I've kept one from you for the last few weeks. Would you like to know what it is, darling?'

When Liz and John opened the door, Charlotte was locked in Meridan's embrace and neither heard as they closed it softly again.

'I'll bet Charlotte has just told him she's expecting a baby!' Liz said, as John's arms went round her, drawing her to him. 'I suppose I'd better tell you, too.'

'Not . . . not *you*!' John said, looking into the bright, mischievous eyes of his young wife. 'Oh, Liz, darling, is it true?'

'Yes, silly, it is!' she whispered, and then they both smiled into each other's eyes, knowing that their cup of happiness was full, too.